PRAISE FOR *THE KIND TO KILL*

"Knife-sharp prose . . . a pressure-cooker of a book"
Hannah Morrissey, author of *Hello, Transcriber* and
The Widowmaker

"A stunner of a thriller"
Danielle Girard, *USA Today* and Amazon #1 bestselling
author of *The Ex*

"As atmospheric and gripping as a Tana French novel . . .
prepare to be transfixed and transported"
Megan Collins, author of *The Family Plot*

"A tense, expertly plotted thriller"
Edwin Hill, author of *The Secrets We Share*

"The complex plot and subtle characterizations elevate
this above similar fare. Wegert remains a writer to watch"
Publishers Weekly

"Wegert does an admirable job of generating mounting
suspense"
Kirkus Reviews

"[Wegert has] rightly earned the badge as one of the finest
talents of the past three years. And *The Kind to Kill* is her
best novel to date"
The Strand Magazine

Tessa Wegert is the author of the Shana Merchant series of mysteries. A former freelance journalist, Tessa has contributed to such publications as *Forbes*, *The Huffington Post*, *Adweek*, *The Economist* and *The Globe and Mail*. Tessa grew up in Québec and now lives with her husband and children in Connecticut, where she studies martial arts.

Also by Tessa Wegert

DEATH IN THE FAMILY
THE DEAD SEASON
DEAD WIND*

* *available from Severn House*

tessawegert.com
Facebook: tessawegertbooks
Twitter: @tessawegert
Instagram: @tessawegert
TikTok: @tessawegertbooks

THE KIND TO KILL

Tessa Wegert

SEVERN
HOUSE

First world edition published in Great Britain and the USA in 2022
by Severn House, an imprint of Canongate Books Ltd,
14 High Street, Edinburgh EH1 1TE.

Trade paperback edition first published in Great Britain and the USA in 2023
by Severn House, an imprint of Canongate Books Ltd.

severnhouse.com

British Library Cataloguing-in-Publication Data
A CIP catalogue record for this title is available from the British Library.

ISBN-13: 978-1-4483-0713-5 (cased)
ISBN-13: 978-1-4483-1005-0 (trade paper)
ISBN-13: 978-1-4483-0979-5 (e-book)

This is a work of fiction. Names, characters, places and incidents
are either the product of the author's imagination or are used fictitiously.
Except where actual historical events and characters are being described
for the storyline of this novel, all situations in this publication are
fictitious and any resemblance to actual persons, living or dead,
business establishments, events or locales is purely coincidental.

All Severn House titles are printed on acid-free paper.

MIX
Paper from
responsible sources
FSC
www.fsc.org   FSC® C013056

Typeset by Palimpsest Book Production Ltd.,
Falkirk, Stirlingshire, Scotland.
Printed and bound in Great Britain by
TJ Books Limited, Padstow, Cornwall.

For Ethan, Michelle, Aidin, and Foster.
Brainstorming has never been more fun

PROLOGUE

It was on the eighth day that I decided to kill him.

Eight days spent largely in darkness, the hours not ticking by so much as unspooling like an upstate highway, no end in sight. All the while, I listened to him talk about his difficult childhood and the bad luck he had to endure. The fatherless home, the mother's paralyzing anxiety, how it all deprived him of the skills and tools he needed to connect with other kids. He never once mentioned the three women he'd abducted and murdered before taking me, or the others before them. Their luck didn't concern him.

I knew who he was by then, not just that he was the suspect I'd been hunting with the NYPD, but that we had history. All week long, I'd been waiting for the moment when he'd show up not with the cheap takeout needed to keep me alive for some purpose I couldn't divine, but with the knife he'd used on those other women. Because history or not, this man was a killer.

But that eighth day was different. For some reason I've never learned, and never will, he was late with the food. I'd come to anticipate the odor of oily noodles as much as the sustenance itself, because that smell blocked out the others. The stink of burning fabric that filled the cellar every time the ancient, dust-caked boiler fired up with a lurch. The musty, wet dog stench of mold spores. The ceiling of that East Village apartment building basement was all exposed pipes, the floor poured cement gone grimy with disuse, but the smells permeated my clothing and hair and I couldn't escape them. That day, my nose was buried in my sleeve and I was huffing what little scent of fabric softener and safety and home remained when I heard the click of a key and the flick of the switch. When the lights came on, my eyes zipped down his body in search of that weapon. There was only the bag of food in his hand.

Bram smiled and said, 'Miss me?'

And then, as one, we turned our heads to the sound of a voice in the hall.

It belonged to a woman, a tenant come to ask for the janitor's help. *Bram's* help. When I met his gaze, I knew: if I made a sound, he'd kill her. He put a finger to his lips. I didn't move. He closed the door on me, and locked it. A beat, and then I was on my knees, cheek flat against the filthy floor, my left eye in the seam of light that shone under the door.

They stood at the other end of the room. He was motionless, his dingy white Converse rooted to the floor. She wore ballet flats and rocked on the balls of her feet as she spoke. She was my way out. I tented my fingers against the door, moving them over dents left by a hundred years of boots, boots belonging to people who had come and gone from this place freely. A dozen escape plans hurtled through my mind, but every one ended the same way. Another woman dead, lying lifeless on that basement floor.

Murmurs. A pleasant lilt, followed by a low, steady drone. Didn't she hear the edge to his voice, that dangerous undercurrent of impatience? *Get out of here.* I squinted at her feet and willed her to hear me. *Go!* When she finally did, I was relieved. Until I remembered what that meant.

For a long time, his feet still didn't move. The woman hadn't seen me. But she'd seen him, and to anyone who knew what the janitor looked like a few months ago, that would have incited suspicion. When my precinct first started investigating Blake Bram, the man who'd been targeting women through a dating app and bringing them here to die, he had dark hair and azure eyes. He was ash-blond now with a buzzcut, hiding from the city in plain sight. On their own, hair dye and colored contacts might not arouse misgivings. Coupled with cagey behavior, they were a tocsin. Did the woman hear it?

When at last he opened the door again, Bram's expression was fiery. 'Fuck.' He spat the word, eyes moving fast around the room. 'I'll be back. Stay right here, I want to hear all about your day.' His grin peeled the lips back from his teeth. *My day.* I'd spent it picturing those toxic spores spiraling down my throat like dandelion seeds to contaminate my lungs, and shivering despite the room's airless heat, and thinking about my family, and wondering if my squad at the Ninth Precinct would ever find me. Bram threw me a wink and began to close the door, but there was a new voice then. It commanded him to raise his hands.

It's dehydration-induced psychosis, I thought. *A fever dream.* I didn't find out until much later that instead of going to her apartment the tenant, sensing something was amiss, burst onto the street and grabbed the first police officer she saw. He was just eight months on the job when the woman sent him down those basement steps. His name became one I would never forget.

I can only imagine what that rookie cop saw when he looked at me, crouching hollow-eyed in that subterranean hell. He was still staring, sidearm drawn and shaky, when Bram made his move.

It happened quickly. Bram lunged at the rookie's knees and toppled him, knocking him backward on the cement floor. There was a thud and a sickening crack. I jolted to my feet. I had trained for this. The air was close and my pulse pounded in my ears, but this moment was mine. I wasn't like the other women he'd taken. I had skills that were designed to save my life, and while I was weak and disoriented from my ragged, endless days in the dark, I knew how to disarm an assailant. I thought, *I can save him.*

You'll fail. You failed once already. Your training didn't help you when Bram slipped a date rape drug into your drink and shuffled you into a waiting car.

I shook my head, but the voice was insistent.

He'll only kill you, too.

So help me God, I listened. Despite all my preparation, all those years of police training and martial arts, when my brain told me to act, my body refused to follow orders. I didn't – couldn't – move.

Before the cop could catch his breath, before he could peel himself off the floor, Bram had his Glock – and that was when I knew. People weren't safe, and never would be, as long as Blake Bram was alive.

I blinked at the scene. Where moments before a woman had fidgeted in ballet flats, a man was now bleeding from his head on the cement floor, and Bram held his gun. I opened my mouth to scream as the shots rang out like canon fire. A whisper in a wind storm. I watched with a disorienting sense of detachment as Bram stepped over the young officer's body and back into my cell.

As he set down the gun, and took my hand.

You're next, said the voice, deadpan.

Am I?

'This is not how I wanted things to end.' Bram's sigh was familiar. Displeased. Childlike. His fingers were tacky with blood, blood that was now on my hands, too. 'His partner will be right behind him.'

The gun. So close that the grip kissed my knee. My eyes traveled from Bram's face, a face I had once known so well, to the Glock. Here, at last, was my chance. The decision was made. But it had come too late.

By the time I looked up, Bram was gone.

ONE

Two years later

The knock on my office door gave me a jolt. Panicked, I stuffed the latest issue of *People* under a stack of papers. Just when I thought the press had finally moved on, an old friend from high school tipped me off to the article inside. If the reporter behind the magazine feature had reached out for a comment, I wouldn't have known it; I'd long since stopped answering calls from numbers I didn't recognize, could hit 'Decline' with record speed. I wasn't responsible for the sordid story on my desk. Still, my cheeks flushed red when I spied Don Bogle hovering in the window.

'We could use you out here,' he said, cracking open the door. The man's voice was grim.

Every now and then, it occurred to me that Bogle had missed his calling. With his clean-shaven head and the height of a retired NBA power forward, he could have made a killing playing a Bond villain or mob movie hitman if he'd only gone to Hollywood. Instead, the poor bastard had stayed in Alexandria Bay to become one of three Troop D investigators who had to take orders from a vilified minor celebrity.

With a nod, I followed Bogle down the hall.

Jeremy Solomon waved me over when he saw me, mouthed the word 'wait.' Ear pressed to his phone, he was jotting notes, interrupting the caller every few seconds. 'Spell the last name . . . Sure, I know it – behind the Admiral? OK . . . Right. Thanks.' He put down the phone, and looked up.

Fleshy-cheeked and freckled, Sol had the look of an overgrown boy who'd spray-painted his hair gray for Halloween, but he aged rapidly when a situation was dire. There were creases around his eyes now. 'That was the Alex Bay PD,' he said. 'Gorecki. Know him?'

Immediately, my mind went to Tim. Tim, who knew almost

everyone in town and helped me navigate the local community. But Tim was out on a criminal mischief case. When I didn't reply, Sol said, 'Ivan Gorecki's a Jefferson County deputy sheriff.'

'What's going on?' I asked. The Alexandria Bay Police Department was small, mostly comprised of part-time officers who worked for other agencies. Officers like Gorecki. The village police took what we called a broken window approach to keeping the peace, shutting down disorder before it got out of control. In little A-Bay, that usually meant noise complaints, security alarms, public intoxication. When a bigger case came in, the state police assumed control. We dealt with narcotics, child abuse, and serial crimes. Felonies. On those rare occasions when our interests overlapped and it was all hands on deck, you could count on it being a major investigation.

A call from Gorecki was a bad sign.

'We've got a missing woman,' Sol said, staring down at the phone in his hand. 'She and her husband were staying at the Admiral Inn last night. Tourists in from Oneida County.'

'They were staying at the *Admiral*?'

A nod. 'Gorecki says they had some kind of argument. The wife stormed out and never came back.'

'I didn't realize the Admiral was open again,' said Don Bogle. Decades of smoking had shredded his voice; he would have done well cast as a timeworn cowboy, too. 'Was it roaches last time they shut down, or rats?'

Honestly, it could have been either. If my family ever came to visit me in Alexandria Bay, a scenario that was looking increasingly unlikely, I'd put them up pretty much anywhere other than the Admiral Inn. Unlike the other hotels and resorts in town, it hadn't been renovated in at least thirty years, but its biggest offense was that the place was nowhere near the water. While the cheapest motel in town was as likely to attract budgeting families as the uncouth, calls about drunken dust-ups on the ramshackle property weren't uncommon.

I listened as Sol explained that, the night before, the village station received a call from the motel's night clerk. Several guests had complained about the shouting, so the couple took their dispute outside. Things escalated after that, to the point where the clerk felt the need to report it. An officer had gone out to the motel, but by then the husband and wife were back in their room. And here we were the next morning, with the husband filing a missing persons report.

Most people think you have to wait twenty-four hours to report a person missing. TV and the movies have hammered that falsehood into everyone's heads, which is a problem because when someone's MIA, a swift response is critical. I didn't know whether the husband of the missing woman knew that was a myth or not, but he'd done the right thing by going to the police. The fresher the trail, the better our odds of locating the wife.

Even so, I didn't like what I was hearing. 'This argument,' I said. 'Was it violent?'

'Seems that way. One of the guests told the night clerk there was some pushing and shoving outside. The husband denies it,' said Sol.

Of course he does.

'But he knows there were witnesses,' said Bogle. 'Right? There's no covering up the fact that they fought. And he went down to the station this morning anyway?'

'Yep,' I said, channeling his thoughts. 'Which means either this guy's trying to play us, or he's genuinely concerned about his wife.'

I leaned against Sol's desk, the sun angling through the nearby window hot on the back of my neck. I still wasn't used to that. Where my hair once curled down past my shoulders, there was nothing now but naked skin that prickled at my touch, vulnerable and unfamiliar.

A month ago, while in the shower, I'd soaped my head and watched with detached horror as a tangle of hair swirled like seagrass down the drain. The stress I'd been under was taking its toll, and my decision was a quick one. Sarajane, who ran a salon in the back room of her weather-beaten bungalow, beamed when she set down her scissors and dusted away the stray hairs. 'Not everyone can pull this off, honey, but you look pretty,' she'd declared, gazing at my reflection in the mirror on the wall. The cut was almost as short as my brother's, and significantly shorter than Tim's, but that was fine. I didn't care about pretty. All I wanted was to look different. A shot at regaining the anonymity I feared I'd lost for good.

'They argued,' I said at length, thinking it through. 'Things got rough. If this woman was afraid of her husband and what else he might do to her, it makes sense that she'd run.' Maybe our missing person wanted to be invisible, too.

At the same time, there was something about the account that sat uncomfortably in my stomach like a creamy, overly rich meal. Far too many victims of domestic violence were doubted and ignored as it was; I couldn't take the chance that this woman wasn't still in serious danger. 'Gorecki's gonna need help locating her,' I said. 'Got a name?'

Sol consulted his notes. 'Rebecca Hearst. The husband's name is Godfrey Patrick Hearst III.'

Bogle raised an eyebrow. *Click. Clack.* He had a habit of cracking his fingers, and Sol winced as his colleague pressed each crooked digit in against itself. 'Seriously? What is he, a lord or something?'

'Godfrey only knows.' Sol's face split into an ear-to-ear grin.

'OK,' I said, rolling my eyes. 'Jesus, guys. And Hearst, he still at the station?'

'He is.'

I nodded. 'Good. I'd like to have a word with him.'

'Thought you might,' Bogle said.

TWO

The air in downtown Alexandria Bay was so humid I could have wrung it out like a sodden towel, and it was a relief to sink into the arctic chill of the Village of Alexandria Bay PD. A squat tan building with a colossal antenna punching into the sky, the place looked like a cross between a radio station and a doomsday bunker, but at least it had A/C.

We'd had record highs for close to a week now, and for some, that was cause for concern. In four days, A-Bay would fill up with visitors from across the northeast, barrel-chested dads in baseball caps and raucous couples in their twenties clogging the streets of the town. They came for Pirate Days, the annual celebration of nineteenth-century smuggler and 'river pirate' Bill Johnston that drew more than a thousand spectators, many from across the border in Ontario. It was part historical reenactment, part renaissance fair, and it brought the tourists in droves. The wigs were heavy, the costumes constricting, and here we were in the middle of a heatwave.

'That's all we need,' Tim had said a few days ago while wincing at the weather app on his phone. 'Pirate week is the busiest of the whole summer. Folks can't afford to lose that income.'

By *folks* he meant the small business owners whose souvenir stores, ice cream stands, and pizza joints lined the downtown streets. They needed the money eye patches and plastic cutlasses would bring – but the word was out about Blake Bram. What he'd done here. Who he was.

Who he'd been to me.

People had made a valiant effort, but it was late to the game. The *New York Times*, the *New York Post*, *Newsweek*, even TMZ had already paraded some variation of the same exposé that readers devoured like buzzards starved for meat. The media relations person with the state police had tried his damndest to create a buffer between me and the press, but the attention was overwhelming, unprecedented, and he was out of his depth. My family was still refusing to talk to the scores of reporters hounding them for an interview, but newshounds found dirt on us anyway by tracking down old classmates, neighbors, former friends. In the process, Alexandria Bay had gone from sleepy river town to national news story.

No one could predict what that kind of notoriety would bring. A serial murderer had terrorized the town for months, and there wasn't a business around that hadn't worried he would leave a black mark that couldn't be scrubbed away. In late May, though, there was a notable uptick in visitors – *at last, thank God* – and the locals grew cautiously optimistic. Memorial Day weekend, and every weekend since, restaurants had been operating at full capacity. The tour boat company had added a new route to their itinerary, and while they weren't so crass as to reference Blake Bram on their website, the excursion took passengers past Deer Island and Dingman Point, both sites where Bram spent time while on the run. For those who didn't have personal history with the man I'd once known as Abraham Skilton, all of this made for an exciting getaway, and the town was currently on track for a record-breaking retail season. Unlike Tim, I didn't think the heat would get in the way . . . but a missing woman?

That was something else entirely.

The Alex Bay PD smelled of floor wax and microwaved tomatoes. On my way to the interview room, I passed a Corelle bowl rimmed with mustard-yellow butterflies, a full can of ravioli upended into its center. A saucy square was growing cold on the fork left behind. Gorecki hadn't managed to get down a single bite of his lunch before Godfrey Hearst III arrived, but I was happy to see a quick response time in spite of the small operation.

I found Gorecki and Hearst in the interview room, a couple near-empty paper cups of coffee on the table between them. My first thought when I saw Godfrey Hearst was that the Admiral was in for a scathing online review. A cheap motel was no place for this man; surely he'd been out for a sail on his father's yacht and taken a wrong turn. The even tan, smooth blond hair with a knife-sharp part above the ear, those coral shorts and clean Dockers . . . it all lent Hearst a collegiate, affected look. I wondered if his wife looked as much like a fish out of water, wherever she was.

When he saw me through the window in the door, Officer Gorecki waved me inside. 'Thanks for coming,' he said. 'I've got a mountain of prep work and could really use a hand.'

The reference to prep work might have puzzled me, were it not for the comment Sol had made as I was leaving the barracks. 'Ivan's gotta be swamped this week. He's head pirate.'

'Head what?'

'Head pirate.' Sol had shot me an incredulous look. 'Ivan's super involved with the event, has been for years. As head pirate, he leads the children's parade *and* the pirate march. His whole family pitches in – his son's a powder monkey in the reenactment, running gunpowder to the musketeers. This is a busy time for Ivan. He'll be grateful for any help he can get.'

Sure enough Gorecki, a sinewy man whose tendons stood out from his arms where he'd rolled up his shirtsleeves, looked as pleased to see me as if I'd come bearing his abandoned lunch.

'This is Shana Merchant,' he told Godfrey Hearst. 'She's a senior investigator with the Bureau of Criminal Investigation. The New York State Police. Missing persons is her area of expertise.'

While I wished that wasn't the case, I had no grounds on which to argue. Between Jasper Sinclair, who'd disappeared from his family's estate on Tern Island last October, and Trey Hayes, abducted from a school field trip to Heart Island, local law enforcement – and the locals proper – had come to associate me with the lost. Time-sensitive investigations and manhunts had become my thing. Given the pride with which Gorecki spoke, I opted not to point out that my track record was far from perfect.

Instead, I said, 'Why don't you tell me about your wife, Mr—'

'Hearst. No relation to Patty or the mass media billionaire.'

The line sounded rote, like the man rattled it off every time he met someone new. Today, he followed it up with a blink, surprised, perhaps, that even in the face of a crisis he could produce a halfway decent joke. In spite of his wit, there were signs of distress in his face, and purple smudges under his eyes that spoke of a long night.

'OK, Mr Hearst-no-relation. I know you probably just got done telling Officer Gorecki here what's going on, but would you mind repeating it for my sake?'

Hearst nodded. 'Yeah. OK. It's like this. My wife is gone.'

'Your wife Rebecca. Same last name as you?'

He nodded.

'Age?'

'She'll be thirty next month.'

'Got a picture?'

'I printed it out,' Gorecki said, opening the folder in front of him and sliding the photo of Rebecca toward me. Dark skin, close-set eyes, tight curls down to her shoulders. In the picture, she wore big hoop earrings and a closed-mouth smile.

'And the last time you saw her?' I asked.

'In our motel room. We're staying at the Admiral Inn, on Route 12?' He made a face, something between disgust and shame. 'She went for a walk last night, late, and I fell asleep. When I woke up this morning she wasn't there, and her side of the bed hadn't been slept in. I don't think she came back last night at all. I don't know where she is.'

'Have you tried calling her?'

He pushed back his shoulders. 'Of course I have – and I sent her, like, ten texts. She isn't answering.'

'Did she leave a note?'

Hearst's expression faltered. 'Not a note. But she did message me last night, while I was asleep. I didn't see it until this morning.' He took his phone from where it sat on the table and swiped at the screen before turning it over to me. I leaned in to study it, the text that was timestamped 2:04 a.m. that morning.

I'm sorry

When I raised my eyes to meet his, Hearst's face reddened, and he snatched the phone away. 'I tracked her,' he said. 'With the tracking app on my cell.'

I nodded, pleased. That would have been my next question for him: are your phones set up to see each other's location? It was common these days for families and couples to activate such apps, a handy way to locate a lost device and protect data. It made the lives of law enforcement professionals a little easier by saving us the trouble of getting a warrant to the wireless network provider. 'And were you able to see her location?' I asked.

'Oh, I saw it, all right. It says her phone's in the river.'

I traded a look with Gorecki. 'In the river,' I repeated.

Gorecki gestured to the phone. 'Load that app again, would you, Mr Hearst?'

When the man showed me his device once more, the Find My Phone app was open and he'd zoomed into a map of the region. I squinted, and leaned toward the screen. *In the river.* The white bubble enclosing a tiny image of an iPhone hovered over a solid ribbon of mallard blue.

'That's Collins Landing,' said Gorecki, using his pinkie nail to draw a circle over the nearby shore, though the words 'Collins Landing' were right there on the map. 'Know it?'

'I know it,' I said. Collins Landing was a small community right on the water, at the mouth of the Thousand Islands International Bridge. I could see the suspension bridge on the screen, too, marked with a highway shield and the number 81. The I-81 crossed the bridge system, which was really five smaller bridges that hopped several islands to span the St Lawrence River, connecting New York State with southeastern Ontario. It was heavily trafficked in both directions day and night; I had the insomnia to prove it. My rental place on Swan Bay wasn't far from the US span, and the constant drone of motorcycles and semi-tractor-trailers made short work of the distance.

'That can't be right, can it?' Hearst asked, his eyes ping-ponging between us. 'I mean, it looks like she's in the water.'

I extended my hand. 'May I? I used this app when I misplaced my own phone. The GPS isn't always accurate. It might get you to the right general area, but there's a margin of error. This could just be a glitch,' I told him, but Hearst wasn't wrong. According to the app, Rebecca's phone appeared to be in the river, almost directly under the bridge.

'Could she have dropped it? In the water?' Hearst drummed the table with his fingers as he spoke, a nervous twitch that set my teeth on edge.

'From the bridge? It's possible,' said Gorecki. 'But the GPS satellites wouldn't be able to locate the phone if it was underwater.'

'Did you rent a boat?' I asked.

'No. Are there any islands down there?' Hearst's eyes widened;

the idea, a flicker of hope, had perked him up. 'Maybe she's on an island.'

'No islands directly under the bridge,' said Gorecki, leaning back in his chair. 'There are a few nearby, but they're private.'

'Let's back up,' I said. Things were moving too fast, and snippets of Sol's phone call with Gorecki still bobbed untethered in my mind. There had been talk of an argument. Shouting outside the motel. 'You and your wife. Where are you from?'

Hearst didn't look especially happy that I wanted to change gears, but the shift away from Rebecca's disappearance relaxed his shoulders a hair. 'Rebecca's from Hollywood, originally – Florida, not California. I'm from Utica, born and raised.'

The pride in his voice surprised me. Utica was no Pleasantville. It was a hardscrabble town with a crime rate to rival Buffalo's and a population in steep decline. A place people tended to leave rather than call home for good. 'And what brings you north, Mr Hearst?'

'We're on vacation?' The sarcasm in his voice was made all the more effectual by the way he tucked his chin. 'Four days off. It was Rebecca's idea. We hadn't been away in a while, and she thought we needed a break. We work a lot,' Hearst said. 'I run my family's network of car dealerships. Hearst Auto Group?' He frowned when I shook my head. 'We've got five dealerships around Utica, in Rome, Oneida, and Little Falls. Chrysler, Honda, Ford, Lincoln. Rebecca works with me.'

The name was suddenly familiar; I could picture a giant 'H' hovering over a showroom the size of an aircraft hangar, the letter checkered like a racing flag. I'd spent some time in Oneida recently, when Tim and I reported to our Troop D lieutenant after the Sinclair case, and again last November when I went in for a psych evaluation following my suspension from the Bureau of Criminal Investigation. Both visits had been rough. It was a wonder I hadn't completely blocked them from my mind.

'What does Rebecca do for you?' I asked.

'Not *for* me. We work *together*. She's in sales,' he said. 'On the floor at our Utica location. She's our top performer. Rebecca's great with customers.'

Great with customers. I jotted that down in the notebook I'd withdrawn from my pocket. It took a certain personality to work in sales, and knowing Rebecca was good at her job told me quite a bit about her character. 'Is that where you met? At one of your dealerships?'

Hearst's eyes darted away. 'We didn't meet there. But I gave her the job.'

'And now you're married.'

'So? Is there some kind of law that says you can't marry someone you hired?'

I shrugged, a single-shoulder lift. 'Just trying to understand your relationship, is all. Running that place sounds like a big responsibility. Making hiring decisions and all the rest.'

'Like I said, we work hard. We both needed a break.'

'Could that be what she's doing right now?' I asked. 'Taking a break? I heard you and your wife had an argument last night.'

These things were all about timing. Show your cards too soon, and your witness might clam up. Wait too long, and you risked missing out on the chance to rattle them. Godfrey Hearst let his upper back fall against the chair. He had known this was coming; he had to. 'There was no *argument*,' he said. 'That night clerk blew it out of proportion. We were talking, that's all. We have loud voices, me especially. I'm a car salesman, for Chrissake. It's practically a job requirement.'

I nodded, and said nothing. Hearst struck me as a man who was used to being in control. He was young to be running a company the size of Hearst Auto Group, and he'd married a member of his staff. Maybe the responsibility – the power – had gone to his head. Big egos were a red flag in the law enforcement business. Big egos bred liars.

'So the night clerk had it wrong,' I said at length. 'Same goes for the guests who complained about the noise?'

'We were talking,' he said again.

'OK. But is it so unimaginable that your wife needed a little time alone? It sounds like she was upset. Could she have gone somewhere – a different hotel, maybe – until things cooled off between you?' I was thinking about her text. 'I'm sorry' could mean a lot of things. It could mean: 'I'm leaving you.'

Even before I finished talking, Hearst was shaking his head. 'No way. She wouldn't do that. You don't understand.' He shoved his chair back from the table and slid his palms up and down his thighs, pressing so hard the sides of his hands flashed white. 'Couples argue. We argue. But this isn't normal. She's never done anything like this before. This isn't right. You don't believe me.' Something happened to his eyes as he said it. His gaze was tighter now, fixed on mine.

'We just don't think it's a good idea to panic,' Gorecki said. 'There's probably a logical explanation.'

For the nebulous text. The GPS signal in the St Lawrence River.

Hearst flinched, and though the movement was small, it opened a chink in his armor. I studied him for a long time before saying, 'Is there a reason to think something could have happened to Rebecca, Mr Hearst?'

For a second he flailed, opening and closing his mouth as if grappling with what to say. He settled on this: 'There was a lot going on with her lately. She was . . . in a bad place.'

'Can you elaborate?'

'Just, things haven't been that great between us for a while. That's why I agreed to come up here with her. Get her mind off things for a bit, you know?'

I could feel the heat of Gorecki's gaze, the urgency in it. I didn't know the deputy sheriff well, but he had to be thinking the same thing I was: I trusted Godfrey Hearst less and less by the minute.

'Most likely she's just simmering down someplace. We'll get to the bottom of this,' I said, and made a move to get up. I'd find Tim, I figured, and we'd try to locate that phone. Have Gorecki obtain a list of friends and family that Bogle could call while Sol took statements from witnesses at the motel. The Admiral Inn was on a main road studded with gas stations and tourist stops, but the streets behind it were residential. A lot of homeowners had video doorbells and security cameras these days, and one of them might have caught something useful. We'd look into it – and in the meantime, maybe Rebecca would come back. 'Missing persons cases are rare, Mr Hearst,' I assured him, 'especially around here. But I'll call in some help, OK?'

I was halfway out of my chair when Hearst's words locked my knees.

'That's not even true. I heard a boy went missing from this town just last year.'

I looked up from the floor and swallowed hard. There were those for whom the Thousand Islands was the ultimate summer destination, but most were completely unaware the fifty-mile strip of paradise existed. I'd been one of those poor uninitiated souls once myself. Hearst lived in Utica, though, just two hours south. He'd know this place, especially once the media started reporting on Bram.

Had Hearst recognized me? The haircut was akin to slapping a Band-Aid on a severed limb. There was no concealing the scar that cut a swathe through my freckled skin from my ear to the corner of my mouth and was visible in every photo I'd seen online. But I was getting good at spotting that dark gleam of realization, and Hearst didn't seem to know me. *This town.* The words had twisted his mouth. Tourists may be flocking in, but A-Bay had a reputation now, a funk that beset those who lived here. That at least one visitor feared might cling to him, too.

'OK,' I said with reluctance, 'that's true. But if you know about that, then I'm sure you know the kid's OK and that the man who took him is—'

'Dead. Yeah, I know. Doesn't mean this place is safe. We're in the fucking boonies,' Hearst said with revulsion, flinging open his arms so fast his heavy watch clacked his wrist bone. 'It isn't like her to do this, to leave in the middle of a-a *conversation* and not come back all night. To not answer her phone.'

'Maybe she lost it,' Gorecki said. 'That would explain why she hasn't responded. Look, try not to worry. Most of the time, these things work out just fine.'

Hearst blew out a breath and nodded, but as he turned over the phone in his hands, that severed connection to his wife, there was something in his expression that I hadn't seen before.

It was fear.

THREE

B ugs flickered in the light of my high beams as the cottage came into view through the trees, all lit up in the gloaming. Music. Laughter. A sense of release as unfailing as a hot shower after a long day on the job. These were the things I'd come to associate with the cottage on Goose Bay.

I wasn't a great cook, despite the way our kitchen table always groaned under the weight of my parents' feasts and their attempts to indoctrinate me into the cult of sourdough starter. That had never mattered when I was at this little house on the water, where Tim sipped local beer and whipped up simple but satisfying dinners. The sagging couch in his living room had a dip in the cushion from all the time he spent reading on weekends, and I loved to sit there and drift off against him, my bare feet on the arm worn soft from the shift of his elbow as he turned the page. I'd tuck my hands into the sleeves of my green UVM sweatshirt, a Christmas gift from Doug back when he was in college. Tim would drop a kiss on the crown of my head. On nights like those, it was like the world narrowed down to a pinprick; I got tunnel vision, utterly fixated on my happiness. But the cottage hadn't felt the same in months, the memories I'd formed there already tenuous as a dream.

It's a pity when a place you consider a second home is stripped of its goodness. There aren't many safe havens to begin with, not for people who populate a netherworld where violence is the norm and death as ubiquitous as a fast-food logo glowing in the night, and I would always mourn the loss of this one. The news stories didn't talk much about Blake Bram's death. His life and crimes and connection to me were far more interesting than his demise. But that demise had occurred right in Tim's back yard, and for us, that wasn't easily forgotten.

The gun. Movement, fast as a whip. That horrible rain of red. For days afterward, until the next April shower, the grass had attracted hard-backed insects that writhed about in a state of ecstasy. They made me think of bedbugs. I'd read somewhere that bedbugs are drawn to dark fabrics that replicate what the creatures crave most. Night. Blood. Those things lured me, too. I spent more time on that blood-soaked patch of grass than I should have, my hours there a strange cocktail of exposure therapy and self-sabotage. I needed to swallow the bitter tincture, but doing so always made me feel worse.

I knew Tim would gladly have sold the place and moved if he had time to transform another waterfront hovel into a home. He'd tried everything to banish the bad memories that lurked outside his door. One afternoon, a couple weeks after Bram's death, he'd driven to a local nursery and returned with a tree. Tim had used a spade to chip away at. the hard dirt between boulders of granite, and tucked the sapling into the earth. The bank of mulch he mounded around it looked like the vestiges of a freshly-dug grave, but I kept that thought to myself and watched mutely as, day after day, Tim sunk his energies into keeping that baby tree alive. He checked the moisture level of the soil, inspected the tenderness of its leaves, but despite his best efforts those leaves had shriveled and curled and fallen to the ground like wisps of my own cut hair.

I tried to push all of that from my mind as I parked, stepped out of my SUV, followed the footpath to the cottage's front door, and fell into my top investigator's arms.

Tim Wellington buried his face in my neck and inhaled as though he needed my scent to survive, as though my skin was oxygen itself. I slipped my hands under his shirt and ran them up his sides, savoring the way my knees went weak at the feel of rippling muscle and rib. Almost four months together, and I still wasn't over the novelty of our love. Only last summer we were struggling to understand each other's investigator methods, to find the rhythm that would prove so vital to our professional partnership. The same bumbling determination had bled into our personal lives, and so far, we were making it work. That might not have been the case if Tim didn't know my ghosts as well as he did. And if he hadn't been right there with me through what could only be described as the most agonizing days of my life, I might never have kissed him back.

Our new relationship wasn't without complications. In theory, there was nothing to stop us from flaunting the fact that we'd started dating. No formal policy existed to prohibit members of the State Police from getting romantically involved. We were, however, expected to behave professionally while on duty, and I felt as helpless in his presence as a finishing nail set before a high-power magnet. It was crazy how often I found myself wanting to reach for him, as if the need to fuse his skin to mine was beyond my control. I knew he felt the same way, had seen him square his shoulders and lock his jaw enough times to understand he didn't like the distance any more than I did, but we had agreed that, at work, we'd keep things on the down-low. We hadn't told Sol, Bogle, or the troopers yet, and didn't have immediate plans to. The sheriff knew – she was as close a friend to me as any I'd ever had – but apart from that, relegating our relationship to home seemed prudent.

If only Tim's home wasn't laced with memories of death.

Tim led me to the couch and we sank into it together, my head on his shoulder, his hand twisted up with mine. My hands looked different these days. Weathered. Since the spring, when the ice cleared off the river, I'd spent hours with Tim in his boat. I called it practice; he called it rehabilitation. Either way, my skin had caramelized to a color that made the moons of my fingernails glow bright white. I was never much for the great outdoors, not even back home in Vermont, but just two months of boating had changed me, and not just psychologically. In the shower, I found myself marveling over the sun's handiwork, the contrasting color-lessness of my belly and breasts. That my entire body had once been pale as chilled milk felt incomprehensible. We were the same now, Tim and I. United by the water.

It didn't take long for me to get him up to speed on Rebecca Hearst and the strange situation with her phone. Tim stroked my arm as I talked, and for all his outward calm I knew his mind was in a full sprint, analyzing every word. I suspected there were very few moments in Tim Wellington's life when he wasn't actively working to make things right.

'I'd like to take a boat out there tomorrow,' I told him. 'Search around for that phone a little more.' The mischief case had taken up Tim's whole day, so I'd driven out to Collins Landing by myself. As relieved as I'd been not to discover a body at the river's edge, I hadn't found Rebecca's cell either, and the GPS signal persisted.

'That sounds like a good idea,' Tim said.

We were quiet a moment, content in our togetherness, until he cleared his throat. 'I thought you'd like to know. Your mother called.'

I sat forward. 'My mother? Called *you*?'

Della and Wally, back in Swanton. My brother, Doug, a few miles from them. Aunt Felicia. My cousin Crissy. Thoughts of my family followed me everywhere. Swanton was in Vermont, just three and a half hours from A-Bay, but reaching them felt like trying to cross a flooded canyon; I didn't even know where to start. I thought of the new *People* story, the headline that took up a third of the page:

NYPD Detective Turned Upstate Investigator Lures Serial Killer Cousin to Town

Memories of the day I had to tell my family about Bram – Abe, as they'd known him when he was a child – will never leave me. I'd driven back to Swanton to do it, because I didn't think my parents would believe me if I told them over the phone what their nephew had done. It had taken a lot of convincing in person, too. They'd stared at me with undisguised horror, the look in their eyes so cold it made me shudder. 'Darling please, think about what you're saying.' My father's words were as firm as a fist on a table. Mom, for her part, had skipped over denial and gone straight to anger. 'Don't be ridiculous, Shana. What is the matter with you?' It was her sister's boy I was talking about, our kin. How could I be so *cruel*?

I felt the sting of their condemnations even now. Online, I'd been called everything from a criminal to a vigilante. In town, when I encountered locals at the Bean-In on James Street, their coffees gone cold in their hands, the whispers were just as savage. 'They were best friends as kids, did you hear? She had to know he was a psycho. It's probably in the blood.' Those words felt like a brand, so blistering hot I could almost hear the sizzle. But hearing them would never hurt as much as having to tell my family what I'd been hiding.

I'd asked my brother to join my parents at the house the night I came clean. I knew how blindsided they would feel.

Fifteen years ago, they hadn't wanted to believe that Abe carved up my face on purpose. Only Aunt Felicia knew the truth about that, but it took her a decade and a half to admit it, and she'd made sure to insinuate that Abe was just reacting to my impending departure. That dreaded decision to leave town after high school. My parents had always believed that my friendship with Abe could endure anything. 'Thank God for Shana,' I heard my mother whisper to Dad more than once. Without me, Abe the Outcast would have had no one. My family wasn't so clueless as to think he was a normal kid. They weren't willing to imagine the alternative, either.

Unlike my parents, Doug's distress didn't stem from disbelief. His was the pain of betrayal. I alone had known what became of our cousin after he fled home at sixteen and I'd been keeping that secret since, like a banished specter, he materialized in an East Village pub. Abe Skilton was Blake Bram, and Blake Bram was the serial murderer who held me captive in New York. Choosing to keep all of that to myself meant lying to Doug by omission. I had deceived him the entire time I was in Swanton last fall, when I returned to be with my family after learning about Uncle Brett's death and ended up piecing together a cold case that couldn't have hit closer to home. The silent treatment I was currently getting from Doug was all about my duplicity. That, at least, I deserved.

My next stop had been Aunt Felicia's, and it was the hardest of all. I sat Aunt Fee and Crissy down and told them the facts as I knew them – and by then, I knew a lot. With the help of the FBI and my former colleagues at the NYPD, I'd learned that Bram née Abe had killed before arriving in Manhattan. He'd spent most of his adult life searching for a woman who understood him the way that I had, a replacement for the companion he'd lost. But there's no replacement for an object of obsessive love, and one by one, they'd disappointed him. These were the details I'd been holding out for, but when it came time to reveal them to Abe's mother and sister, possessing those elusive truths didn't make things any easier. For years, I'd been telling myself my family would want to know why. Why did he become a murderer? Why did he kill those women? In the end, all Fee and Crissy really wanted to know was how I could live with myself.

'You should have told us,' they said. 'You owed us that.' I didn't know how to explain that Bram's blood lust was matched only by my determination to take him down before he could harm anyone else. His own family included.

I listened as Tim told me about the call with my mother. 'She just wanted to make sure you were OK.'

'Then she should have called me directly.'

'It's a step in the right direction, though, yeah?'

I tensed in spite of myself. Tim was on my side about most things, but this wasn't one of them. He believed that to get past their feelings of betrayal, my parents needed to work through their pain. I'd had months to absorb the barbarity of my cousin's crimes, he said, while to them, his violence was still abstract, reality as raw as a stitched-up wound. And I was the embodiment of all that hurt.

My outlook on the situation was a little different. It was me who'd watched my cousin fall. Me whose name was currently being dragged through the mud. Me who'd been held prisoner for eight hellish days. My family hadn't seen Bram's stomach-turning handiwork, or had to console the ravaged parents of his victims. I hoped they would remember how much I'd suffered in New York and come to understand what I'd been through since, but to acknowledge that was to acknowledge the horrors they still hoped were just a misunderstanding, some freakish waking nightmare that couldn't be real. I'd been trying to spare them. I had done it out of mercy. Yet here was my mother, so shattered she couldn't speak to her only daughter on the phone. Did she even understand the message her silence sent?

'Your mom sounded rough, I'll be honest,' said Tim, hooking a finger behind his ear where a dark curl of hair had gone astray.

'Well, that makes two of us.' He gave me a look, and I sighed. 'I don't like that she's suffering, obviously. It's just hard, knowing she feels more comfortable calling you than me.' As far as my parents were concerned, Tim was a work friend. A colleague forced to play middle man.

'Your mom's really close to your aunt, right? Maybe her reluctance to talk to you is about feeling like she's betraying Fee. I mean, Bram was Felicia's son.'

'Bram wasn't her son,' I said. 'Abe was. And Abe's been gone a long time.'

'Not to her.'

I looked down at my hand, still wrapped up with Tim's. Bram had been a cousin, a brother, a son. He'd been as much a part of the Merchant-Skilton family as I was, once. But he was also a killer, one of the worst New York State had seen in decades. I *couldn't* have told them, not while he was still alive. But in keeping it from them, I'd lost the thing that mattered to me most.

'They'll come around,' Tim said, his voice hopeful. 'They just need some time.'

It was what I'd been telling myself, too. *Time heals all wounds.* But I was starting to wonder if that was true. The wounds I'd inflicted on my family were deep, the kind that wouldn't heal easily.

The kind that left a scar.

FOUR

The search for Rebecca Hearst commenced on a muggy August morning under a sky the color of a gas flame. I didn't expect to be the one driving the police boat, but there I was behind the wheel of the Boston Whaler, water slapping against the hull as we sped toward the Thousand Islands Bridge.

When I left the A-Bay PD on Monday, I had believed there was a good chance Hearst's wife would turn up at a superior hotel in town, where she'd quietly been enjoying all the amenities the Admiral Inn lacked and taking some time for herself. Now, twenty-four hours later, we were boots on the ground.

In large part that was because of the weekend night clerk, whom I'd interviewed the previous afternoon. The incessant noise of my finger on the buzzer to his apartment in town had woken Jon Embers from a dead daytime sleep, and I'd questioned him on a plaid couch the color of Flamin' Hot Cheetos in a room that reeked of pot and BO. The argument Godfrey and Rebecca Hearst had was nasty, he told me, knuckling the crust from his eyes. A screaming match straight off reality TV.

'Guy was smashed,' Embers said. 'When they checked in on Sunday, they asked where they could eat and grab some drinks. I told them Bay Point Grill has good steaks. Bar there's open till eleven, too.'

Hearst had given me the same story, minus the part about being drunk when Rebecca disappeared. When I asked Embers what they were fighting about, he cited 'typical marriage stuff' in the world-weary voice of a man who'd seen it all, though he still had acne and the spotty facial hair of a high school freshman. 'He didn't like her giving him lip. She thought he was too controlling.'

'Controlling how?' I asked.

'The usual. She accused him of never letting her see her friends and said he was always criticizing. She didn't like that at all.'

A crude theory had occurred to me after that, the idea that Rebecca hadn't lost her phone so much as thrown it in the river. Rebecca must have known Hearst could track her. Maybe she got rid of the device so her domineering husband couldn't find her.

Rebecca wasn't tight with her family and didn't have many close friends in Utica – at least according to Godfrey Hearst's list. She'd moved up north from Florida in her teens, and was the only member of her family still living in New York State. Bogle had called every name on the list – and then he'd called every inn, hotel and resort in a forty-mile radius. The woman's height, weight, hair and eye color, tattoos, marks and scars had become the basis for a missing adult alert, and as of this morning, news of the disappearance was all over Jefferson County. It was a short ride from where we docked our police boat to the Thousand Islands Bridge and the location of that curious phone icon on Hearst's screen.

It was worth a look.

The wind whipped my bangs back and forth across my face, but I relished the momentary reprieve from the heat. This was why the Thousand Islands had attracted America's elite at the turn of the century, and all those Gilded Age industrialists in the decades that followed. August in Upstate New York could be brutal, especially on the mainland, but on the water it was always blissfully cool. With just the two of us on the boat, Tim leaned toward me and tucked a strand of wild hair behind my ear. The heat of his fingers on my skin made me smile – that, and the thrust of the two hundred-fifty horsepower engines at the stern of the boat. This was nothing like driving Tim's antique Lyman, the nautical equivalent of a 1950s Chevy Impala. The police vessel was built for speed, and speed was what we got when I nudged the throttles, the vibration of the dual handles zinging up my arm. Above us, the pale green bridge soared 150 feet toward that cloudless summer sky.

'If the phone was in the water, there wouldn't be a signal,' Tim said as I slowed down the boat. We were in the vicinity of the icon on Hearst's map, and there was nothing around us but river. Shoals were common in the St Lawrence, but not here in the channel, which served as a seaway for freighter ships traveling to the Great Lakes, sometimes all the way from Europe and Asia.

'Gorecki said the same thing at the station. But the signal's going strong. The phone has to be close.' I gestured to the device in Tim's hand, which we'd borrowed from Godfrey Hearst before heading out on the boat, and together we looked from left to right, studying the land on either side of us as our boat nodded in the water. The shore was crammed with houses, each with its own weather-worn dock extending into the river. The water was gloomy here, navy even in the daylight.

'So what are we thinking?' Tim asked, fingers gripping the bar of the T-top. The sleeve of his State Police jacket whispered in the breeze. 'The phone's around here somewhere, and she threw it from the bridge?'

Bracing myself against the pilot seat, I leaned my head back and gazed skyward. The underside of the bridge was so high I couldn't make out a single detail. It was an expanse of solid darkness above us. A highway in the night.

'Wouldn't be the craziest idea,' I said, 'if she was afraid of her husband.' But that was the piece of the puzzle that didn't quite fit, no matter how much force I used to mash it into place. People didn't like to part with their phones. If she was like most, Rebecca's cell was her lifeline, the chain that linked her to family, friends, coworkers and everyone in between. Studies showed going a single day without a mobile phone could make people anxious, and the younger their age, the more connected they were to their device. It would take a lot for someone like Rebecca to give hers up.

'It has to be here,' I said, eyes on the water once more. 'But where?'

Tim said, 'Head over to that island.'

To the left of us was Wellesley Island, one of the largest in the area and home to several residential communities, multiple golf courses and two popular state parks. Tim was pointing toward the mainland from which we'd come, opposite the river from Wellesley. There was an island there too, this one smaller, just off New York State's northern shore.

With a nod I swung the boat around, my own unzipped jacket flapping like a flag. As I drove, I tried to remember the island's name, but it was too small to stand out in my mind. Home to nothing more than a summer cottage that faced the channel, perched atop rocky terrain. I would need to look it up, though, because as we approached, I caught sight of an object gleaming at the edge of the shore.

'Well, I'll be damned,' Tim said when I'd pulled parallel to the island. There, on a patch of scraggly grass an arm's length from the water, its screen glinting in the sun, was a smartphone.

FIVE

I docked at the island and Tim jumped out, crossing the lawn in seconds flat. Hearst had given us a description of the item we were looking for – an iPhone 11 with a purple case. The phone on the grass had a splintered screen, but otherwise matched it to a tee.

Tim looked from the phone to the bridge and back again. 'Well. This is interesting.'

It certainly was. 'If her goal was to dispose of the thing,' I said, 'she would have aimed for the water. The river's a big target. Hard to miss.'

Tim was holding the phone with the hem of his shirt, and it lit up in his hand. The battery was low, but the fact that the damaged device was still working was a huge win when it came to tracking down our missing woman. 'The grass is pretty mossy here. Spongy.' Tim bounced a little on the balls of his feet. 'Whatever she was aiming for, it got a soft landing.'

'Maybe she didn't toss it. The screen could have gotten cracked some other way. Could she have been here, on this island? Maybe she knows the owner.'

'Hearst said this was their first visit to the area.'

'His, maybe. It's possible she came pre-marriage and didn't tell him.' I tapped a fingernail against my teeth. 'Let's talk to the homeowners. See what they know.'

No sooner were the words out of my mouth than I noticed a woman hurrying across the lawn. Her hands were clad in gardening gloves – which explained the flowers. A lush bed of red petunias encircled the house and ran along the edge of the entire island.

'Hello!' she called. 'What's going on?' Up close, the woman – early-fifties, disheveled bun, soil smudged across her cheek – looked like she hadn't slept in days. She introduced herself as Allison Novak, and we divulged what little information we were willing to share about how we came to be on her property.

'Do you know how this phone got here, Mrs Novak?' I asked.

'That's a question for my girls, but they're still sleeping. My daughters had a party out here last night. It must belong to one of their friends.'

'How old are your kids, Mrs Novak?' said Tim.

'Twenty-one. They're identical twins, juniors in college. One's at Ohio State and the other's at UConn. They're legal,' she reminded us, because she could see that I'd spotted the fire pit at the side of the house. The colorful Adirondack chairs that encircled it, and the empty beer cans littering the grass.

'How many people were here last night?'

'Six, I think,' she said. 'My two, and a few local friends.'

The odds that Rebecca Hearst from Utica, age twenty-nine and married, would somehow hook up with a group of college kids seemed unlikely. But then, finding her phone out here had seemed unlikely, too. 'Does the name Rebecca Hearst mean anything to you?' I asked.

'Rebecca?' She shook her head, bun bobbing. 'No. I know all the kids my girls hang out with here. No Rebeccas.' I watched as she processed what that meant. 'This Rebecca,' she said slowly, 'she was here last night?'

'That's what we're trying to find out,' said Tim.

'Who is she?'

I said, 'We're just gathering information right now. Any idea when the party started last night? How long it lasted?'

'Ugh, *late*. We sleep with the windows open. No A/C,' she explained. 'They didn't even get here until ten, and they were carrying on until almost three. Rick and I – that's my husband – we barely slept.'

Three o'clock. The text Hearst received from his wife had a time stamp of 2:04 a.m. If she was here, on this island, Novak's children and their friends would surely have seen her. The island would have been crowded with trees, once, but it had long since been clearcut. Aside from the small cottage, where the Novaks had lain awake fuming, there was no place to hide. Could Rebecca have texted her husband from somewhere else and come to the island after the college kids dispersed?

'Did you talk to your girls before they went to bed last night?' I asked.

'One of them, just briefly.'

'No mention of a stranger in your yard? African-American woman in her late twenties?'

She shook her head. 'This woman.' Novak looked wary now, and she plucked at the cuff of her teal Bermuda shorts as she spoke. 'You're trying to find her?'

'We're going to need to talk to your daughters,' I said.

As Tim and I waited for the woman to wake our potential witnesses, I let my gaze trail back to the river. The current moved so swiftly in the channel that it was visible to the naked eye, a rippling strip on the surface that swept past the island and upriver. If Rebecca was here last night, she had to have come by water, but aside from our police boat there was just one vessel tied up at the island's dock. Its name, painted along the side in the exact shade of red as the petunias, was *A Perfect Match*.

Tim's mouth was a tight line across his face, his eyebrows graded toward his nose. 'Why would Rebecca come here?'

The words were out before I could stop myself. 'Maybe it wasn't by choice.'

A year ago, before I joined the State Police, homicide would have been the farthest theory from any A-Bay investigator's mind. It wasn't that murder was unheard of in these parts, but it was definitely uncommon. Then came the Sinclairs. My first big case on the new job had been brutal; it was as if the Thousand Islands had saved up its horrors for decades and unleashed the reserve onto me. There was more violent crime to follow, culminating in Bram's death. I'd been no stranger to homicides back in New York. My mind was preconditioned to expect murder and mayhem.

Tim Wellington's mind was another story.

'Those girls could come out here in a minute and tell us they met Rebecca Hearst in town and brought her to their party,' he said. 'Right now, from where I'm standing, there's no evidence of foul play here.' For a second I was back on Tern Island, mouth agape as Tim tried to convince me that, with blood on the scene and a half-dozen motives aside, the Sinclair family's prodigal son had skipped town of his own volition. No matter how many atrocities befell his long-time home, Tim would never give credence to the cruelest of theories about his fellow man unless he had no other choice. I used to wonder if, as a detective, that was a knock against him, but I'd long since come to realize it was a plus. Because he was disinclined to jump to the blackest of conclusions, Tim's investigative methods were especially thoughtful. 'I hate to say it,' he went on, 'but there might be another explanation for what happened to Rebecca Hearst.'

High above us, the blare of a car horn resounded from the road. I dragged my gaze up to the bridge.

'She and her husband hadn't been getting along,' Tim said. 'From the sound of it, they fought a lot. And didn't the night clerk tell you he overheard Rebecca saying Godfrey isolated her from her friends? Her last message to him was "I'm sorry," no punctuation, no explanation.'

I'm sorry. There was a finality to the text that I found disturbing. 'You think she jumped,' I said.

Tim's eyebrows, dense as a thatch of grass, drew together. Like me, he couldn't keep his eyes off that impossibly high crest of green metal in the sky. He said, 'It would explain the phone's location and cracked screen. The Novaks' island is close to the bridge. Hitting it would be a long shot, but not impossible.'

'You're saying she dropped the phone while she was falling.'

'Or threw it in a panic.'

'When was the last time someone jumped off this thing?'

'It hasn't happened since I've been with the BCI,' he said. 'But it has happened. Honestly, I don't think there's a bridge in the country that hasn't enticed some poor sod having a dark night of the soul. I read somewhere that someone jumps off the Golden Gate every two weeks.'

I'd read that, too.

'Suicide,' I said, contemplating the idea. And by some stroke of luck – I wasn't sure if it was good or bad – the phone hadn't made the plunge with her.

Like a flash bulb igniting, something Tim said on Tern Island last fall came back to me. 'I know you're used to crazy cases in the city. Around here, the explanation's usually pretty simple.'

Except this time, where Rebecca Hearst was concerned, the simplest of possibilities was almost as terrible as the worst-case scenario Tim wished he could ignore.

SIX

A marine patrol vessel cruised soundlessly down the channel, its fractured blue lights glittering on the black water. On board, one of the two officers operated a military-grade searchlight that skimmed over the river's surface and penetrated the shadowy trees on the shore. To anyone watching, every movement the beam of light made would have looked like a wink, as if the boat was transmitting a message in Morse code. If any island residents noticed the boat that night, repeatedly snaking its way up and down that stretch of the river, we didn't know it. Back at the barracks, all hell had broken loose.

The vanishing of Rebecca Hearst had made the lead on Tuesday's five o'clock TV news, her photo stamped with the words '**Tourist Missing**' in bold black type. The BCI often relied on the media's help when it came to cases like this one, but there were times when that felt less like a helpful strategy and more like a necessary evil. In this case, that had a lot to do with Godfrey Hearst. I had no desire to terrify the public with talk of foul play, especially if this was a suicide, but Hearst was quick to don a fresh shirt, pose for the cameras, and throw around words like 'thin air' and 'without a trace.' I'd seen glimmers of real grief at the A-Bay PD. Now, Hearst's demeanor smacked of defiance.

'She didn't kill herself,' he said when Tim and I called him to the barracks, the sentiment punctuated by a fist slamming down on the table. Our intention had been to prod him for more information about Rebecca's state of mind, work in the questions that were used to screen for suicide risk, but Godfrey caught on and flew into a rage. He liked what we had to say next even less.

When Allison Novak's daughters emerged from the house bleary-eyed and still stinking of booze, they assured us there was no way they could have missed a stranger on the small island. That had left us with the Thousand Islands Bridge. As a border bridge it had webcams, the footage from which Tim and I were able to obtain and review. While there was no evidence of a jumper, there were a couple of blind spots, and it was feasible Rebecca could have occupied one of them. Erring on the side of caution, I'd sent Bogle and Sol back out in the boat to do a more thorough search of the shoreline.

They found it floating next to the dock at the Price Chopper, where islanders tie up their boats while shopping for groceries. A woman's flip-flop, sunny pineapples embroidered on the pink strap. It matched the description I'd taken from Godfrey Hearst back at the A-Bay station.

The shoe belonged to Rebecca Hearst.

Things moved quickly after that.

The day had dawned clear again, a bluebird morning so scorching hot even the air above the water wiggled, and the underarms of my button-down were soaked through by eight a.m. Summer was my least favorite season. That had a lot to do with my job. Sure, there were the boat rides and glasses of Sauvignon Blanc sipped in angled Adirondack chairs designed to enforce lounging. In the North Country, lawns were shorn within an inch of their lives, but they abutted fields of yellow and purple wild-flowers so vibrant they seemed unreal, and the river – cold, fresh, wild – always beckoned. Those things, I'd come to enjoy, but I had never gotten over the trauma of summers spent in the city, navigating streams of garbage soup and trying not to think about what fattened up the flies now big as bumblebees, their bodies meat-hungry and hairy. To me, at least to some extent, summer still meant needing to find the dead as fast as possible so they didn't have to rot alone in the merciless sun.

That Wednesday morning, daybreak brought not just blue and bird calls but the *thwack-thwack* of chopper blades reverberating across the water. The helicopter was the new Bell UH-1 Huey added to our North Country fleet, painted navy, white and gold. It looked completely out of place against the natural beauty of the river. So did the police boats with divers on board. This was nothing like that covert night search. Calls flooded in from the islands up and down the channel when they arrived, first to the PD and then, when the dispatcher remained tight-lipped, to the *Thousand Islands Sun*. The whole of Alexandria Bay was abuzz with talk of the missing tourist.

The divers were muscled and tattooed and wore grim expressions, all business as they yanked wetsuits over their sturdy bare torsos with a smack. 'Hell of a job,' Tim muttered under his breath as we watched. If we were lucky – the word made me cringe – the men in their dive masks wouldn't leave this place empty-handed.

While they readied themselves for the plunge, my gaze drifted to the nearest island. Four adults and a gaggle of kids had gathered on its shore, an extended family with their eyes on the divers. One of the women took out her cell phone and held it steady, videoing the scene on her doorstep. It wasn't so unlike rubbernecking a car crash, considering the unusual activity on the river, but the sight of that phone and the kids pointing excitedly at the chopper above sickened me all the same. I kept staring, and eventually the lady with the phone noticed me out on the boat. We locked eyes. She lowered her arm. Turning swiftly away from the water, she ushered the children inside.

What would happen if one of those children discovered a corpse today, broken and bloated, hideous in every way? The current ran downriver from the bridge, the St Lawrence wending its way around rocky shorelines and under docks gray with age. We'd found Rebecca's shoe next to just such a dock, and Tim had told me other things tended to get stuck under them, too. Fallen branches. Beach balls. The troopers had checked the docks nearest to the bridge and found nothing, but I was still on edge.

All morning long the calls kept coming, not viable tips that might lead us to our victim but inquiries about the helicopter, a rare and curious sight. Some of the callers asked if they were witnessing a training exercise. Only those watching closely, like the woman on the island or any residents who might have seen that boat in the night, knew the truth. Helicopters and divers and search boats like ours had only two jobs, and this was no training mission.

It was a mission to recover a body.

SEVEN

I t was late morning by the time we got back to the barracks, and someone was waiting for me in the lobby, chatting up the uniform sergeant who manned the phone line to the dispatch center in Oneida. The man's eyes lit up when he saw me. 'Got a second?' he asked, standing too close. 'It's about all this fuss with the missing tourist.'

I'd had little interaction with Chester Bell since arriving in A-Bay. All I really knew about the guy was that he owned Sir Robert Peel Boat Tours, named for the British steamer plundered off Wellesley Island following the war of 1812. Bell, as it turned out, was also president of the Alexandria Bay Chamber of Commerce Pirate Days Committee. And he wanted to talk.

It took some time to get Bell into my office. He and Tim first had to exchange pleasantries, Tim remarking on Bell's slimmer middle. Apparently, at the behest of his wife who insisted that heart disease ran in the family, Bell had taken up biking. He'd lost twenty pounds as a result, and had never felt better. Cherub-faced with squinty eyes and pouty lips, Bell was a hard man to take seriously. I'd seen him outside the charter office before and always thought of him as unremarkable, but toward the middle of last year, Bell had acquired a full, dark beard and grown out his hair. He had a pompadour now, swollen and slick, and was wearing a vintage bowling shirt. As I listened to him chat with Tim, I wondered if Bell's transformation had anything to do with A-Bay's recent notoriety. I wouldn't have been shocked to discover he was trying to parlay the town's fifteen minutes of fame into a Discovery Channel reality show in which he'd play a starring role.

'I assume you know why I'm here,' Bell said once finally seated in front of my desk. When I lifted my eyebrows, he added, 'Pirate Days. I'm in charge of making sure it goes smoothly.'

'That's great.' Truth be told, I didn't envy the man his job.

Managing sword-fighting marauders and sandcastle building competitions sounded like a royal pain in the ass.

'Pirate Days is big,' he explained, tetchy now. 'Huge, in fact. Sometimes we attract more than a thousand people. We're talking massive crowds. These are the busiest days of the year for merchants here in town.'

'Including your tour business, I bet.'

Bell colored. 'Well, yes. Pirate Days benefits everyone.'

'How can I help, Mr Bell?' I said, suppressing a sigh.

'Well, we all know about the woman who went missing from the Admiral Inn.'

'Yes. There's a search and rescue mission underway.' I sounded more confident than I felt. We'd brought out the cavalry, and so far we'd failed to recover more than a single shoe. We'd searched, yes. But rescues were scarce.

'That's good,' said Bell, 'because we don't need some family from Michigan or a kid on a jet ski stumbling on to a –' his flush deepened as he struggled to find the words – 'a *missing person* with their rental pontoon.'

So that's what's eating at Bell. When the troop commander in Oneida deployed the helicopter and dispatched the divers, Pirate Days was the farthest thing from my mind. But Chet Bell was thinking of it now – had been, probably, since he first heard about Rebecca Hearst. While the celebration was concentrated in downtown A-Bay, Pirate Days didn't only play out on land. I'd been concerned that a local might stumble across her remains, but at that very moment, incoming tourists from Buffalo, Plattsburgh, and beyond were transporting their bass boats and Sea-Doos north to frolic in the St Lawrence, right where our operation had set up shop. There was the antique boat show to think about, too. It had taken place last weekend, the race boat regatta long since passed, but a lot of owners stuck around to cap off their vacation with street beer and buccaneers. This time of year, especially on days as hot as these, boat traffic on the water could triple, the usual trickle engorging to a steady flow. I'd seen boaters zipping around our divers just that morning, showering us with their wake as their heads turned our way. Whether Rebecca Hearst had jumped off the Thousand Islands Bridge or drowned by some other means, the evidence suggested that her body was in the St Lawrence, and it needed to be recovered fast.

'I can assure you we're doing everything we can to find her,' I said, and meant it.

'To be honest, ma'am, that's not my only concern.'

'It's not?'

He held my gaze in a way that suggested the man believed he held sway over me. As if he'd somehow forgotten I was leading this investigation. Bell was smirky and self-important, and that combination always boiled my blood. 'It's the negative press, you see,' he said. 'I'm really hoping we can keep the incident as quiet as possible.'

'The incident.' Like we were talking about a kid stealing a Hot Wheels car from the supermarket checkout lane.

'The missing girl,' he said. 'Before the national press gets ahold of it, I mean. What's happening out there, with the helicopter and all that police activity under the bridge, it's not exactly subtle. I've been keeping an eye on social media – the whole chamber has – and two videos of your search boats and divers are already up online. *Two*.' Bell's fingers popped up in the shape of a V. 'By the time I found them, they had a total of eight hundred views.'

I thought of the mother on the island, filming us while her children looked on. 'Unfortunately, that kind of thing happens. Especially these days,' I said. 'Everyone has a phone, and a lot of people like to think of themselves as citizen journalists.'

Stroking his beard, Bell said, 'That may be, but the last thing we want is for the press to sit up and take notice, because we both know where that leads. They'll make the connection between this unfortunate event and your cousin. I'm sure you're not interested in being thrust back on to the front page.' With a pitying look, he added, 'It's been quite a year for you here, hasn't it?'

Quite a year. That was one way of putting it. Like everyone else in the state, and many beyond its borders, Chet Bell had heard about my connection to Bram. It made sense that local merchants would be reading all those features about Bram's life and his link to A-Bay as they waited to see how the spotlight would affect their sales. But Bell's comment about the past year felt like a personal affront. I'd solved the Sinclair case, yes, but I wasn't proud of my behavior on Tern Island, which could have resulted in a law suit, or worse. And then there was the recent murder of Hope Oberon, and the horrors that followed. If Bell thought he was the only one who wasn't happy with my track record, he was sorely mistaken.

'We're on it,' I said, chin lifted, gaze thin. 'My last few cases have been a challenge. I don't deny that. But this is different.' I folded my lips in on themselves, searching for the right way to explain. 'The climate around here, it's changed. Certain . . . dangers have been neutralized. There are fewer uncertainties. There's no such thing as a typical investigation, and I don't think it's prudent to assume this one will be entirely without surprises. But right now, Mr Bell, there's no reason to think this case will be anything other than standard procedure. Tragic, yes, but quickly resolved.'

Bell thought about my response for longer than I would have liked. At length, through an ersatz smile, he said, 'Listen. I know you can't control everything. Crime happens, you respond and do what you need to. I get all that. But it hasn't even been four months since . . .'

Blake Bram. Abe Skilton.

'. . . since *that man* was removed from the equation. We're just starting to get back on our feet, here. Revenue is up, but we're coming off a winter that could have ruined us. Our merchants need Pirate Days to be bigger than ever. We're doing everything we can to make that happen – the money we've spent on advertising would make your head spin. This upcoming week is the last hurrah, our only other chance to bring in profits before Labor Day, profits we sorely need to make it through the off-season. None of us want to see our efforts to rebuild this town's reputation derailed.'

Did he imagine we were dragging our feet on finding Godfrey Hearst's wife? That our divers were laid out on the decks of those search boats, working on their tans? 'What exactly are you asking of me?' I said.

Chet Bell put up both hands and smiled. 'All I'm asking is for you and your team to move quickly on this. It's the least you can do for this town.'

It's the least you can do . . . after your cousin turned this paradise into a killing field. I heard the insinuation in his words loud as a cigarette boat's V8 engine.

'Mr Bell. I appreciate the position you're in, and I have no doubt ensuring a successful Pirate Days event is every bit as critical as you claim,' I said. 'But I need to remind you that a woman is missing, presumed dead. Her husband is still here in town, waiting on pins and needles for news, living in the worst state of limbo you could imagine. We all want to find Rebecca Hearst and put this case to bed.'

'It's Wednesday,' Bell said, hands spread on his knees now, already halfway out of his chair. 'Most folks won't get to town until Friday. I have every confidence that you'll be able to wrap this up before then.'

Wrap it up. Like a missing persons investigation was an unwanted street performance, the disappearance of a tourist a pothole to be filled. The tops of my ears were red-hot. I didn't answer to Bell, with his hip hairstyle and self-serving demands. He had no authority over me or my work. My knee-jerk reaction was to tell him off and kick his toned ass out of my office, but I couldn't bring myself to do either, because I did owe it to A-Bay to help the town recover.

And I didn't want a woman's mysterious disappearance in a place that would forever be associated with Blake Bram to go viral any more than Chet Bell did.

EIGHT

'Christ, that man can be myopic. God forbid a recovery effort should get in the way of celebrating a pirate who's been dead for a hundred and fifty years.'

On James Street, baking in the full noon sun in clothes that felt dense as velvet with my phone slippery against my ear, I listened to Sheriff Maureen McIntyre rant. There were only two people in A-Bay I trusted implicitly, and the call I'd made to Tim on the drive downtown had gone unanswered. It was just as well, because Mac wasn't so much a friend as a mentor and savior, all rolled into one lanky quinquagenarian with a puff of feathered blonde hair that would look more at home on a daytime soap than in the Jefferson County's sheriff's office. She was the first person I'd opened up to about my abduction and post-traumatic stress. I didn't need to explain to Mac how bushwhacked I felt by Chet Bell.

'Ignore everything he said,' she told me. 'It's only going to get in the way of your work.'

I paused on the sidewalk to catch my breath. My skin was damp all over, my button-down glued to my stomach as rivulets of sweat pooled between my breasts. 'I'm trying, I really am, but the last thing I need is this guy shaking my confidence.'

'Chet's a talker, always has been,' said Mac. 'He's been involved with the Chamber of Commerce since back when I had your job, and he's good at rallying the troops. People know him, and some may blame you for things beyond your control – the town's reputation, the downturn in hotel bookings, Chet's goddamn boat tour ticket sales. But none of that matters right now, OK? You just focus on finding this woman.'

McIntyre wasn't one to shy away from conflict, but Bell's demand had clearly put her on edge, and that made me nervous, too. How much power did this guy have around here? Enough to make sure I was a permanent outcast? I was an investigator with the plainclothes detective branch of the New York State

Police, and Alexandria Bay was in my jurisdiction. It was also my home. I needed this community to trust me, but I'd be damned if I was going to cater to Chet Bell's whims.

'You're right, as always,' I told Mac, hoping I had managed to keep the doubt out of my voice. 'I've gotta run. Quick stop at the Bean-In to grab some lunch for the team.'

'Well, at least you're eating. Small victories, right?'

I thanked her, hung up, and turned toward the coffee shop. On the sidewalk to my left, I saw something that caused me to stop. I made my hand into a blade to shade my eyes against the sun.

I'd noticed the car parked on the next block, a dented blue sedan with New York plates, upon pulling up. When I first passed it, the engine had been running, windows down despite the hundred-degree heat. I remembered the meaty arm flung over the side. The open palm slapping out a hollow beat against the vehicle's driver-side door. Now, the car sat abandoned and its occupants stood immobile on the sidewalk. Staring straight at me.

'Can I help you?' I asked as they peeled their feet from the gum-sticky sidewalk and came closer. Neither one of them was familiar. I took them for Hispanic, with hair and eyes a deep shade of brown, and there was enough of a resemblance between them to make me wonder if they were kin. The woman's hair was long and loose, the man's so thoroughly shorn it looked like a black skull cap.

For a second, I wondered if they needed help. I rarely wore my State Police jacket in summer if I wasn't on the water, but if they'd been watching, they might have noticed my unmarked Chevy Malibu across the way, the lights in the back window dark. Even as that thought passed through my mind, though, I knew I was wrong.

I wasn't used to the awkwardness of being recognized in public, and probably never would be. Was this what fame felt like? Was I destined to live out my days as a sideshow attraction? I didn't bother to glance over my shoulder in case the people with the aggressive stances and stormy expressions were here for someone else. I knew better than to hope for that. My image belonged to the masses now, my face and story up for grabs, and even before we were toe to toe I knew the couple had come to challenge me. It was in the slant of their mouths and the intensity of their stares. These two had read the papers, and they were not on my side.

'It's you.' The woman ran her eyes down my body. 'You're Shana Merchant.' It was an indictment, the words both confident and disbelieving. They almost sounded rehearsed.

'That's right,' I said, already defensive and working to keep that out of my voice. 'Do you need something?'

'Need something?' The woman's laugh was dark. 'It's a little late for that.' There was nothing intimidating about her, in theory. She was dressed in a fluttery cap-sleeve shirt, high-waisted jeans and sneakers, with skillfully-applied make-up. She had the look of a thirty-something new mother, youthful and curvy in the bust and hips, and had she been smiling she would have seemed very approachable. That tone, though. The daggers in her eyes were sharp enough to skin a cat, and they were aimed directly at me.

There were a few ways I could play this. The first was to shut her down. Whatever the woman thought of me, however she felt, I didn't need to hear it. What I needed was to focus on finding Rebecca Hearst, just like Mac said.

There was another track I could take. A decade of working in law enforcement had taught me it was sometimes better to give people the stage. Let the nonsense they spew roll right off my back – especially if it had to do with Bram. 'You don't owe them anything,' Tim had said when the stories started hitting newsstands, 'not an explanation or an apology. They don't know the half of what you've been through.'

I went for option three: the obliging benevolence that I strived for in my everyday job. 'Why don't you start by telling me your name,' I said calmly, 'and then you can tell me why you're here.'

For a split second the woman's face opened up in surprise, only to shutter again. 'You don't even know who I am. I told you, and *mamá*, too. She doesn't even recognize me.' This she said to her companion – her brother, apparently, who hadn't so much as blinked since she started talking. Tattoos wound around both of his wrists, two black links of chain.

I studied their faces again, but I was certain I couldn't place either of them. *Should* I know them? What made them think I would? As I racked my brain, a vein in the man's forehead bulged.

'We're not stupid,' she told me, the words a hiss. 'We know we can't touch you. I bet you wish we would. Then you could retaliate, right? It doesn't take much these days for people like you to cry self-defense.' Chin raised, she shook her head. 'God, I can't even believe I used to defend people like you.'

'People like me.' She'd said that twice now.

'Cops.' Her eyes flashed. She wore a long gold necklace that disappeared into her tank top, and she plucked at the chain as she spoke. 'It used to break my heart when a story about a crooked cop hit the news. I told myself those were the bad apples. There were plenty of good guys out there who'd sooner die than hurt someone or their department, who would give their life for a fellow officer. I *believed* that.' She made a fist and thumped her breastbone, so hard it had to hurt. I saw tears in her eyes now, pain writ large across her pinched face, but that did little to veil her rage. 'But not you, *Shana*.' A chill trickled down my spine, turning me cold. 'You put that evil bastard first and let him kill an innocent man.'

'Enough.' Shoulders pinned back, I took a step forward. A small crowd was gathering around us: a biker couple covered in tattoos; a family holding ice cream cones that were rapidly melting, trails of rainbow sherbet snaking down the children's scrawny arms. I raised my hands in warning. 'I don't know who you are or why you're here. I'm sorry, but I have work to do.'

'Who I am?' Again the woman laughed, the sound weighted with menace. Her smile turned black. 'I am Estella Lopez, wife of Jay Lopez, the man you left to die in that basement. And I'm here to make your life a living hell.'

NINE

You don't owe them anything.

I wanted to believe Tim when he said that, to accept I'd done the best I could even if others didn't see it that way – but how could I? There were people out there who'd lost a loved one to Blake Bram, and with Bram gone, they had no one to blame but me. My cousin took something from them that couldn't be replaced, and the way I saw it, I *did* owe them. If lobbing obscenities at me online provided even a shred of comfort to the friends and relatives and siblings of the dead, I'd take their virtual punches all day long.

Somehow, it never occurred to me that I might have to look one of them in the face.

Jay Lopez was a stranger to me before the day he stepped into my basement cell. He'd been a beat cop fresh out of the academy, a husband and father of three with rakish curls and a cheerful demeanor that I didn't get to witness but read about in the news after his death. Lopez's paternal grandfather had been on the force in Puerto Rico, one of just ten thousand officers who served more than three million citizens there. The man had been a hero to Lopez, and he'd wanted nothing more than to follow his example. Bram robbed Jay Lopez of his dream. Punched a hole into an unsuspecting family. And now, his widow wanted retribution.

I felt clammy and off-kilter on the drive back to the barracks, like I was coming down with a nasty bout of the flu. I had thought about Jay Lopez's family many times in recent months, and spent countless hours wondering whether I should track down his widow and beg forgiveness for failing to stop Bram from killing her husband. Stop him from ever killing again. After I was rescued, I hated myself for what I'd failed to do. I'd walked out of that basement on my own steam, but I'd left so much behind.

It was Carson Gates who talked me out of contacting Lopez's wife, back when he was still my therapist, before he became my fiancé. 'You shouldn't feel guilty, Shana,' he'd said, chin in his hand and one leg crossed over the other so his pantleg slid up to reveal a pair of Sriracha sauce socks, the red bottles lined up like soldiers at the battlefront. 'You were under Blake Bram's spell. Spending eight days in captivity with only a charming psychopath for company will do that to a person. You may be a police officer trained to prevent violent crime –' he'd graded his body toward me then, narrowing the gap between us – 'but you can't be blamed for putting your own safety first.'

I had blamed myself, though. That day, and every moment since. And when Carson, like so many others, lost his life to Bram despite my efforts to keep my cousin's violence in check, I realized I always would.

'She's not wrong,' I told Mac and Tim in my office as I pinched a hangnail between my teeth. I wasn't one to gnaw at my cuticles, but lately they were ragged as a torn hem. 'I was NYPD back then, and so was Lopez. We were the same, he and I, and I let him die.'

'Shana.' This was the tone Mac used when she expected more from me. 'The woman's entitled to her pain. Looking for someone to blame for a death . . . that's as natural as tears at a funeral. Estella Lopez's pain has nothing to do with you,' she said. 'You didn't shoot her husband. You were as much of a victim as he was.'

I hooked a finger behind my ear in search of the hair I used to find there, and felt the familiar jolt of shock that came from realizing it was gone. The cut had been a bad idea. It only made me feel more exposed.

Tim knelt beside the chair I'd slithered on to like a discarded scarf. 'You tried,' he said softly. 'I know you blame yourself for not being able to follow through with detaining Bram, but you need to remember your trauma made that impossible. And if you *had* killed Bram that day, all those other women he snuffed out along the way would still be cold cases. Their families wouldn't have answers. You couldn't save Becca, Lanie, and Jess. You couldn't save Jay Lopez. But you were able to give those other families some peace,' he said, 'and I'm sure Lopez's wife will come to realize that.'

'Tim's right,' said Mac. 'What happened to her husband, it's all fresh in her mind again because . . . well, because Bram's finally gone. You can't change that – no one can. Coming up here to avenge his death may feel like the right thing to her right now, but that won't last. Pretty soon, it's going to sink in that you're not your cousin, and they'll let it all go.'

'I don't know,' I said as I scoured my eyes with the heels of my hands. 'Estella seems pretty determined to "make my life a living hell".'

'That's not going to happen,' said Mac.

'An empty threat,' said Tim.

I wasn't so sure. I had run the plates on the blue sedan as soon as I got back to the barracks. The car belonged to Javier Barba, Estella's brother, and he lived in Flatbush. Jay Lopez's family, I knew, lived in the city, too. These two had driven all the way from New York, five-and-a-half hours not counting traffic, just to look me in the eye as they condemned me. 'They tracked me all the way up here like bounty hunters with a hot tip. They're not just going to quietly slink back home again.'

Mac said, 'How the hell did they find you, anyway?'

The news stories had been thorough. My profession, the recent relocation to A-Bay, my hometown in Vermont, all featured in the narrative that had sold papers by the bundle. So far, though, I'd managed to avoid getting doxed. My home address, phone number and license plate were known only to friends and locals, and I didn't think it likely that Estella and Javier had any other connection to bitty A-Bay. I would have known if they'd followed me from the barracks. I didn't spend as much time looking over my shoulder as I used to, but my senses were still finely tuned to suspicious behavior. After years of hypervigilance, I doubted my surveillance skills would ever go away. 'They were parked outside the Bean-In when I got there,' I said. 'Almost like they were waiting for me to show up.'

'That's weird,' said Tim. 'How would they know where you like to get your lunch?'

Call it intuition, one of those hunches that nips the back of your neck and twists until you take notice. I pulled my smartphone from my pocket, typed my name into Google, and hit News. 'Holy shit,' I said, staring at the words on the screen.

A Criminal in our Midst.

The title stopped me dead. It was a letter, an opinion piece published by the *Watertown Daily Times*. The timestamp on the post was August seventh. *Yesterday.* I chewed my bottom lip as I skimmed, key words and phrases leaping off the screen.

Former NYPD . . . Captor was her first cousin . . . Relocated to our beloved town of Alexandria Bay . . .

By the time I reached the middle of the letter, I was tasting blood.

> Ms Merchant wasted no time inserting herself into the local community, a place she is expected to protect as a senior investigator with the State Police's Bureau of Criminal Investigation. It's unclear exactly how Ms Merchant passed the time at the State Police station while Blake Bram was terrorizing Jefferson County, but any local will tell you that in recent months, you'd be as likely to find her kicking back at hangouts like the Bean-In and The Dot as investigating her cousin's ungodly crimes.

A wave of nausea rose in my throat and I felt my hands start to tremble.

> One wonders why Ms Merchant, who spent ten years studying martial arts in New York City and currently trains at Shaolin Kempo of Watertown, was unable to defend herself against Blake Bram when a fellow police officer's life was at stake. One thing is certain: the BCI would have to be asleep on the job not to immediately terminate Merchant's employment and charge her with obstruction of justice.

The letter was signed Gracelyn Barlowe. *What the hell?* This wasn't an op-ed, it was an exposé, incendiary and cruel, and it put my entire life in A-Bay on display. It hadn't even been up for twenty-four hours, and in that short time it had provided Jay Lopez's family with all the intel they needed to know.

Tim and Mac had come to stand beside me and were reading the letter over my shoulder. 'This was written by Gracelyn Barlowe?' Tim said it quietly. 'I think that's Juliet Barlowe's mother.'

Juliet Barlowe – she'd kept her maiden name – was Don Bogle's wife. That made Gracelyn Barlowe my fellow investigator's mother-in-law. 'I feel sick,' I said, slapping the phone down on my desk. More than that, I felt wobbly. I recognized the sensation for what it was: a panic attack, sharpening its claws on the desktop. Preparing to pounce.

Anxiety is a cheap wine glass shattered on a tile floor. You can try to clean it up, but there's always a chance that you'll step on a stray shard. After a few days you grow complacent, sure the threat is gone. All the while a splinter has been festering in your heel, so deeply imbedded that you wonder if it's part of you now, for good.

'Unbelievable.' Mac had picked up my phone, and there was fire in her eyes. 'I swear that woman's got more nerve than Boldt Castle has bricks.'

'They couldn't have known for sure you'd be at the Bean-In today,' said Tim. 'They must have been actively looking for you.'

'Oh, God.' There was a vice around my lungs. The idea of Jay Lopez's family prowling around town for days was suffocating. There was no shortage of people who, if asked, would gladly have given me up. Had Estella Lopez questioned them? Stopped them on the street to tell them I was an accomplice to murder?

Tim was watching me closely. 'OK, let's just calm down. I'll talk to those two from New York.' He put a hand on my shoulder. 'It's going to be OK.'

'Is it?' I pulled away so fast I sent my wheeled chair wobbling across the room. 'Bram's crimes? My abduction? They're never going away.' They were a finger trap clamped to my nails. It was not going to be OK.

I bit back the desire to cuss and scream. I drew a breath and said, 'You don't know what it's been like these past months. The sneaking around I've had to do just to get to the bank or the Price Chopper for a damn bag of groceries.'

'I can help with all that,' said Tim.

He could. A-Bay loved Tim Wellington like a prince, and that wasn't hyperbole. Tim had emerged from the day of Bram's death like a venerated cowboy. He'd taken a bullet for his town, while I'd been exposed as a traitor. Judas Iscariot in State Police gear.

'I'm a curse on this place,' I said, pacing the room like it was a cage. 'I can't live this way. The judgment. The hiding. I didn't think it mattered. But it does.'

My breath was coming in gulps. I hadn't felt this way since Tern Island. I wanted to go home, where I was free to wallow without scrutiny or fear of judgment. The way it ought to be.

'Shana,' Tim said, making a shushing noise under his breath. 'Breathe, OK? Just like Carson taught you.'

Before Carson Gates was killed, Tim would rarely utter his name. He hated the scheming, duplicitous man who'd once been his closest friend. Hated the way Carson gaslighted me throughout our relationship even more. Was there *anything* Bram hadn't changed?

I closed my eyes. Imagined Carson telling me to 'connect with the breath.' All I could see was another victim I'd tried and failed to save.

'I need some air,' I said.

TEN

Neither Tim nor Mac tried to stop me when I made a dash for the door. Beads of sweat sprang from my forehead within seconds of stepping into the heat, and between the atmosphere indoors and the humidity out, there was a weighted blanket on my chest. Standing on the steps of the barracks, I stared at the brittle field that stretched beyond the parking lot. *This place.* It was so rural, the village down the road a glitch in a desolate landscape of corn fields and tumbledown barns at the northernmost edge of New York. I hadn't known it was possible to feel claustrophobic in a place so bereft of life.

'You look like you could use a smoke.'

Hand to my heart, I spun around toward the side of the building.

It didn't matter that I'd seen him a hundred times before; Don Bogle was just as startling as the first day I met him. At six foot six with that shaved head and skin so deeply pocked he could have studded his cheeks with Smarties, Bogle wasn't the calming presence I needed.

The pack of cigarettes in his hand, however, was another story.

'Give me one of those,' I said as I slid into the shade of the building. I hadn't had a cigarette in years, was only a social smoker to begin with, but all I cared about right then was quieting my nerves and getting my mind off the image of Jay Lopez's uniform sodden with his own blood.

Bogle raised his eyebrows and looked down at me. 'You sure? I was kind of kidding.'

'I'm sure.' I accepted the pack and tapped out a smoke. The act felt foreign, the cigarette's papery firmness unfamiliar, but I tucked it between my lips and leaned toward the lighter in Bogle's hand. Smoke clawed at my throat as it went down. I closed my eyes and let the nicotine do its work.

'Bad day?'

I gave Bogle a look that turned him serious.

'Sorry. Dumb question,' he said.

The cautious anticipation in his expression took me back to the spring, when I'd confessed everything about my history with Blake Bram. Inside Tim's cottage I'd found the men waiting, the table set for four, three seats already taken. The air swam with the residual heat from the oven, and my vision swam with it.

'No more secrets,' I told them after I'd taken my place. 'I've been living that way for too long. It's all out in the open now, and you're going to read some damning stuff about me. You probably already have.' Sol and Bogle traded a glance that told me I was right. 'I want you to know the full story. The real one.'

I looked to Tim then, who gave a nod. I took a breath, and began.

'It was on the eighth day that I decided to kill him.'

It had been the only way I knew of to divest myself of my sins. To live with what had happened. To *live*. I wasn't Catholic, but I imagined that unburdening was similar to what went on in a confessional booth. Nowhere else was there a complete record of my whole experience, gaps plugged and questions answered. The secret I'd worked so hard to conceal from my family, my colleagues, the world, was out, and I wanted my team to know the truth. That night, Bogle had listened without judgment. He did the same now.

'Please tell me you didn't know your mother-in-law was going to skewer me in the local press,' I said after explaining about Estella and her brother.

'Wait, what?'

'That's how they found me.' When, blowing out a hot stream of smoke, I paraphrased Gracelyn Barlowe's opinion piece, Bogle's eyes went cold. 'What the fuck,' he said, 'was she thinking?'

I could only shake my head.

'Gracelyn's a loose cannon,' he said roughly, flicking ash from his own cigarette with a yellowed thumb. 'I don't like to talk shit about Juliet's mom, but that woman has always felt entitled to take what she wants. It kind of runs in the family. It's not right, what she did. I'm sorry, Shana.'

'Not your fault. But I guess I'd better start thinking about getting a new routine.' The exposure wasn't only an issue where Lopez's family was concerned. There were a lot of crazies out there, and I didn't like the idea that any one of them could track me to my favorite hangouts at will.

'And her husband was that guy from New York?' Bogle said, changing the subject back to Estella. 'The rookie Bram killed in the basement?'

'That's right.'

Watching me, he ran a flipper-sized hand over his skull. 'They threaten you, boss?'

'They're angry,' I said simply. 'What Gracelyn wrote isn't entirely wrong – but it's also nowhere near the whole story.' I thought about the *People* magazine piece. The writer had reprinted a photo that the *Watertown Daily Times* ran of me after the Sinclair case, when I first started actively looking for Bram. Tim and I had been in Oneida, taking our licks at headquarters, and I'd known that Jared Cunningham, a beat reporter for the paper, was keen for a scoop. The candid shot Cunningham used in that *Watertown Times* feature had served a purpose for me, too: it was the first step toward flushing Bram out of hiding by luring him back to me. But I'd forgotten the physical toll the hunt had taken on my body. In the photo, which now filled half a page in a magazine with a circulation in the millions, I looked like a beaten-down loser who'd abandoned all hope. That did little to help me argue the case that I was a consummate pro.

'All these news stories,' I said, rolling the cigarette between my fingers, 'they're just so . . . incomplete. They don't talk about the hail of shame I feel for letting Bram live freely for as long as he did, or the guilt over hiding his crimes from my family. From everyone.'

'So, what, these people blame you for a murder you had nothing to do with?' Bogle pushed back his shoulders as he said it, and I was grateful he'd been nowhere near Estella and Javier when they confronted me. His looks were his primary means of intimidation, but the man oozed alpha male energy, and I didn't know him well enough to gauge his ability to keep his cool.

I said, 'They have a right to be angry.'

'Not with you, they don't. Look,' he said, 'if my wife did something terrible, would you hold me responsible?'

'Depends. Were you standing right there when she did it? Did you try to intervene?'

'All due respect, you're missing the point. My wife and me, we have personal autonomy over our lives. We're free to make our own decisions, independent of anyone else. So are you. And so was Bram.'

I looked down at the cigarette in my hand, its poppy-orange cherry aglow. I didn't know if it was the smoke or the stress or the unbearable heat, but I was woozy all over again. 'Thanks for this,' I said, pinching what was left of the cigarette between my fingers as I prepared to grind it out.

'Not like that.' Bogle plucked it away, tapped the cherry against the building's shaded wall, and folded the butt into my hand. 'In case you need it later.'

'Somehow I don't think this is going to solve my problems.'

'Well, it can't hurt.'

I smiled. Thought about telling him taking up smoking actually could make things worse, and decided to hold my tongue. I slipped the butt into my pocket and said, 'Thanks for the talk, Don.'

'Anytime. And if you ever need me to lend a hand – more than usual, I mean – I got you. Hey.' He caught me by the arm. 'Lopez's family? They're here because you're all over the news right now. You're an easy target. I know you don't need me to tell you this, but you should watch your back.'

'Watch my back?'

'If this situation shows us anything, it's that these guys aren't messing around. It takes balls to come up here and confront an officer of the law without an ounce of concern for the consequences. I didn't see how this thing went down, but confronting you doesn't read like a spontaneous decision. You said Estella was calm, yeah? The brother, too? That tells me they had time to prepare for the moment. To plan. Which means they might be planning other things, too.'

I blinked at him through the lingering, liver-colored smoke. Took in Bogle's flat face and drooping eyes. I saw only sincerity in both. Don Bogle had made no effort to console me. Instead, his advice was to prepare for the worst. Face facts, and armor-up.

It wasn't exactly what I wanted to hear. As much as I'd resisted Tim's sympathy, I hoped his theory would prove out, and that the visitors would quickly realize being here with me wouldn't change a thing. At the same time, Bogle's warning rang true. By all indications, Estella Lopez and Javier Barba had been anticipating the opportunity to provoke me. They wanted me riled, or better yet, scared. And maybe I should be.

The more I thought about it, the more I found myself resenting Tim a little for being so quick to placate me. He hadn't seen the spark of savage rage in Estella's eyes – but he did know what it was like to lose someone to Blake Bram. To some extent, he knew what Estella was going through. Tim was my partner, in every way, so if he really wanted to protect me, shouldn't he be building me up rather than encouraging me to let down my guard? Ten minutes with Don Bogle and I felt energized. Tim just made me feel weaker.

As I walked back inside, I felt for the cigarette butt in my pocket.

I might be needing another smoke after all.

ELEVEN

The headquarters of the *Watertown Daily Times* were on the second floor of a boxy, sixties-era building of cinderblock gray. On the drive over, I'd occupied myself by imagining all the ways I could storm the building: loudly, shouting expletives as I went. Furtively, with canines bared. I felt like a coastal shark on Labor Day Weekend, nose twitching toward a swirl of blood.

I didn't expect to be able to walk in off the street, but when I told the security guard at the entrance I'd come to see the editor, I was issued a visitor's badge and directed to the stairs. I was pretty sure the curious, stealthy looks the guard kept giving had a lot to do with the ease of entry. For once, I was grateful for my famous face.

The newsroom was a labyrinth of desks, all outfitted with shelving that doubled as cubicle walls. There were newspapers everywhere, in yellowing stacks that listed toward the floor or folded and tucked under binders, kraft mailing envelopes, well-thumbed dictionaries missing their covers. The adjoining conference room featured, of all things, orange shag carpeting worn flat from years of foot traffic and sensible shoes. On the newsroom wall, a blue-and-red banner announced that I'd arrived at 'Northern New York's #1 Newspaper.' Underneath it, a man seated before a black Dell computer raised his head.

I'd never met Jared Cunningham in person, but he spent enough time covering the recent corruption scandal that had spilled over into A-Bay for me to recognize the thinning strawberry hair that held the lines of a pocket comb, his lean lips and colorless eyebrows. Where his collar was open, curls of fine red hair bubbled up toward a hastily-shaved neck. Cunningham had been a thorn in my side for nearly a year, and he was finally sitting right in front of me.

In the aftermath of the case on Tern Island that led to my month-long suspension, he'd written article after article suggesting, with little subtlety, that while I did solve the case and charges were in fact brought against the perpetrator, the investigation had been botched. That, mind you, was *after* I'd thrown him an exclusive tip. It didn't matter that the resulting story had served my purposes as much as his. I had helped the little weasel. And in return, his paper had sold me down the river.

'Detective Merchant,' he said with something much closer to alarm than surprise. 'What—'

'Relax, I'm not here to see you,' I said. 'I need to talk to your editor.'

'My editor?' Eyes wide.

'That's right – and I'm willing to bet you know why. Need me to jog your memory? Your paper published an op-ed that reads like a goddamn smear campaign. That letter was a personal attack against an employee of the state of New York, and it exposed aspects of my life that are personal and private.'

'I don't need my memory jogged.' He stared down at his slipper-style loafers, the leather laces of which were frayed. 'That letter made false accusations against you. It should never have been published.'

'Oh.' What was happening here? Was Cunningham actually on my side?

'I'm sorry,' he said, looking up. 'Truly, I am.'

Cunningham, I realized, had a North Country accent. It was unreliable, fading in and out like an FM radio signal, but I could pick up those short As and Es now and then. *Truly, I aim.*

'That's great and all,' I said, 'but because of that letter I was accosted on the street today by two somewhat threatening people who had a good idea of where I'd be. Would your editor like to publish pictures of my house next so all the stalkers can find their way to my front door? What the hell have you people got against me?'

When he spoke again, his voice was grave. 'You shouldn't be here. In a few minutes, I won't be either.'

It was only then that I noticed the box on his desk. It contained a nearly leafless jade plant protruding from a mug that read *Happy Birthday, Son!* and an open box of cinnamon granola bars. There were books inside the box as well, titles splashed across their spines in black and red. *True Crime Tales. American Murder. A Social Study of Serial Killers.*

'I quit.' Though Cunningham said it lightly, the shrug that accompanied his statement didn't look especially carefree.

'You quit the paper?'

'Went out with a bang, I guess you'd say. It probably wasn't the best idea to fling accusations on my way out the door, but what can I tell you? I was pissed.'

He was pissed? 'About what?'

'About the same thing you are. That letter.' He shook his pink head. 'When it came in, Rudy – Rudy Stuart, he runs the editorial page – showed it to me. He said he wanted my opinion, since I knew you best. Professionally,' he added. 'By way of my previous stories. I told him not to publish it, because you're right, it was inflammatory.'

'So how the hell did it end up in the paper?'

His eyes darted around the room. 'I am *not* making excuses for him,' he said, 'but Rudy's old school. He comes from a world where there are good guys, bad guys and nothing in between. You're a detective who's related to a known killer, who lives and works in the same town where he wreaked havoc, in the community Rudy happens to call home. A kid got snatched. There have been more homicides in Jefferson County since you got here a year ago than over the entire last decade. And Rudy blames you.'

'Tell him to join the club.' The joke fell flat, and I felt my cheeks redden. 'Look, I appreciate your support, but to quit your job over it . . . that's a big deal.' Cunningham had always struck me as ruthless when it came to his work, willing to do whatever it took to get the scoop, and now he was leaving the paper because his coworker didn't give me a fair shake? It was completely out of character, on top of which I didn't want to be responsible for killing a man's career.

'I don't regret what I did. This isn't just a story, it's your life. The shit he pulled? It's like he thought he was working for a tabloid or something. This is a newspaper brand with a century and a half of history, a sterling reputation. But don't worry, Rudy's leaving too – and not by choice. Oh, boy.'

Cunningham's gaze slid to the left, and I followed it to find two men in sport coats watching us from across the room.

'Crap,' he said. It sounded like *crepe*. 'Here come the big guns. I might have made a bit of a scene. Time to go.' He hoisted the box from the desk, its sad contents clattering, and nodded at the door. 'Follow me.'

TWELVE

I trailed Cunningham out the building's glass doors and into the brutal sunlight. A row of trees separated the headquarters from Washington Street, and – no discussion necessary – we made a beeline for the shade.

Blinking in the daylight, Cunningham set down the box and propped himself against a maple. With no preamble at all, he said, 'I've been reading about serial killers.'

Great. At least being outside would make it easier for me to cut and run.

'That started long before I heard about Bram,' he went on before I could tell him I had no interest in hearing about his sick hobby, none at all. 'Crime reporting, it's my job.' He cast a glance at the building behind us. 'And it won't *stop* being my job just because I no longer work here. It's what I know, and what I care about. I want to see justice served.'

There was a sheen of sweat on Cunningham's neck, already blotchy from the oppressive heat. 'When I found out who you were – who you were to him, I mean – I got curious,' he said. 'I started looking into the families of notorious serial killers. You're not alone in this, though it may feel that way. You realize that, right?'

This guy was raising my hackles something fierce. 'What is this, a therapy session?'

'Casey Mitchell. Know her?'

I sighed, and shook my head.

'Casey Mitchell is the daughter of Mike Mitchell, also known as the Blind Creek Killer. Mike Mitchell killed seven people over the course of three years and dumped them all around Florida's Blind Creek Beach. His daughter went on The Maury Povich show in the nineties, where she submitted to a brain scan. She was entirely convinced she'd inherited her father's psychopathic traits.'

'Did she?' I asked, in spite of myself.

Globules of perspiration had appeared on his part. As if my

stare made him itchy, he ran a hand through his hair. 'She did not. Her brain was totally normal. But her father spent years trying to persuade her, and everyone else who'd listen, that she was just as insane as he was. How about Noah Remus?' Cunningham went on, hardly pausing to breathe. 'Noah's brother, William, strangled ten people in Houston over ten years, taunting the media with gruesome photographs all the while. It took Noah nine of those years to realize his own brother, whom he was close to, was the murderer the entire city was looking for. When he did, he provided the police with the evidence that led to William's arrest and execution.'

When I swallowed, I found my mouth dry as sand.

'In an interview with the *Houston Chronicle*, Noah was asked how a sibling can ever get over a betrayal like that,' Cunningham said. 'How could poor Noah ever come to terms with what his brother had done? Noah's response was that, while he'd never forgive William, he didn't believe he deserved to find happiness or love ever again after what he'd done to his brother. His friend.'

Cunningham did pause then, and met my eye.

'Though he had nothing to do with his brother's crimes, Noah was instrumental in William's capture, and felt an immense amount of guilt over the dark mark his brother left on the city they both called home. Casey Mitchell and Noah Remus are innocents,' he went on. 'But every time a new true crime series starts streaming, or a nonfiction writer recounts the tale of bloodlust in Baltimore, Boise, the Bayou, people like them are traumatized all over again. The media takes possession of their pain and repackages it as entertainment. No permission asked, none granted.'

Listening to Cunningham recount the stories of Casey Mitchell and Noah Remus was like an out-of-body experience. I didn't know these people, had never heard of them in my life, yet something about them felt disturbingly familiar.

'I'm a reporter.' Cunningham faltered as he said it, and his gaze flicked to the building at our backs once more. There was a good chance he was having an out-of-body experience of his own. 'Sometimes, that doesn't feel so different from turning crime into a narrative. Putting a salacious spin on a story that – though I don't mean it to – glorifies the villain while the victim's family suffers, forced to go about their days avoiding reminders of their living nightmares. Why don't the families of all those victims have the right to keep their trauma private? That kind of pain doesn't belong in the public realm.'

I shook my head. I didn't know what to say.

'Over the years, many of those families have begged producers not to go ahead with a film or a series about the killer in their bloodline, only to be ignored. They don't deserve that. They shouldn't have to live that way.'

After my own abduction, the media had respected my privacy – or more accurately, they weren't allowed to print my name thanks to the handiwork of the lawyer hired by my department. The lives of Bram's victims and their families, though, those had been fair game. Cunningham was right: it wasn't fair that they should have to suffer in public, neither when the crime occurred nor months later when some eagle-eyed producer took a shine to their story.

'The victimization doesn't stop with the grieving mothers and brothers you see on TV, Shana,' he went on. 'What I'm interested in is the people on the sidelines, the ones who get overlooked. We're fed images of the victim's family at a press conference, pleading with the public to bring their baby back or crying at a vigil once they realize their little girl's gone for good. But there are two families involved in every crime: the victim's, and the killer's. More often than not those sons and daughters, siblings and cousins had nothing to do with the way the killer turned out, yet they're all lumped in together. What happened when they discovered the person they loved and trusted is a monster? What about when that person's apprehended, and the whole world knows the truth? *Those* are the stories I want to write.'

When Cunningham looked down at his feet again, I did the same. 'The truth is,' he said, 'I've been thinking of leaving the paper for a while. I have a plan. I want to start an online magazine devoted to the families of notorious killers. It's not true crime the way others have been doing it, with all the focus on the murderer. My stories will be about the victims, starting with the killers' own families. Starting with you.'

I gaped at him, my head swirling with questions. I wasn't so delusional as to believe I was the only person in the world linked to a human stain, but never once had I thought about the fact that there were others like me. I'd been too busy dealing with my own pain and separation from my parents and brother.

But here was Jared Cunningham, about to build a content hub on the backs of the people my cousin had killed – because in spite of Cunningham's righteous stance and insistence that his pieces would be different, there could be no story without the dead. Unshackled from the paper, with no editor to keep him honest, there was no telling what this man would write.

At the same time, what he'd said about the daughter who doubted her sanity and the brother who didn't believe he deserved happiness eddied around my mind.

When I looked up from the hard-packed patches of earth where the heat had fried the grass, Cunningham locked me in a gimlet-eyed stare.

'Talk to me,' he said. 'Share your experience. What I write . . . it will humanize you.'

'I'm plenty human as it is, thanks.'

'You know what I mean. The people out there reading about Bram feel no empathy for you because they don't know Shana Merchant. They hear words like "cousin" and "cop" and draw their own conclusions. The media would have you believe Casey Mitchell and Noah Remus went public with their stories because it helped them heal, but by the time Casey signed on with Maury, she'd received thirty-three death threats from total strangers, and before Noah talked to the *Chronicle* he was recognized and attacked outside a Burger King around the corner from his house. Eleven stitches to the forehead. He still has a scar.'

I reached for my cheek and ran my fingertips over the crimped skin.

'Rumors, celebrity – it changes people,' Cunningham said. 'Once the press has you in its jaws the opportunity to defend yourself, to tell your side of things, is all but gone. Pretty soon, people are going to lose interest, but not before locking in their votes. Your chance to change their minds is slipping away.'

'And why would I want to do that?' I asked, because I really wanted to convince myself I didn't care. What the public thought of me. What they'd been led to believe.

'There's one reason I can think of, above and beyond the

possibility that you could get jumped in a fast food parking lot.'
I felt his stare on my scar. Tried not to flinch. 'That reason is your
job. I have to imagine being a senior investigator with the BCI
requires a lot of respect. You've worked your whole career to earn
that from your colleagues and superiors. More recently, you've
earned it from the community over which you have jurisdiction.
But you read that op-ed. That Barlowe woman, she isn't alone.
How prepared are you for the possibility that you're going to lose
everything you've worked for because you happen to be related
to a serial killer?'

When I first arrived in Alexandria Bay with Dr Carson Gates,
I knew no one. My fiancé's hometown had felt insular. Possessive.
Were it not for Tim working by my side, I have no doubt that
witnesses would have been far less willing to answer my questions. Over time, the community grew accustomed to my
presence. I proved my worth by solving one case, then another.
Over the past two years, I'd cut a path through a forest where
the trees were packed in tight. Most importantly, I'd established
a relationship with Sheriff McIntyre and Lieutenant Jack
Henderson at Troop D headquarters in Oneida. With Jeremy
Solomon and Don Bogle. With Tim.

Cunningham had a point. But I didn't want to see it. Just being
that physically close to the guy was making me feel antsy. He
was a newsman who dealt in truth and facts, black and white,
but my cousin was all gray. He'd been average, and evil. He'd
perpetuated the trope of the murdered girl and stoked our culture
of fear, only to turn around and protect me against a perceived
threat. Even at the end, he would have given his life to save
mine. About that, I was certain. Bram was an unsolvable puzzle.
Maybe, in a way, I was, too.

'I can help you, Shana,' Cunningham said. 'Let me help you
be the architect of your own story.'

There was a coin newsbox in front of the building, and I
watched as a woman who was walking her dog leaned over to
read the headlines. My name was in that paper in the box – mine,
and that of my cousin. Estella Lopez and Javier Barba were only
the beginning. Shana Merchant was no longer a senior investigator
with the state police. She was the cousin of a killer who failed
to save a fellow cop's life and concealed information about a

notorious suspect. Shana Merchant could no longer be trusted to do the right thing.

Lifting the toe of my shoe, I dug my heel into the hard-packed dirt.

It didn't give.

THIRTEEN

There were three text messages on my cell when I got back to my car, all of them from Tim.

Just checking in. You OK, hon?

This isn't as dark as it seems.

Call me, OK? I'm here for you. Always.

I pictured him in my office, soft and eager. *Breathe, OK? Just like Carson taught you.*

I didn't want to think about Carson, especially after talking with Cunningham. I couldn't do that without picturing Carson as portrayed by Robert Pattinson in a Hulu Original series about Bram's decades-long killing spree. So instead, as I started the ignition, I found myself thinking about Gil Gasko.

Gasko and I had bonded last year over cream-no-sugar coffees, black tea, and murder. As my state-appointed counselor, he'd guided me through my lingering PTSD and fresh pain toward recovery, and single-handedly got me reinstated post-probation. I owed Gasko a lot, and he'd been overjoyed when I contacted him again after Bram's death. Especially once he got a read on my mental state.

'I don't want to call it a relapse,' he'd said gently, stabbing at the log jam of ice in his sweet tea. With his face lowered like that toward his cup, the widow's peak in his hair had looked like the beak of a large, black crow. 'Recovering from a trauma-induced condition isn't a linear process,' Gasko told me. 'There are triggers – sounds, smells, images – that can take you back to that place. Think of PTSD as a bad case of eczema. Yes, there are treatments, but it can always flare up again – so with all this publicity, when you're so exposed, trust is more important than ever.

'It would help to have friends' – here, he gave me a meaningful look – 'who simply listen without trying to shelve your feelings or dish out easy answers. You should feel safe to share as much as you need to, over and over again, without worrying that you'll bore or annoy them. Do you have people like that in your life, Shana?'

I thought about that question on the drive from Watertown back to A-Bay, the landscape a blur of electric green. *Do you have people who make you feel safe?* I did. I had Mac, always willing to lend an ear. But I didn't have my family anymore, and I didn't know when – if ever – I'd be getting them back. I had Tim – but the vision of him stroking my hair or my hand and telling me it was 'going to be OK' loomed large in my mind. Bram's last victim had been someone Tim and I both knew well, who'd once meant a lot to us. Many a night we'd awoken to dueling nightmares about Carson's murder and mashed our chests together, waiting for the drumbeat to slow. That's how I pictured our hearts in those moments: as kettle-drums. Tim's youngest stepbrother played percussion in the school band, and he'd explained about something called sympa-thetic resonance, where one drum could be made to vibrate by striking another nearby. Time and time again, Tim and I would absorb each other's pain – but with the speed of a hammer strike, it always came back again.

As close as we'd gotten, and as much as I cared for him, I sometimes wondered if Tim would ever really understand how I felt. Tim was a fixer. When I was sad, he asked what he could do to make it better. When I was frustrated at work, he'd blithely brainstorm possible solutions, his eyes lighting up at the chal-lenge. There was a lot to love about his white knight personality. Tim cared about people, and genuinely wanted to help. But Gil Gasko had another theory about him, one that had been needling me since my tantrum in the office.

Gasko hadn't come right out and said it – Tim was a fellow employee of the state police, after all, and he and Gasko had never met – but I got the distinct feeling that he didn't think Tim was good for me. I'd told Gasko I was seeing someone, and that the guy was so determined to help that it sometimes left me feeling suffocated and even more alone. Gasko said he knew the type. 'People like that, the rescuers of the world, often can't grasp that there are those who just need time to heal at their own pace and on their own terms. To your boyfriend, that lack of happiness means something's defective. In need of repair.' Gasko didn't fail to point out that a fixer mentality was sometimes indicative of insecurity. Those driven to patch up pain were often carrying around some of their own.

Tim hadn't had it easy, either, with a childhood best friend determined to derail his life just for kicks, who then returned as an adult to torture him all over again. I knew the guilt Tim felt over Carson's death would linger. Which begged the question: could two people with so much competing pain really find a way to heal together?

You're not alone in this, though it may feel that way.

At least Cunningham was half right.

FOURTEEN

I t was just past eight a.m. on Thursday morning when the call came into the barracks, minutes after I'd stepped through the door. Tim was the one who answered, immediately arranging his face in an expression of grave concern.

'There's been a development,' he said. There was no more talk of Estella Lopez or my panic attack, just as there hadn't been when, upon returning to the barracks the previous day, I'd told Tim I was sleeping at my place. There was no time for any of that now.

As soon as he lowered his gaze, I knew.

'Where?'

'LaFargeville,' Tim said. 'The quarry.'

Quarry. Whenever I hear that word, I picture a craggy, prehistoric pit punched into a rock shelf, a place miles from civilization and abandoned by time. I see the eerie teal gleam of the quarry lake from *Stranger Things*, a show Henrietta, my niece, introduced me to a couple of Christmases ago, and the abandoned granite quarries that feature in Dennis Lehane's *Gone, Baby, Gone.* In that novel, Lehane refers to their holes as a dumping ground for everything from stolen cars to bodies, and that description always stuck with me. The terrible image pushed itself to the forefront of my mind once more as Tim and I made our way to the Cape Quarry in LaFargeville, New York.

The view that appeared before us as our car lumbered over cracked, crumbly earth was a flat expanse of clear-felled forest dotted with towering mounds of gravel, sand and stone. The piles looked like giant anthills from a sci-fi movie, home to overgrown alien insects with bulbous bodies and legs that were longer than Bogle was tall. We drove, then walked, between them, boots crunching on the dense gravel under our feet. I swatted at flies as I breathed in the earthy, mineral scent of morning-damp stone and prepared myself for what we were about to see.

'Coroner got delayed, but he's on the way. A mason found her first thing this morning.' Bogle had been working an assault case at Fishers Landing, and had beaten us to the scene. 'A customer showed up bright and early,' he explained, 'looking to fill his truck with stone dust for a patio project. The mason pointed the guy to this pit, and as soon as he dug in, he found this.' Bogle swallowed, the bulge in his neck bobbing like a river buoy.

I could see it even from a distance. Fabric mottled light and dark, splashed with colorful lettering. The kind of shirt you'd find at one of the souvenir shops in town. Tim and I ducked under a taut strip of crime scene tape and made our way toward the mountain of stone dust as high as Tim's cottage, and the T-shirt black with blood. Sticking out of it now, a slack human limb. Rigor mortis was complete. She'd been dead at least a few days. Probably since the night she disappeared.

'All that time spent looking at the river,' I said, my mouth a grim line, 'treating this like a suicide, and she was here all along.' *All that time wasted.*

'We were playing the odds,' said Tim. 'We didn't know. We couldn't have.'

Maybe not. But it still felt like failure.

'Where's the mason now?' Something I knew about stone workers: they had strong hands, strong enough to overpower a grown woman.

Bogle blinked a few times before jerking his head in the direction from which we'd come. 'The office. It's in the building you passed on your way in. He was pretty shaken up – a little green, if I'm honest. I thought it would be best to keep him close, though.'

Bogle looked a little green himself. 'Nice work,' I said as, absurdly, I heard my mom's voice in my head telling me to give credit where credit was due. Between Jeremy Solomon and Bogle, Bogle was the one with brass while Sol was built to observe and react, but I wouldn't have accused Don Bogle of being overconfident. Though he got the job done and knew how to follow orders, he wasn't proactive, often needing a nudge.

Bogle had done a good job of protecting the crime scene, though. Defending against the creation of artifactual evidence

– footprints, fingerprints, matter that hadn't been present before – was crucial. It was clear someone had tried to move the victim; the customer or the mason, probably, to check if she was alive. Whoever it was, they'd let her body fall back against the dust, causing it to shift and cascade back over her like a mini avalanche. Visible now was her torso, half her face, and her right leg, the latter jutting out of the black matter like the twisted appendage of a discarded doll.

'Those look like stab wounds to me,' I said, drawing a circle in the air above the motionless body.

'You OK? Do you need to sit or something?' Tim's hands were busy, roaming the space between us. He cast a glance around us and added, 'You need to be careful. Something like this, the similarity to Bram's victims, it could give you flashbacks.'

Bram's victims, all of whom were stabbed. 'I'm fine,' I said, a little too harshly, and returned my attention to the woman.

Discovering a homicide victim isn't something you get used to. Most often, the violence of the act is etched in every square inch of the victim's body, from the unnatural angle of their head to the pallor of the skin, so waxen and lusterless it would be right at home at Madame Tussauds. *Chamber of Horrors was right.* My first time finding a body wasn't on the job, but it *was* in New York City. I'd been walking through Chinatown in search of bubble tea and had paused at the mouth of an alley to answer a text message on my phone. I didn't intend to linger for long. The alley stank of hot garbage, sour milk, and something especially rank that rushed my mouth, filling it with so much saliva I thought I might choke. Funny, how the body reacts the same way to the cloying stink of decay as it does to the aroma of a good meal. It didn't take me long to realize there was something very wrong about that smell. Because I was a new rank-and-file member of the NYPD, still feeling self-important and invincible, I took it upon myself to investigate.

Not three steps into the alley, the floor of which was wet despite the lack of rain, I saw him. Back propped against the wall of the shop with the Hello Kitty purses in the window that I had just passed. Head flopped over to one side. There was a gash on the man's forehead so ferocious I saw exposed bone, a ghastly sliver of white. No doubt inflicted by the unidentifiable hunk of metal left next to his thigh. His face was red and black and sticky. His hands too, from hopelessly groping at his deadly wound. The man looked homeless, and I guessed his attacker was, too. The few possessions that remained had tumbled out of a dirty shopping bag on to the ground. A few items of stretched-out clothing, a bent spoon, a water-damaged paperback, its pages curled up like a pill bug.

I'd stared at him for a long time before dialing 911, forcing myself to look. I was days into a lifetime of police work, and I knew I'd see hundreds of bodies like this one, many of them more gruesome still. There was something else that rooted me to that alley floor, too. Like his belongings, this man had been cast off. Most likely, he had died alone. As hideous as he looked, and as hard as I had to fight not to compromise the crime scene by bringing up my shrimp fried rice, I had an innate understanding that I needed to stay. To be with him, even though I suspected his broken face would haunt my nights for months.

I was wrong. It had haunted me for years. But had I known that would be the case, I wouldn't have changed a thing.

I peered down at her face now, the woman in the dust. Dark skin, those curls skimming her shoulders that rock powder had dulled to the color of river silt. The hollow of her exposed eye was filled to the brim with dirt, but even without confirming eye color, I knew the woman matched Godfrey Hearst's description of his missing wife.

'Let's get Charlie out here,' I said, motioning to the tread marks on the ground. 'Looks to me like someone drove right up to the pile to dump her.' Tire tread impressions were invaluable in scenes like this one. A forensic investigator could use them to determine everything from tread design, wear and the make of the tires to the dimensions of a suspect's car and possibly even the vehicle model. The morning dew was drying fast, the impressions clean. It would take too long to hear back from the lab in Albany, which sent its reports as certified documents that didn't usually come in for weeks, but we had a trooper in our unit who was trained as an evidence tech. In addition to collecting evidence and photographing the marks, I hoped he'd be able to make an unofficial determination on the spot.

We got busy then, taking notes and photographs while we

waited for the coroner to arrive. As we moved, Tim shook his head and said, 'Chet Bell is going to lose his mind.'

He hadn't raised his voice. He didn't mean to be insensitive. In fact, Tim was probably right. Four months since the murders of three locals, ten since the death of two others up river from Alexandria Bay, and now this. There was no way to keep another homicide in Jefferson County under wraps. Tourists making plans to travel upstate this weekend would learn about it on the news, and those who'd already arrived would startle at the whispers. Another woman was dead. Bram was in the ground, and somehow people were still losing their lives. 'Doesn't mean this place is safe,' Godfrey Hearst had said, and he'd just been proven right. But nothing was farther from my thoughts in that moment than pompous Chet Bell, and as I looked down at the body of Hearst's wife, Tim's words soured my stomach.

Our focus now was to find out who did this. Bram's death was supposed to set this place free, return it to the peaceful village it had once been. Instead, yet another person had lost their life on Jefferson County soil. And I couldn't help but wonder if that was a bellwether of the trouble to come.

FIFTEEN

Godfrey Hearst III cried when he ID'd the body, the kind of full-body sobs you feel in your own gut. He made no effort to stifle his emotions as he wore a rut into the morgue's hallway floor, fists clenching and unclenching against his thighs, hopelessness yanking every nerve in his body taut as wire.

'Start again,' I said. 'Why did you and Rebecca come to Alexandria Bay?'

Hearst had calmed down a little by the time we reached the barracks. He'd declined legal counsel, opting instead to sit rigid in a chair and answer our questions for hours. There was much about Hearst's story that still flummoxed me.

'Whose idea was it to come upstate? Why the Admiral Inn?'

The trip, the motel – according to Hearst, it was all his wife's doing. She'd picked the place and booked the room, acting on a recommendation from a friend. When I asked for the referrer's name, he said he didn't know it. Rebecca hadn't told him, and he hadn't asked.

Tim had questions of his own. He inquired about Rebecca's friend group, whether she'd recently talked about anyone new. Hearst's job was scrutinized as well, because this was a man who ran a small empire, a thirty-three-year-old with considerable power. Godfrey Hearst maintained there was no jealous lover who might have seen Rebecca as an obstacle to his fortune. He insisted that he'd loved his wife, despite the occasional arguments. That they'd been happy together.

'There are three ways of looking at this,' I said later that evening, once Hearst had been released and Tim and I were gathering our things, preparing to leave work but not wanting to look like we were leaving together. 'It could be the husband, for any number of reasons. Rage or distrust. Jealousy.'

Tim took the empty cup from his desk and spun it on to the mouth of his Thermos. There had been chili in there earlier, leftovers from the dinner we'd shared a few nights ago. 'Hearst wasn't seeing someone else,' Tim confirmed. 'Don made the calls, talked to everyone in the guy's orbit. Isn't that right, Don?'

Bogle nodded, bobbling the cigarette that was pinched behind his ear. I'd delegated assignments at the scene, and our investigation was well underway, with Sol taking depositions from witnesses: the quarry worker, and a neighbor who'd since surfaced. She lived behind the Admiral and had heard the squeal of tires on Sunday night. Despite the help we were getting from the troopers in Utica, who were following leads down there, Bogle had put our incendiary questions to Rebecca's parents and sister, Hearst's family, and their coworkers. 'It doesn't look like this was an attempt to end his marriage and start fresh with someone new,' he said. 'And no. As of now, there's no evidence that Hearst was having an affair.'

I said, 'No evidence linking him to the crime scene, either.' Charlie, our resident evidence tech, had analyzed the tire tracks both at the quarry and behind the motel, and determined they were Goodyears belonging to a truck. Either the truck was new, or the tires were; the tread showed minimal wear. Hearst drove a 2016 Lincoln Aviator from his own lot. A luxury SUV outfitted with Pirelli tires that were three years old.

'OK, second possibility,' I went on. 'Our perp followed her up here, and when she went out for a walk like Hearst said, she was taken. It's conceivable that someone was watching her, waiting for their chance. Rebecca was on the sales floor in Utica, right? That's a very public position. Maybe she had a secret admirer who couldn't stand that she was married to the boss, or she rubbed a customer the wrong way. Look into that, will you, Don? Check out the sales Rebecca made in June, July and August. Maybe we'll find a link that way.'

'OK,' Bogle said, the word scratchy in his throat. 'Will do.'

'You know,' said Tim, 'it's also possible the person who took her was already here.'

'And that's door number three. We have to ask why she was targeted,' I said. 'If it's some sicko with a grudge against women, there are plenty of single out-of-towners around right now. Why complicate things by choosing a woman with a husband in tow? To me, that suggests he had his eye on her already. We could be looking for someone who already knew her, but who's also a local. Somebody she's been concealing from her husband.'

Bogle said, 'But how probable is that? It's summer. We get people passing through all the time. Isn't it more likely she was killed by a random tourist?'

'I vote for that theory,' said Tim. 'I know Shana said Hearst called this place the boonies, but come on. We're not all Children of the Corn and banjo-strumming mountain men.'

'Maybe that should be the town's new motto,' Bogle put in. '"Not all murderous kids and sadistic mountain men." Could be just the PR angle Chet Bell's looking for.'

The vision of Bell looking the fool as he waved a sign that X'd out both movie casts was strangely satisfying. I hadn't wanted to think about him, but I knew I couldn't avoid a confrontation for much longer. Rebecca Hearst's death was going to hit this community hard. Small towns tend to insulate themselves against the world's hard edges, and when the world finds a way to pop that bubble, the shock can be a doozy – even when it's not the first time violence has managed to seep in. That's why the story of a kid missing from Fruitland, Idaho, population 5,000, will trump a similar tragedy in LA or Chicago every time. It's about the breaking of some arbitrary set of rules the locals established to protect their own. In places like Alexandria Bay, people make a pact with God and expect to be rewarded. Fewer sins in exchange for a home free from harm.

But it had happened again, in a place where it shouldn't. A killing. A woman abducted from the safety of her life and hauled kicking and screaming toward oblivion. It had happened on a warm summer Sunday night, when Rebecca Hearst should have been listening to the crickets chirp outside her motel window and wondering whether she should add a side of bacon to tomorrow's breakfast at the DineRite. Her murder was an open hand slap. Chet Bell wasn't going to take the blow lying down.

'Bogle's right, though,' I said. 'The perp could be someone in town for the summer, or just for this week. The season's almost over. If they're visiting, it'd be easy to kill her, pack up, and leave.'

'Well, the word is out,' said Bogle. 'Her photo's all over the news.' We'd put out a plea to the public, too, asking anyone with information about Rebecca Hearst's murder to contact the state police. 'If that theory holds water, the killer could already be gone.'

Up close, Bogle's shaved skull was lumpy, hills of bone protruding more in some places than others. His philtrum was off-center, knocked a little to the right, and that made him look rough, like a biker who'd been in more bar fights than he could count, though I knew he'd sooner grill ribs and watch football at home than brawl in some filthy dive. I sometimes found myself wondering what he'd looked like with hair. Had it softened him? Did Bogle always emit this threatening energy, or was that just about his hairlessness and hulking Frankenstein form? One day, I might ask him. But not today.

'There's something weird about this,' I said, locking him in my gaze. 'Can you see it?' It was a test, one that I needed him to take. To his credit, Tim stood by in silence.

Bogle pondered my query for a long time, idly pushing his wedding band around a heat-swollen finger. 'She wasn't very well hidden, for one thing. The attempt to conceal her body feels . . .'

'What?' I pushed.

'. . . sloppy, I guess. Like the killer was in a hurry.'

'Is that the only way to read the scene?'

'It could have been intentional,' he said after a few slow blinks. 'Like, the person who did this wanted her to be found.'

'It's the timing that bugs me,' I said. 'Pirate Days kicks off tomorrow. There are a million places he could have dumped her where she might not be discovered for weeks, if ever.' I pictured the divers on the back of the police boat, preparing to search water that went on for miles and brimmed with more seagrass than a forest has trees. 'The river, or the woods. Instead, he picked the quarry.' In truth, it was a miracle Rebecca's body hadn't been found sooner. There were countless piles of stone there for customers to choose from, but in summer – construction season – the quarry was a busy place.

'So maybe he wanted us to find her?' Bogle mulled that over, pleats of skin on his naked brow. 'Why?'

'That's the question. In New York, those homicides . . .'

Reflexively, I glanced at Tim, knowing he'd be watching me. He was.

'One of the women was left at a construction site,' I said. 'An empty lot cluttered with just enough lumber and machinery to provide the cover he needed to dump and run. He wanted us to find her, too. In that case, he was making a statement. I wonder if we could be dealing with something like that again.'

'What kind of statement, though?' Bogle's eyes were wide. Alert.

'Well, I'll tell you what I think. In spite of what her husband believes, Rebecca Hearst might have been seeing someone else.'

Tim had been quiet up until that point, but now he said, 'Meaning she planned to meet someone up here?'

I shrugged and said, 'Could be. Maybe she instigated the fight with her husband so she had an excuse to get away, and rendez-voused with her lover somewhere near Collins Landing. It would explain how her phone ended up by the bridge. And maybe her love interest is from these parts. Why else wouldn't Rebecca tell her husband who recommended the Admiral Inn?'

'Because it was her guy on the side,' said Tim.

'It fits,' I said with a nod. 'Explains the fight she had with Hearst, and why she took off afterward, too. It explains why they ended up at a crappy motel with no security cameras on the outskirts of town.' It was the motel that had me so convinced. Godfrey Patrick Hearst III was an unlikely guest at a two-star highway motor lodge, especially when there were a half-dozen waterfront resorts within a few miles' drive.

'I wouldn't recommend that motel to my worst enemy,' said Bogle, reading my mind.

'Exactly. There are other options in town, but they're all *in town*. The Admiral backs up to those residential streets, streets that would most certainly be empty at night. It's the perfect place to meet someone if you're planning on leaving your husband.'

'So you think she was going to leave him,' Tim said. 'She's meeting her guy – but it doesn't go the way she expected. And what, he gets violent? Tosses her phone and then kills her?'

'If her phone's in the water, or busted from landing on the shore, the husband can't track her. Maybe,' I said, turning the idea over in my mind, 'the relationship was still new, and Rebecca got cold feet. There's this thing that happens sometimes, when a woman who's spoken for is interested in someone else. It's flirtation, at first. Good clean fun. She tells herself it's harmless, and keeps playing along. The guy reads her enthusiasm as consent. Inevitably, they reach a point where the guy wants to take things to the next level.'

'It's do or die time,' said Bogle slowly, his gaze on the floor. 'Teasing banter is one thing, but extramarital sex . . . there's no going back from that.'

Score another point for Don Bogle. 'If that's what he wanted from her, and she denied him? That could piss him off,' I said.

'So, he kills her.' A pause. Bogle's forehead wrinkled. 'Or someone else does.'

I pointed a finger at him. 'Yes. A crime of opportunity. Someone sees her over by the bridge, distraught and alone, and pounces. And if it *was* someone else, Rebecca's side boy may soon come forward waving an alibi. A homicide on the front page of the paper is sure to tip him off to the fact that he's a suspect.'

'Wow,' Bogle said, and my eyes slid to Tim. Tim, who looked sullen standing between us, hands clamped to the edge of the desk and his shoulders up around his ears. I felt a little guilty for enjoying the ease with which Bogle and I were spitballing. It was a feeling I'd come to associate only with Tim.

'Let's not get ahead of ourselves,' I said. 'We can theorize all day long, but without any physical evidence of a boyfriend or motive for murder, we're nowhere. We need to shake a suspect out of the bushes. Since Rebecca's friends and family don't seem to know anything, I think we should look at social media.' It was an avenue we explored often, and I was optimistic that we'd hit paydirt. We'd wasted no time poring over Rebecca's recent calls and messages, and I'd managed to get her phone records as well, but we hadn't yet done a deep dive into her social accounts. 'If she *was* two-timing her husband, she had to be in contact with him somehow. Nothing suspicious on her call and text history means we move on to Facebook and Instagram.'

'I can work that angle,' Bogle said quickly. 'If there are messages there from another guy, I'll find him. And I can see if the Bay Point Grill has any cameras outside, too. Hearst said they were there on Sunday from six to just before ten, right? We might be able to find some witnesses who know something useful about Rebecca's behavior that night.'

'That's a great idea, Don.'

Beaming at me, Bogle slipped the cigarette from behind his ear and began rolling it idly between his fingers. 'I could use a smoke break. OK if I cut out for a sec? Two minutes, tops.'

'Go for it,' I said.

'Wanna join me, boss?'

I gargled out a nervous laugh as my eyes darted to Tim. I felt hot and ashamed, like a teenager trying to fleece her parents, and somehow that angered me. 'I'm good,' I said, trying to sound casual. 'Take your time.'

When Bogle was gone, I turned to Tim. Chin tucked and head bowed, he was leafing through a stack of papers on his desk. His hair was just long enough that I couldn't see his eyes.

'What's up?' I said. 'You on to something over there?'

'Not yet, but I'm working on it. *Boss.*'

'Whoa,' I said. 'Why do you sound pissed?'

Tim raised his eyebrows, comically thick. 'You've been smoking,' he said, his tone flat. 'I could smell it on you yesterday.'

'So?'

'*So?* So, you don't smoke. Was this Don's idea? What the hell, Shana?'

I knew why he was upset. Tim's dad had smoked when Tim was a kid, all the way until his parents split up, and Tim hated it. But one cigarette wasn't the same as a lifetime of addiction, and anyway, I was an adult. If I wanted to smoke, well then, I would. It had nothing to do with Don Bogle.

I was preparing to condemn Tim for treating me like a disobedient child, my heart rate already rising, but instead of scolding me, Tim took my hand.

'Look, I get it, OK?' he said. 'It's the stress. Not gonna lie, I don't like it. It's not good for you. But if it helps right now, with what you're going through, I'll support you.'

No reproach. No argument. Tim was tender as ever, his hand holding mine as delicately as if it belonged to his frail grandma.

That almost made it worse.

SIXTEEN

'It is the case that's bothering you? Or is it something else?'

We were spooning, Tim's long body molded against mine, me facing the wall of his cottage where my half-open eyes were riveted to a knot on the wood paneling that looked like a face. I had stayed late at work and met him at his cottage, mostly because spending another night apart would lead to *a talk*, and I didn't have the energy for that. But now here we were, talking anyway.

In the wake of his questions, the room filled with the sound of bubbling water. Back in June, Tim had bought me an essential oil diffuser as a gift – two, actually, one for his place, the other for mine. All night long the orb would gurgle in my ear, slowly infusing the air with the scent of rose and citrus. It was supposed to reduce feelings of anxiety. Tim said certain oils could interact with the nervous system and brain to alter my mood. To me, it felt like sleeping behind a department store perfume counter, forever on edge as I awaited the next unsolicited spritz.

What was bothering me was that Rebecca Hearst was dead. Would she still have ended up in that quarry if I'd been quicker to react to Hearst's abduction theory? If Tim and I had found her phone a few hours sooner, and realized its location smacked of foul play? Questions like those didn't dummy up when you lay down to sleep. In the midnight silence, they were louder than ever.

When Bram died, Alexandria Bay had breathed a collective sigh of relief. The wolf was slain, the sheep free to roam again, complacent in the knowledge that they were safe. I'd done the same, assuming the nightmare was over and that we could all slip back into our halcyon dream. I don't mean to suggest erasing one lawless individual can completely eradicate crime, but the terror that had metastasized over time, the sense that Bram was forever preparing to pounce . . . surely that would change after the man who'd done the terrorizing was dead?

It had taken me four months, up until the moment we found Rebecca Hearst, to realize it hadn't. Evil is a mushroom in the

woods; pick one, and all it takes is a hard rain for more caps to
punch through the earth, stems twisting skyward as their jelly gills
unfold like paper fans. It can happen overnight. In fact, it had.

Tim's bare chest was sticky against my back, his breath moist
on my neck, and I tensed when I felt his nose nuzzle my skin.
Years of living alone had made me hypersensitive. The creak of
a mattress spring, the soft *pfff* that slid from Tim's parted lips
for a full hour after he fell asleep, these things took getting used
to and I wasn't quite there yet. If he'd been sleeping just then,
I would have headed for the river, barefoot through the buggy
night. Down to the spot where Bram fell.

Tim had always talked about building a staircase down to the
boathouse someday, but for now there was just a steep footpath
of bald spots rubbed into the grass. The path tested my balance
every time, and I'd lurch as I made my descent, picking my way
down the rutted terrain. Lately, the night had the quality of a
stuffy room, the air warm and close, but while I sometimes found
it hard to breathe, I went anyway.

Tim rarely woke when I went to that spot. He had my back,
told me so ten times a day, but more often than not he slept
deeply, no doubt luxuriating in his escape from the trouble I'd
brought to his hometown. Tim had no idea how much time I
spent beside the river, replaying Bram's death in my mind.
Reliving the moment that spray of blood from his head hit mine.

Without turning over to face him, I said, 'I need to tell you
something.'

'It's the popcorn thing, isn't it.' A huff of breath on my ear.
Tim was laughing. 'I know it's weird, but my sister started doing
it when we were in high school, and as dumb as I thought it was
at first, it kind of makes sense. Keeps your hands clean, see? But
if it really bothers you—'

'Ah, no.' The popcorn thing *was* weird – who eats popcorn
with a spoon? – but Tim's bizarre snacking habits were the
farthest thing from my mind. 'It's about the Hearst case. I don't
think you should work it with me.'

Silence. At length, I peeled away and flipped over to face him.

Not everyone has an expressive face. Some people are in
complete control of their features and can wipe emotions away
like smudges on a night-dark window, leaving behind a view

that's utterly blank. Tim isn't one of those types. Inches from me, his face was a Mardi Gras parade of thoughts and feelings, bewilderment and doubt.

A few weeks ago, he and I reached a milestone: one whole year of working side by side for the BCI. It had been his idea to commemorate the event with a fancy dinner. Lobster and a strip steak cooked over charcoal on his Weber, grilled pineapple with a dark, sugary rum sauce for dessert. One year ago, I'd arrived in A-Bay, and all the platitudes were true: it felt like yesterday. Time had, indeed, flown.

Looking back, I don't know what I was thinking when I applied for the job. My abduction had left me dazed and emotionally pummeled. I was broken in ways that couldn't easily be mended. I'd left the city to put some distance between me and my ordeal, and immediately rushed headlong into a job investigating the very atrocities I was trying to escape. Tim had been aggravating at first, with his side-eye glances and Eugene Levy eyebrows lifting warily at my every move. He didn't know what to make of me, nor I of him, and so we'd clashed, most famously mid-investigation while trapped on a private island.

That experience had also brought us closer together. We'd been forced to cooperate. We'd become trusted colleagues, then friends. Now we were something more.

I scrubbed my face with my hands. 'This case . . . it's the first homicide since we became a couple.'

'And?'

'And that worries me.'

'It worries you.' He was ruminating now, poring over every moment of the past few days in search of the anomaly, a word or act that had seemed so innocuous at the time but in fact pulled the pin on a grenade. It was terrible to watch.

'It's nothing you did,' I said quickly, immediately hating how that sounded, as if Tim was an insecure kid afraid of getting his hand slapped rather than a competent – no, exemplary – investigator. 'What we found out at the quarry, it changes things. This isn't a suicide or a wife on the run. Foul play means a high-profile investigation, especially in the middle of Pirate Days. It means me on TV and in the news. More than usual, I mean.' I waited for a sympathetic groan. When it didn't come, I went on. 'A woman has been murdered, and there's no way the media isn't going to draw a parallel between that crime and Bram's. The scrutiny I'm going to be under with this . . . you can't begin to imagine.' Frankly, neither could I. 'And the reporters who cover this thing? They're going to descend on us like vultures and pick this story clean.' Not to mention the true crime podcast hosts and crime-obsessed Murderinos for which Cunningham had such distaste. 'For the next few weeks,' I said, 'nothing about my life will be secret or sacred. Including my relationship with you.'

'So what?' he said. 'So they find out. We aren't breaking any rules.'

I shook my head. On paper, our relationship may have been above board, but would the press see it that way when they discovered I'd worked a case involving a member of my family and then promptly started dating my partner? 'Tim—'

'Shane.' Tim usually threw out the nickname he'd given me when I first came to town, a reference to an old Western movie, as a joke, but there was no laughter in his voice now. 'There's no policy that prohibits us from dating. We've been totally professional this whole time.'

'And yet we haven't told anyone at work other than Mac. Why?'

Tim was silent.

'I'll tell you why,' I said. 'Because people make assumptions. There will be those who are convinced what we've got will interfere with our ability to do our jobs. You don't think the media will assume the same thing? It's just more ammunition for them to use against me, and I'm already on the firing line. And it's not just that.'

'Oh great, there's more.'

Yes, there was more. And this was the hard part. 'Lately I've been feeling a little . . . smothered.'

Two pink coins appeared on Tim's cheeks. When, chagrined, I lay my hand on his bare chest, it was like touching a propane flame.

'I get that you want to help me. I *love* that,' I said. 'Sometimes it feels like you don't think I'm capable of helping myself.'

He thought about that for a long time. And still, he said nothing.

'I'm going to need a lot of confidence going into this situation.'

'And I sap your confidence,' he said.

'No! No. I just doubt myself a little more when you coddle me, that's all.'

That cut to the quick, and I knew it. Behind me, the diffuser burbled.

A person can get used to just about anything if they do it often enough. Isn't that what they say? Over the years, I'd learned how to endure lots of things I don't particularly enjoy. Cauliflower. Clothes shopping. Death notifications. Staking out a suspect from a spring-slick field in shoes so wet my feet stay crinkly and bloodless for days. There were some things, though, I knew I'd never get used to. Hurting Tim was one of them.

'What happens with the case?' He was dry-eyed, doing his best impression of a man who couldn't care less. 'Are you just going to, like, assign it to somebody else?'

'I'm giving it to Don.' It was a split-second decision, one I hoped would pay off. I didn't want Tim to feel like bottom dog, but even taking into consideration the lingering nausea from the cigarette, I had felt more relaxed and focused standing outside the barracks with Bogle than I had in weeks.

You can't erase what happened here. That's what I'd told Tim when he planted that tree in his yard only to yank it a week later, gray and shriveled, from the ground. And if it couldn't survive there . . .

What did that say about us?

I stopped talking then, and allowed myself to sink into the horrible, bog-like truth of what I'd become. I was a dark cloud in Tim's blue-sky world. I'd never be rid of this pain, not completely. The scars would always remain. If my parents couldn't get over the feeling of betrayal that led them to distance themselves from their only daughter, what did that mean for me and Tim? I didn't know, and that scared me – because after all this time, and all we'd been through, I had thrown our mutual trust into jeopardy all over again.

'OK. Sure.' Tim forced some good humor into his voice. 'Hey look, whatever you think is best. I trust you.'

He kissed my nose, smiled, and turned his back on me.

And once again, I faced the knot on the wall.

SEVENTEEN

I left the cottage in the pale light of morning, long before Tim woke, so I could shower at home before work. There was no valid reason for that, since Tim had long ago insisted I leave half my clothes in his dresser, emptying three whole drawers just for me. It would be obvious to him that I was taking the easy way out, but I didn't think I could face his thinly-veiled disappointment in me. I'd be seeing enough of it at the office soon enough.

Route 12 turned into East Riverfront Road, which led to the private drive at the end of which stood my rental. Through my SUV's open windows I could smell the musky, petrichor scent of the river. On weekends, live music from the mobile home park across the bay bellowed through the silence, performed on a makeshift bandstand at the river's edge for the couples and families who, for the next few weeks, would call those campers home. It was Friday, the first day of the pirate festival, and Mac had warned me the kickoff would be wild. At the moment, the bay was still quiet. As I approached the house, it was something else that disrupted the morning calm.

There was a small parking space abutting my rental, and it was the first thing I saw every time I pulled up. I never used it, preferring to park in the ground-floor garage, so it's where I kept my trash and recycling bins, both tucked into the shade of the roofline and freckled with lichen. The trees encroached on the parking spot so aggressively that, twice a year, its paved western edge was sticky with pollen and leaves. It was here that I eased my SUV to a stop. I got out and stumbled across the cracked asphalt, the heat of what I knew would be another sweltering day already baking into the ground and curling up around my ankles. The front of the rental was in my sights now. Something had been spray-painted on my garage door, a single word made up of ruler-straight lines that glowed poker-red in the creeping sunlight.

Guilty.

Immediately, inevitably, my mind went to Bram. It was habit, predicated on years of expecting my cousin to blindside me at every turn. Even as kids, back when our days were spent solving neighborhood mysteries, I hadn't known it was my bestie Abe pulling the strings. He'd gone from orchestrating classroom crimes to hijacking women's lives while I stood on the sidelines, fumbling for my gun. He was a master of the hoodwink. Hypnotic. Always a beat ahead. It couldn't be Bram this time . . . but that word. It was an accusation, as blatant as a shove.

A-Bay had a year-round population of about a thousand, and I was currently its most famous resident. Any number of locals knew where I lived, because you could be damn sure there was gossip. It hopped like a tick from shop to home to motel, growing fat on the chatter's blood. Still, I didn't think I had a resident to thank for defacing my door. This message, delivered with a steady hand, felt personal.

I had all but forgotten Estella Lopez and Javier Barba since learning Rebecca Hearst was dead, but there wasn't a doubt in my mind that they were responsible for this. They found my rental and made good on their word to harass me. 'I'm here to make your life a living hell,' Estella had said.

Get in line, I thought as I slammed a closed fist against the metal door.

EIGHTEEN

The medical examiner's preliminary autopsy report was waiting for me when I arrived at the barracks, and the details of the murder were grisly. There were four major wounds on the victim's front torso: three four-to-five-inch lacerations to her abdomen, and another near her left breast. The latter had punctured her lung, but the cause of death was listed as exsanguination due to sharp force trauma. While we hadn't managed to locate the murder weapon, the ME had a pretty good idea of what it was. A garden-variety folding pocketknife, brand new, the edge of the blade so sharp it could cut glass.

The medical examiner had also found scratches on Rebecca's body, several incised lacerations across her neck. While those cuts were shallow, they were just as disturbing to me as the wounds that spoke of unbridled violence. They suggested torture, inflicted merely to cause fear.

As expected, Bogle was delighted when I told him he'd be taking Tim's place as the lead.

'I'm about to make my first contribution,' he said, a flush of excitement in his cheeks. 'A tip just came in, from a woman who ate at the Bay Point Grill on Sunday night.'

'Tell me.' Bogle had already reported that the restaurant was a dead end, no cameras inside or out, and like every other place in town it was bustling the night Rebecca and Godfrey Hearst dined there. While several diners remembered seeing the couple around, nobody recalled any unusual behavior.

'It was mostly tourists there that evening, so they wouldn't have noticed,' said Bogle, drawing out the big reveal, 'but the witness who called is a local.'

'You're killing me, Don.'

He chuckled. 'OK, OK. The night Rebecca ate there, so did Chet Bell.'

'Bell? That can't be right.' Chet Bell and I had talked extensively when he ambushed me on Wednesday. He hadn't mentioned anything about crossing paths with Rebecca, let alone eating dinner at the same restaurant. 'Did they interact at all?'

'According to the witness, they had a full-blown conversation.'

'But Rebecca was there with her husband.'

'Who spent most of the night at the bar. You've eaten at Bay Point, yeah? There are two sides to the place, the restaurant and the bar.'

This was true. The bar and dining room had separate entrances from the street, but there was an adjoining doorway inside. It wasn't a bad business concept; serve the people dinner, then herd them to the closest pub, which happens to have the same owner and is just a few steps away. 'So Rebecca stayed in the dining room?' I asked.

'Nursing a glass of white wine while her husband chatted up a group of women having a girls' night. Our witness saw him on her way to the bathroom.'

I pictured the layout of the Bay Point Grill, the orientation of the dining tables. 'If you're in the restaurant, you can't see the bar, can you?'

'Nope, and vice versa – which may be why Rebecca had that long chat with Bell.'

A cold trickle of disquiet slithered down the furrow of my back. 'Chet Bell asked me to downplay the investigation,' I told Bogle. 'That was before we knew the victim was deceased, but he was adamant that her disappearance would negatively impact profits from Pirate Days.'

Bogle's eyes bulged. 'Seriously? And he never mentioned that he talked to her?'

'Nope. Even if he didn't catch her name that night, he would have seen her photo in the paper and on the TV news. There's no way he didn't know what she looked like when he was so concerned her disappearance might spoil A-Bay's big week.' And yet, he'd kept his *tête-à-tête* with Rebecca to himself, even now that he knew she was dead. 'This goes to the top of our priority list.' I reached for the phone on my desk. 'There are a lot of other businesses around the restaurant.' That part of downtown, near the public dock, was wall-to-wall tourist traps. 'I know you said Bay Point doesn't have cameras, but call up those other places and see if they have security footage from that night. I'm going to track down Bell and find out why the hell he's been keeping this from us.'

'Before you do that,' Bogle said, looking suddenly uncertain, 'there's something else I need to tell you.'

Phone receiver hovering in the air, I paused. 'Yeah?'

'It's about the brother and sister from New York.'

Estella and Javier. I set the phone down in the cradle. 'What about them?'

'The guy. Javier Barba.' Bogle frowned at me. 'I hope you don't mind, but I looked into him. Listen, I only scratched the surface on his background, but he's not the kind of dude you want to mess with.'

That got my attention. I'd spent the drive into work wondering how I was going to explain the vandalism to my landlord. 'What do you mean?'

'Guy's got a record,' said Bogle. 'Conspiracy to robbery with a dangerous weapon. Back in 2000, he and a buddy broke into a private residence in Tribeca. Javier Barba did thirty-eight months at Rikers.'

At 400-acres located in the East River, Rikers Island was New York City's principal jail complex and a common place for criminals serving short sentences to end up. At any given time about eighty-five percent of its inmates haven't been convicted, and are either being held on bail or remanded to custody. Thirty-eight months was a fairly short sentence for conspiracy to armed robbery – a Class D felony – but I didn't love what it said about Javier Barba's character.

'It shows a history of violence,' said Bogle. 'It suggests—'

'You think he's dangerous.'

'Don't you?'

I thought about the greeting I'd received that morning, the literal and proverbial writing on the wall. 'They're just upset,' I said of the man and his sister, though I was starting to wonder why I kept defending them. At the same time, twisted as it was, it felt like I'd gotten off easy. Estella had lost her husband, Javier a brother-in-law. If I knew with certainty that accusing me of being complicit in their loved one's murder would bring them even an ounce of comfort, I'd have invited them to go full Banksy on the cottage and even supplied the paint. This kind of retaliation, I could handle. Maybe even deserved.

'It's not just the charge that worries me,' Bogle said. 'I found out where they're staying up here.'

I tilted my head. 'And?'

'You probably know my in-laws own the inn on Carlson Island.'

I flashed to the op-ed by Gracelyn Barlowe, and gritted my teeth. 'I might have heard that,' I said. Carlson was a mid-sized island close to Cape Vincent, not thirty minutes from A-Bay. I'd passed it a few times by boat when Tim and I were working the case on Wolfe Island, which required some ferry trips. Most likely it was Tim who told me about Bogle's connection to the inn, though I couldn't remember when. Regardless, I had paid attention. It was my job to protect the residents of Jefferson County, and that included those on the islands. This one in particular had a history that piqued my interest. 'Are you telling me they're staying at the Carlson?' I asked. For a visit perpetuated by vengeance, it was an opulent choice.

'They are. Checked in last Sunday morning – and it isn't their first visit north. I talked to the concierge, and she remembers them saying they couldn't find a free room anywhere else, "unlike last time." I made some calls. Estella Lopez booked a double at the Admiral for a couple of days in early July, staying through the Fourth. That makes two trips up here in one month.'

'The Admiral, huh?' I bit my thumb. Was it actually possible Estella and Javier had come to A-Bay twice just to find me? Could they have been staking out the town since July? I didn't like the idea of that at all.

Begrudgingly, I told Bogle what I'd found on my garage. He sighed heavily as he shook his head. 'There's no shame in getting an order of protection, you know.'

I laughed out loud. I couldn't help myself. No self-respecting police officer – no officer I knew, period – would agree to a restraining order. If we couldn't defend ourselves against a threat with the amount of training we had, not to mention the weapon we carried, what good were we to anyone?

When my brain conjured the cellar in the East Village, I quickly banished the thought from my mind.

The notion that Barba might be following me did put me a little on edge. His presence at my home felt like an invasion of everything that was holy: privacy, safety, freedom. I had no desire to live in a state of suspension, not knowing when the sudden appearance of a dangerous man would yank me from the tedium of my day and send me spiraling toward peril. This wasn't the first time I'd suspected someone was on my tail, but it was the first time that person was somebody other than Bram. I can't explain why, but after leaving that basement I never truly believed my cousin would threaten my life. While he'd hurt me in the past, he didn't ever want me dead. Could I say the same about Javier Barba?

I wanted to move on from talk of a stalker, to focus on ferreting out Rebecca's killer, but Bogle wasn't done. 'He confronted you in public,' he said, 'and tracked you to your home. His behavior, his aggression . . . Shana, it's escalating.'

'It was graffiti.'

'Sure. But what will it be next time?'

I chewed the inside of my lip. Javier's history wasn't exactly comforting, nor was the discovery that he'd been in A-Bay before, but if he or his sister intended to hurt me, would they not have done it when I was still oblivious to their presence? Instead, they'd exposed themselves, making sure I knew who they were and why they'd come.

Still, loathe as I was to admit it, I knew Bogle was right. Estella and Javier's presence in town didn't begin and end with graffiti.

Their visit was about something else.

NINETEEN

The sun was a bucket of scalding water on my back, and it made the skin under my dark shirt pucker and itch as I left the dock owned by Sir Robert Peel Boat Tours. The harsh light gave everything a white sheen: the windshields of cars parked along James Street; the sloping road; even the river it dead-ended into. When I got back to my car, I yanked my sunglasses out of the center console and spun the dial on the A/C to max.

According to the girl who answered the phone when I called the ticket booth, Chet Bell would be in a meeting until noon. When, at twelve thirty p.m., I darkened his doorway, the same leggy teen in jean shorts said he'd gone to lunch, location undisclosed, return time undetermined. 'Pirate Days has everyone real busy. He probably won't be back today at all.' The way she said it, you'd think Bell wasn't commemorating a dead-and-buried rum-smuggling rebel so much as launching a civilian space flight to the moon.

No part of me believed there was a simple explanation for Bell's decision to conceal his interaction with Rebecca Hearst. Chet Bell was respected in town, married to a woman named Mavis who'd insisted he start biking to stave off heart disease. By all accounts – even Sheriff Mac's – he was a man who'd devoted more than a decade to bettering the Village of Alexandria Bay. There had to be a reason for his disinclination to become a material witness in a homicide.

Frustrated, I started to make my way back to the station. Pirate Days hadn't been on my radar last year; I'd only just arrived in town, and street festivals were never Carson's bag. From what I'd heard, the main attraction was Sunday's Grand Parade, but there were dozens of other events too, and I could see I'd made a mistake by taking James Street to Miller. Even after Mac's warning about the noise, and even though I'd been listening to Tim and Bogle and Sol speculate about the incoming crowds for weeks, I wasn't prepared for the madness that had descended on A-Bay.

Day one, and the streets teemed with blue-tongued children wielding plastic swords, grown men in cheap felt tricorn hats, women in Jolly Roger shirts cut down to their sternums. Festival goers hauled Styrofoam takeout containers of leftover clam linguine and chicken fingers stiff with cooled fryer oil, and none of them gave a shit about traffic. A-Bay's main drag wasn't closed to cars, but pedestrians didn't seem to care. My speedometer barely topped five miles an hour as I rolled along behind a mammoth Chevy Suburban with Pennsylvania plates that paused every few feet to let an overstimulated family wander into the road.

Seeing the crowds hit me with a profound sense of dread. Five days ago, a woman much like the brunette in the frayed cut-offs to my left or the busty friend laughing into a strawberry cone had been carved up like a joint of beef. I slapped the dashboard vent, redirecting a blast of icy air on to my face, and stifled a shiver.

My car was crawling past The Dot when the glint of a sunbeam on a long, dark braid caught my eye. The patio was cluttered with wrought iron tables and chairs with curling arms, every one of them occupied. In summer you could often find live music outdoors at The Dot, and today was no exception. I could hear it even through my SUV's closed windows. The indie rock was coming from a man strumming an acoustic guitar before a standing mic. A few tables away, the woman with the braid ignored him as she sipped the dregs of her drink, which by the look of her plastic cup was one of the bistro's notorious wine slushies.

Behind me, a driver leaned on his horn. I rolled down my window, flung out an arm to wave him around. Both sides of the street were parked full. There was a lot around the corner, but the two plates on Estella's table looked like they'd already been licked clean.

Estella and her brother hadn't been far from my thoughts since my conversation with Bogle. Their repeated visits to town, the confrontation outside the Bean-In, the message on my garage door; it ate at me. I needed to know why they were here, and if I wanted to catch Jay Lopez's wife, I'd have to be fast.

Punching down the button for my hazard lights, I turned off the engine.

Despite the two mammoth maple trees that flanked the patio's entrance and dappled it with shade, it was only marginally cooler beside the restaurant and I was sweating again by the time I reached Estella's table. 'Mrs Lopez,' I said, removing my sunglasses so the woman could see my eyes. 'Can we talk?'

Estella looked up and shrunk away from me. 'Javier's in the bathroom. He'll be right back.'

'I got your message,' I said.

Her face went slack. 'We were just leaving.' She reached for the Coach purse that hung on the back of her chair and looked over my head for her brother.

Estella had been bold when she confronted me on the street, unflinching. Without Javier for backup, she almost looked afraid. This was a reaction I wasn't used to. People were generally too busy judging to fear me. I hated the gossip and undisguised stares, but I hated the look on Estella's face now even more.

Before I could stop myself I reached for her arm, my palm slippery against her skin. 'I'm not like him.' I had to make her understand, to distance myself from Bram's violence. 'I am *nothing* like my cousin.'

Estella shook me off and stared me down. 'I don't care what you are, OK? I only care what you did.' She closed her eyes, just for a second, before going on. 'You're a cop. You were NYPD back then, trained to disarm suspects. You were taught to keep your head. You think I don't know how it works? Jay was a cop, too, and he would have laid down his life for you.'

I wanted to tell her he'd done exactly that, but I couldn't find the words. Now it was me closing my eyes against the sun and Estella's burning accusation. How could I ever explain? It wasn't just about the week I'd spent in captivity, or the trauma bond I'd formed as a result, but the decade and a half Abe and I lived together as family and best friends. Estella couldn't know what any of that was like, or that I planned to kill him anyway, or how quickly Bram reacted to Lopez's sudden appearance on the stairs, or how addled my mind was when he did.

I'm sorry. I'll never forgive myself for your husband's death. I opened my mouth to say it. That's when I felt the heel of a flexed hand connect with my breastbone. Winded and shaken I stumbled back into a nearby table, scrabbling to gain purchase while scattering plates and silverware on to the floor.

'Javi, *no!*' Estella's voice was a screech.

'The fuck you doing here?' I could feel his spittle on my cheeks, my lips. 'You threaten her? Did you? Get the fuck away from my sister.'

By now, the patio had fallen silent. Every diner had abandoned their syrupy wine to watch the commotion. Even the guitarist was looking wary, a grimace on his face as he hesitantly played on. Beside her brother, Estella looked as stunned as I felt. That changed when I reached for my cuffs.

The moments that followed were swift and hard. Whether he didn't expect the response he got or my martial arts training was finally paying off, Javier was facedown on the table in an instant. Over the years, I'd heard many an officer jokingly use the expression 'cuff 'em and stuff 'em,' a catchphrase from *The Dukes of Hazzard*, but it wasn't inaccurate. No sooner was he immobilized than I dragged him down the patio steps and shoved him in the back of my car. Estella shrieked at the sight of her brother in handcuffs, and for a second I thought she was going to take a swipe at me too, but she only trailed us to the street.

'Your brother will be at the state police station,' I told her as she swayed on the sidewalk, fingers quivering against her glossed lips. 'I hear this isn't your first time in town,' I added coolly. 'I'm sure you can find the way.'

TWENTY

When Estella Lopez arrived at the barracks it was with an attorney, a local ambulance chaser who was all too happy to take her cash. She needn't have bothered. Javier Barba was released with a summons to appear in court, but not before I'd grilled him about his presence in A-Bay.

'We're here on vacation,' he told me, tattooed arms folded on the table. Standing his ground. 'That's it.'

'And you just happened to bump into me at the Bean-In.'

Javier faltered. 'Estella read that letter in the paper. But we didn't think we'd find you.'

'No? What about all that stuff about making my life a living hell?'

'She was pissed.' He said it with a shrug. 'She got every right to be.' As for the graffiti, Javier swore he wasn't to blame.

When at last Estella led her brother out the door, she shot a look at me over her shoulder that could have split rock.

The confrontation with Javier, coupled with several nights of poor sleep, had me dragging. My limbs felt like they'd been dunked in wet cement. I had planned to track down Bogle for an update, and was hoping I'd bump into Tim on the way. I hadn't seen him all day, didn't even know if he'd heard what happened at The Dot. We hadn't talked about the previous night either, and that nagged at me. The feeling I had when I thought of him now reminded me of where our relationship was months ago, that agonizing charade of going about our days wearing simulated smiles and pretending everything was OK when in fact I'd rejected him in the worst way. I needed to find him, and soon. Instead of searching the barracks, though, I took a left into my office, pressed the door closed behind me, and reached for my phone. There was something I had to do first.

My brother's voice in my ear was a balm on my soul. 'It's you,' he said. The words had an echo. I pictured Estella on the sidewalk, her face a mask of awe and disgust. This time, though, it wasn't Jay Lopez's wife who'd said it, but Doug.

He and I had barely spoken since I told him the truth about our cousin. As much as that stung, I'd respected his request for time. But Estella and Javier's arrival in town had changed my outlook on things. Javier had driven all the way upstate with his sister to confront me. He'd put his freedom on the line to protect Estella and defend his fallen brother-in-law. It may not have been smart, but the loyalty he'd displayed was fierce. Would Doug have done the same for me? I didn't know if he was ready to talk, but I had to try.

We'd always been close, Doug and me, especially after Abe skipped town as a teen and we were left with the terrible knowledge that an amoral boy of sixteen had been unleashed on the world. I often wondered if there was anything we could have done about that, but we didn't know where Abe had gone, or that he was already becoming Bram, and even if we had, we possessed no definitive proof of his darkness. Doug once confessed that he never fully trusted our cousin. He didn't like Abe's possessive attitude toward me when we were younger, or that he was always driving a wedge between me and my friends. But when he ran away, we both chose to turn a blind eye to what he'd done. It was easier for Doug, I think, than for me, doomed as I was to look at the pale, pinched scar stretching from ear to mouth forever more.

I'd called Doug because I hoped he would remember we were once on the same side. I thought that maybe this time he'd listen when I told him everything I'd done was to protect him, our aunt, Abe's sister, our folks. If Doug could understand that, then maybe the rest of our family would, too.

'How are you?' I asked when my brother fell silent. The question sounded oddly formal and forced. I cleared my throat, adding, 'And Josie and Hen?' What had Doug and my sister-in-law told Henrietta about their aunt? I couldn't imagine.

'Everyone's fine,' he said. Then: 'It's good to hear your voice, sis.'

I went boneless, letting my forehead loll against the office window, which was icy from the A/C vent above. 'God, it's really good to hear yours.'

'You're OK?' There was guilt in his question, and the bones of an apology, too. Until Bram, the troubles I'd had to shoulder without my big brother's support were few and far between. 'We saw that letter in the paper online.'

'Ah.' I hadn't been expecting that, but then why wouldn't my family have read Gracelyn Barlowe's op-ed? They were watching the news just as closely as I was, praying the press would lose interest so we could all vanish into the ether. It occurred to me that my family might be using the news to keep tabs on me, too. 'I'm sorry,' I told him, 'I'm sorry for everything. You know I didn't mean for any of this to happen, not like this. You know that, Doug.'

Once again, there was silence on the line. At length, Doug said, 'We need more time, Shay.'

Early on in my new life upstate, before I was used to the pull of the current and the heave and tumble of the SP boat, my stomach used to flip at the mere mention of water. That sensation returned when Doug confirmed my worst fears. Strangely, my mind went back to Jared Cunningham. I was thinking about the people he'd mentioned: Casey, whose psychopathic father tried to convince everyone she was as crazy as he was; Noah and his murderous sibling, whom he himself turned in. What did the other members of their families think of them? When Casey and Noah came home, were they welcomed? Or did mothers and sisters, cousins and aunts, tell them they "needed more time?"

Even under the arctic blast of the building's central air, I could feel the sun baking the window. I pictured the glass reaching its melting point and drooping, Dalí-like, over the frame. And me, with no protection from the outside world at all.

'You got it,' I said, ignoring the sting behind my eyes as I ended the call.

TWENTY-ONE

'You look beat.'

Bogle stood at the door to my office rubbing circles on his scalp with a free hand as he gazed down at me from underneath a rutted brow. Like the knuckle-cracking, this was another tick of his that I'd detected over time. We all had them, but this one was the most conspicuous. Hard to ignore a habit that drew further attention to Bogle's extreme height and baldness, the forbidding severity of his looks.

'It's been a day,' I said, slumping into the chair by my desk.

'Understandable. I was just hoping you had some energy left.'

'Yeah? Why's that?'

'I've got a bead on a party tonight.'

'A party.' On the Pirate Days schedule circulating around town, I'd seen that the festivities were set to kick off tonight with something called a block dance that ran from eight to ten. It was the last place I wanted to be, especially in the thick of a homicide investigation. But Bogle had something else in mind.

'It's at my in-law's place. The Carlson?' His face reddened as he said it. His neck, too.

'Oh.' A party at his in-law's hotel? After Gracelyn Barlowe gleefully eviscerated my reputation? Bogle rarely spoke of his wife or her family, which I'd taken as a sign of professionalism. All I really knew about Juliet was that she and Bogle had been married five years. They'd celebrated their anniversary in the spring, at a rustic Italian restaurant across the border in Gananoque.

The Carlson was said to be an architectural treasure, but it wasn't always that way. It was built in the late 1800s by a tycoon with E. Remington and Sons, the first manufacturer of commercial typewriters. Back then the house was called Wyckoff Villa, and it was 15,000 square feet of Richardsonian Romanesque Tudor-Revival perfection. When its owner died the day after moving in – what I wouldn't give to know the rest of *that* story – the property was acquired by General Electric, which intended to use it for corporate retreats. Then came WWII, and plans, along with the home itself, were abandoned.

When I looked the place up sometime last spring, I'd lucked onto an old real estate listing packed with original black-and-white photos of the home alongside contemporary images that put its crumbling plaster and lath on full display. The manor on Carlson Island wasn't the only extravagant Gilded Age home in the area to fall victim to desertion, but according to Tim, it was one of the last to be revived. Five years ago, a local family – Juliet's family, the Barlowes – purchased the historic property for less than half a million dollars. Three years later, they opened the doors to an inn, the renovation supposedly so impeccable it inspired articles in the travel sections of the *Boston Globe*, *Globe and Mail*, and *New York Times*. The Carlson had risen from the ashes like a phoenix, and it had the high nightly rates to show for it.

'The party, it's for Pirate Days,' Bogle explained. 'Invitation only, to get business owners and locals hyped about the festival. Gracelyn and Morton have it every year – but don't worry, we'll steer clear of them. I wasn't going to go, but I've reconsidered.'

'I bet it's quite a place.' I was already scrambling for an excuse to reject his invitation, because I was pretty sure this was an attempt to curry favor with the boss. Bogle was doing good work on our case, but he was ambitious, and likely after more responsibility. No doubt he also wanted to convince me he should hold a senior investigator title someday.

'Juliet does all the PR.' Bogle rolled his eyes as he said it. 'You wouldn't believe how many times I've heard the words "Jewel of the Thousand Islands."'

'That's . . . nice,' I said, preparing myself to hurt his feelings, 'but . . . what? What's funny, Don?'

It was his expression. Bogle's face had broken into a wicked grin. 'Relax, it's not a date or anything,' he said with a chuckle. 'Chet Bell will be there.'

Well, I'll be damned. 'You're kidding me.'

'Hand to God. The Chamber of Commerce never misses it. It's become a tradition,' he said. 'Dance, mingle and toast to the lucrative week ahead.'

I couldn't help but smile. It felt crass, considering an invitation to a party at a palatial manor when Rebecca Hearst's family was in mourning, the woman's killer still at large, but I hadn't managed to connect with Bell, and I still considered him a key witness. I was very interested in hearing what he had to say about his conversation with our victim.

I was about to congratulate Bogle on his quick thinking when it occurred to me that a party at the Carlson meant people. Residents and visitors who read the news and would know who I was.

'If you're worried you'll be bombarded, don't be,' Bogle said as he studied my face. 'I mean, look at you.' He paused for a beat and in spite of myself, I blushed under his admiring gaze. 'I barely recognized you with that new haircut. Leave the state police jacket at home and you could be a different person.'

A *different person*. How good would that feel, to be someone else for a night?

'I do own a dress.' It was my one and only, a simple black sheath I only trotted out for funerals, but Bogle didn't need to know that.

Again, his face broke into a smile. 'Great. There's a dock on the mainland, near Burnham Point State Park.' He grabbed a snatch of paper off my desk and jotted down an address as he spoke. 'Look for the boat that ferries guests back and forth. Come anytime after seven. I'll be waiting on the island. Chet Bell is in for quite a surprise.'

As it turned out, so was I.

TWENTY-TWO

Tim hadn't been happy to hear about my Friday night plans. 'You know Gracelyn Barlowe will be there, right?' he said when I called him after work. 'The woman who wrote that letter?'

'Yup. It's going to be awfully tempting to clock her, but I'll try to resist since I'm on the job.'

'I was hoping to see you tonight.' He was keyed up; I could hear the telltale shiver of concern in his voice. After talking to Bogle I'd come straight home, missing my chance to reconnect with Tim. There was a chasm opening between us, and I knew he felt the distance as much as I did.

'I want that too,' I told him softly. 'But this is my chance to get at Bell.' As I spoke, I gave myself a final once-over in the bathroom mirror, still faintly steamy from my shower. Rather than tucking my short hair behind my ears, I reached for the tin of pomade Tim kept in my medicine cabinet and slicked my bangs straight back. The style accentuated my eyes, but more than that it emphasized the sickle-shaped groove along my jaw. I tilted my head. *Maybe you're on to something, Shay.* If calling attention to my scar made me look more intimidating, all the better. 'I could come to the cottage after, if you want?'

'I want.'

I smiled. 'Done.'

'This is your first time over there, yeah? To the inn?'

'Yeah.' I stepped into my heels and headed for the door. 'I hear it's really something.'

'You heard right. It's got a lot of interesting history. The guy who built it, the one who made a fortune off the company that sold the first commercial typewriter – which, by the way, was the same outfit that made Remington guns – died in that place the same night he moved in. His wife had passed not a month earlier. After that, it was stripped for materials during WWII and sat empty for decades, right up until it was bought by the Barlowes. People

like to say it's haunted, which Juliet and her mom play up in
interviews to get more press. Every now and then, you hear a story
about a guest who felt like they were being watched.'

'I'll give your regards to Casper,' I said as I reached for my
purse. 'And the wicked witch, too.'

I thought I was prepared. I'd seen pictures of the mansion post-
renovation both online and around town. There wasn't a Thousand
Islands travel brochure in existence that didn't include an aerial
photo of the handsome manor set at the western end of Carlson
Island. Still, when the skiff that was used to ferry guests made
its approach, I felt my jaw unhinge. It was Tern Island all over
again, only even more juiced up – and this time, I actually felt
a twinge of excitement. Thanks to Bogle, I had an opportunity
to explore a historic island home while also squeezing the truth
out of wily Chet Bell.

The Carlson was, for all intents and purposes, a castle.
The tower that once rose from the edge of the house had long
since been torn down, but the fifty-room inn still boasted fairytale
turrets and arches, a majestic marble staircase, and oriel windows.
The ferryman, a bearded man in his sixties named Len who had
a chest so broad his arms hung away from his sides, told me all
about the place on the ride over, in a boat painted navy with
brilliant gold trim.

'The interior had to be rebuilt almost entirely from scratch,' he
said as we glided away from the dock next to the Barlowes's well-
lit boathouse. The night was muggy, my neck slippery with sweat,
but I was too focused on Len to care. 'The exterior is a true replica
of the original, but the inside is modern and bright. I'll be honest,
the Barlowe family took some heat for that decision from history
buffs and traditionalists who wanted to keep the build as authentic
as possible, but they all came around. You'll see why.'

'That must have been expensive,' I said. 'All that space, all
those rooms crumbling to dust.'

'I'll say. The home was in a real state of disrepair – which
explains why it took seventy years to sell. Imagine dealing with
that listing? It paid off in the end, though.' At that, he chuckled.
It wasn't just his chest that was broad; the man had the neck of
a powerlifter, his lateral muscles like two ribeye steaks. 'There

were other interested parties over the years,' he said, 'but once they saw the house for themselves and found out what it would cost to renovate, they skedaddled. Island construction costs about thirty percent more than projects on the mainland.'

'The Barlowes took on quite a project, then.'

'Indeed they did. They had some help, though,' said Len. 'When the New York Historical Society got wind of their plan to open a hotel, they kicked in some money for renovations. In return, the Barlowes run paid tours a couple days a week. That money goes back to the society.'

'Mind if I ask what the Barlowes do? What they did before this, I mean.'

'Ah. That would be shipping. Morton Barlowe is top dog of the St Lawrence Seaway Corporation, president and CEO. All those freighter ships you see chugging through the channel? His company supplies the pilots who navigate tankers through the St Lawrence Seaway, from St Regis, New York to Port Weller, Ontario.'

'Ah.' I imagined there was money to be made from that kind of work. My rental cottage had a view of the channel of which Len spoke, and tankers passed by it more often than an Amazon delivery truck. Not a day went by that there weren't ships making their way from Montreal to the Great Lakes or vice versa, moving iron ore, coal, grain, cement. I'd even seen ships carrying wind farm turbine blades longer than the wing of a Boeing 747.

'It's a lucrative business,' Len said. 'Morton Barlowe has been in it for decades. But Morton's wife, Gracelyn, wanted a project of her own, and people like the Barlowes don't do anything halfway. The hotel took off right away. It's Gracelyn and the Barlowe offspring, Amos and Juliet, who run the place. It's only open seven months of the year because of access issues' – he waved his stubby fingers at the river, which I knew would start to freeze as early as November – 'but most summer weekends are booked solid, sometimes up to a year in advance.'

'I'm guessing this weekend is one of those,' I said, wondering how Estella and Javier managed to score a room.

As the boat coasted up to the dock Len grinned and said, 'Arrr.' His pirate impersonation wasn't half bad.

Bogle promised to meet me upon my arrival, and true to his word, he was waiting on grass so green and plush it looked like new carpeting. His eyes bugged when he saw me and he muttered something under his breath that I didn't quite catch, though I thought I heard the word 'pretty.'

'You weren't kidding about this place,' I said, looking up at the brightly lit manor before us. 'It's a stunner.'

Bogle's grin was conspiratorial and giddy. 'Wait till you see the inside.'

It was so chilly in the hotel that goosebumps rose on my arms, but it wasn't the artificial cold of airport terminals and walk-in freezers. The humidity and summer heat had been muscled out by rough-hewn stone walls, polished marble, heavy doors that sealed in the perfumed air and deadened every sound. The place smelled of lilies and vanilla and citrus and cash and it was by far the grandest island home I'd seen yet. Len wasn't kidding about the décor; while those turn-of-the-century bones remained, its interior was bright and clean with glossy navy-checkered floors, taffeta upholstery, silk drapes like poured cream. Everywhere I turned, artfully arranged bouquets of flowers spilled from vases of cut crystal that could cave in a table. Someone had done a beautiful job here, and it was all I could do to stay focused on finding Chet Bell.

The event was already well underway, and the main floor bustled with guests in summer cocktail attire. I hadn't been expecting a pirate theme – this wasn't a kid's birthday party – but I spotted several Jolly Rogers on the walls, and more than a few guests had accessorized with bandanas. One woman wore a silver dress with ruffles down the back that made her look a little like a sturgeon. I recognized a few faces as local business owners rubbed shoulders with hotel guests in nautical dresses and crisp sport coats. Coral, the precise shade of Godfrey Hearst's shorts, was as pervasive as white and navy, which appeared to be the hotel's signature color scheme. On the check-in counter, the stack of business cards was emblazoned with a navy-and-white logo, an antique typewriter spitting out a sheet of paper shaped like a wave.

I scanned the nearest clot of guests as Bogle and I headed into the sitting room, taking in their good cheer and boozy smiles. Had the Barlowes considered cancelling the event when news of the homicide reached them? I had to wonder. There would no doubt be whispers tonight about 'another murder, another killer on the loose.' For the moment, though, the guests were doing a good job of feigning ignorance and drinking their way to oblivion.

Bogle's eyes trailed a server with a tray of champagne flutes, and before I could stop him, he was pressing a glass, cool and fizzing, into my hand.

'We're on duty,' I said.

'For appearances only. The trick is to act casual.' He flashed me a quick wink as he touched the rim of his glass to mine. 'We don't want Bell thinking we're here for him, or he'll bolt.'

The man had a point. 'We'll mingle,' I said. 'Looks like we're starting right now.'

A man in khakis and a red seersucker shirt was walking our way. I watched as the stranger gave Bogle a fist bump. The two exchanged a fleeting hug. 'Shana Merchant,' said Bogle, pivoting back to me, 'meet Amos Barlowe.'

'Barlowe.' *Shit*. I showed him my gritted teeth. 'Hope you don't mind me crashing the party.'

'Not a bit,' said Amos. 'Any friend of my brother-in-law's is a friend of mine.'

When I turned back to Bogle, he was swallowing a mouthful of champagne. There was an energy between the men that didn't sit right with me, a strange tension running through their words. 'Amos is Juliet's brother, the baby of the family,' Bogle explained. Then, to Amos: 'Shana and I work together.'

Amos raised his eyebrows at that, the act shifting the thick hair on his scalp. 'So *you're* Shana,' he said, looking me up and down. 'In that case, you don't need to be Don's plus-one. Always good to have some state police muscle around.' He leaned toward me, cupping a hand to his mouth. 'You never know when a grab for the last mini crab cake might come to blows.'

While I put Amos in his late twenties, he lacked the slipshod looks and unearned swagger of other guys his age, the ones currently wandering downtown A-Bay wearing low-slung jeans as they slugged their tallboys. He looked a lot like Juliet, whose picture I'd seen on Bogle's desk; both brother and sister were brunettes with strong jaws and twinkly smiles. I suspected that Amos was the same breed as Godfrey Patrick Hearst III; it was clear the man was brought up with money. I doubted the Barlowes had struggled to make ends meet in decades, not with their patriarch heading a company that offered a critical service to the active shipping business. Wealth was a surefire way to put some spit and polish on just about anyone – but money was no guarantee of joy, and I could see Amos wasn't wholly content tonight. It was in the eyes.

'Amos is in the business,' Bogle said as I scanned the crowd for Bell's distinctive pompadour and outlandish outfit of the day, maybe something in a floral print. We needed to keep moving. If Bell was here, there was no telling how long he'd stay, and I didn't want to miss the chance to question him.

'Freighter ships or hotels?' I asked as I searched.

'Welcome to my office.' Amos spread out his arms and grinned. 'Eleven bedrooms, seven acres, and a hundred and ninety-eight feet of water frontage. Five years of running this place, and counting. Never thought I'd end up working as a hotel manager after getting a degree in economics from Princeton, but here I am. That's my wife, Tarryn.' He gestured to the woman in the skintight silver dress I'd seen when I came in. 'She did the decorating, used to work for Martha Stewart's magazine. You wouldn't believe how much effort it takes to keep this place on-trend. My sister, Juliet, handles PR. With a little help from Mom.'

Amos jerked his chin in the direction of the lobby and I saw Juliet Barlowe in the next room over. Despite her dark hair she had fair, creamy skin that must have been a battle to defend in summer. Juliet was taller than I expected, and incredibly fit; her navy flats and sleeveless white shirt-dress with the collar turned up oozed nautical chic, but the outfit also showed off toned arms and legs. Beside her, a woman in her late sixties with a silver-streaked bun whispered something in Juliet's ear. Gracelyn Barlowe laughed, glossy red lips yanked wide. I cringed at the sight.

'It's a family affair, then,' I said, as politely as I could.

'Well, not for everyone. Right, Don?' Amos chuckled. 'We never could convince him to pitch in, the scamp. But then, he does have a pretty interesting job. You, too.'

'You could say that.'

Amos shook his head and said, 'I heard about the homicide. That poor, poor woman.'

'We can't say too much about it, I'm afraid.'

'Right, of course. I guess you're both going to be pretty busy this weekend.'

'Amos and I play pickleball on Saturdays,' Bogle told me, 'at the TI Club. But yeah, I'll be a no-show tomorrow, man.'

The Thousand Islands Club was as fancy as it got in the North Country. 'Who's the champ?' I asked.

Bogle said, 'He wins every time. Refill?' Somehow, his champagne flute was empty. 'Wait right here,' Bogle told me. 'I got you.'

He grabbed my glass, the wine still an inch from the rim, and started to weave his way through the crowd.

'Pretty sure he could have flagged down a server,' said Amos. 'It's not like the guy's hard to miss. My youngest calls him Green Giant.'

'He does stand out,' I said as I watched Bogle go.

'I'm glad he came tonight, though.' A shadow passed over Amos's face. He'd angled his body away from me to look out the nearby window, but all I could see there was the two of us, reflected in the dark glass. 'We were all sure he'd skip it.'

'Because of the investigation?' I didn't want Amos knowing why we were here. People like to talk, especially at parties. Especially in villages like A-Bay.

'Because of Juliet. Sorry,' Amos said, turning back to me and lifting his glass to his lips. 'This is awkward. You working with him. Him being married to my sister. Honestly, we're all just grateful they don't have kids.'

I felt my brow furrow. Amos lowered his drink without taking the sip.

'You didn't know,' he said.

Bogle and his wife were having problems? It was only a few months ago that he'd been excitedly planning their anniversary dinner. 'I'm sorry,' I said, looking past him to make sure Bogle was still out of earshot. 'No, I didn't know.'

'Juliet tried everything,' he told me. 'The thing is we all saw it coming, watched him slowly spiral out of control, but he was in denial – still is – and there was nothing we could do. We're all hoping it's still fixable, but he's in a bad way. The man needs to get his head straight, you know?'

I didn't, had no clue what Amos was talking about. It must have shown in my expression, because Amos blanched.

'Shit, you're his boss, aren't you. Christ, forget I said anything. The guy doesn't need trouble at work, too.'

He glanced over my shoulder and immediately dropped his gaze. I swiveled my head, and saw what he'd seen: Bogle, chatting up an older man by the bar. Both champagne flutes gone and a tumbler of something amber-colored near-empty in his hand.

Swift as a gear shifting into place, I understood. I hadn't seen any evidence that Don had a drinking problem, not in all the months I'd known him. Our interactions took place during work hours, and I didn't spend time with him outside the barracks the way I did with Tim, but I would know if he was a high-functioning alcoholic, wouldn't I? Still, Amos's implication was clear.

'How long?' I asked.

He studied me, weighing his options, before shaking his head. 'Since it's been this bad? Three, maybe four months. We used to joke about it, which in retrospect was a shitty thing to do. When Don starts drinking, the alcohol turns into truth serum – Canadian whisky, especially. He blurts all kinds of ridiculous things. Last Thanksgiving, over dinner at my parents', he accused my mother of bribing Juliet not to marry him. Caused quite a scene, actually; Jules had to drag him out of the house. Half the time he doesn't even remember what he said. It used to happen once or twice a year at most, then suddenly he was pouring Jules a glass of wine in the evening and finishing the rest of the bottle himself. Now? He's tying one on four, five times a week, and drinking in the daytime, too. Juliet was worried, at first. Then she got scared. He's been following her.' Amos tented two fingers over his eyes and rubbed his temples. 'Showing up at the bars and restaurants she goes to with friends and acting all surprised that she's there, too. One time, she caught him outside her girl-friend's place, watching them through the picture window. I'm sure you can imagine, doing what you do for work. It's freaking her out.'

It made no sense. The Don Bogle I knew was thoughtful and considerate. He'd defended me when it felt like the whole town had turned bitter. He had my back. And it didn't feel right, listening to his brother-in-law accuse him of being a drunk. I knew I should take the declaration with a grain of salt. Amos was Juliet's brother. Presumably, his allegiance was to her. Even so, the possibility that he was being honest about Bogle's current condition concerned me.

There was something else that bothered me about Amos's story. If Bogle and his wife were separated, why had he been so insistent about coming to her family's party? Even knowing the event might present us with an opportunity to confront Chet Bell, being here put Bogle in an uncomfortable position. In the forty minutes that we'd been inside the Carlson, I hadn't seen him make an effort to find anything other than the bar.

'Look, don't get me wrong, Don's a great guy.' Amos's face twisted, and I suspected he was starting to realize how much his confession could hurt Bogle professionally. 'He just hasn't been himself lately. Everyone goes through phases like this, right? And Don knows how to compartmentalize. Cops, detectives, they're trained to put their emotions aside. Right?'

'Right,' I said, even though leaving work at the barracks wasn't nearly that simple. The emotional toll crime took on us could bleed into every aspect of our lives. It was the reason so many cops succumbed to addiction. We lived in a near-constant state of stress and fear, the polar opposite of suspended animation. Our days were live wires come loose from their groundings, and we were forever at risk of being fried. If we weren't mentally fit for duty, people like me and Tim, Don and Mac could lose our lives or endanger others. I knew that better than almost anyone. And here was my investigator's brother-in-law telling me Bogle needed to 'get his head straight.'

I thought about my conversation with Bogle outside the barracks. The good work he'd been doing on our homicide case. 'Whatever he's going through right now,' I said, 'I trust him implicitly.'

Amos stood very still for a moment before adjusting his expression and the collar of his shirt. 'Then you're a braver person than I am,' he said.

And that's when I saw him.

Chet Bell.

TWENTY-THREE

From where I stood in the overcrowded parlor, I had a clear view of both the foyer-turned-lobby and the adjoining lounge, which boasted a fifteen-foot ceiling and so many books it could have passed for the New York Public Library's Rose Main Reading Room. With oiled hair and a striped three-piece suit, Bell was coming down the stairs from one of the upper floors of the inn with a woman on his arm who looked the right age to be his wife. He was gladhanding before he even stepped onto the lustrous checkered floor, waving at some guests and winking at others on the way to the bar. Reveling in his station. I hadn't fully understood Mac's concern over his visit to the barracks until I saw him swarmed by other business owners. Bell was a man with clout.

And at the moment, he was standing just a few feet away from Don Bogle.

A single guest separated Bell and Bogle now, and I watched dumbstruck as my investigator chuckled with the paunchy man on the other side of him, not noticing the witness within arm's reach. Lifting his drink to his lips yet again.

'I have to go,' I told Amos. There was a clear path from me to the bar, but that wouldn't last. The guests whirlpooled around each other, forever in motion. I stepped past Amos Barlowe and collided with a woman in enormous anchor earrings. 'Excuse me,' I said, 'coming through,' but the crowd shifted now in earnest, everyone moving as one toward the lobby where Gracelyn was preparing to give a speech. My gaze swept back across the room to find Bogle. His collar was askew now, his dress shirt stained. He laughed as he leaned toward a woman two decades his senior who looked like she couldn't abide the fug of his breath for another second. When he clapped her frail shoulder, white wine sloshed from her glass onto the polished floor. He and Bell were still just inches apart, but Bogle wasn't paying attention. He didn't see.

Bell turned his head in my direction. The man froze, and then his attention tripped past me, just as if he hadn't noticed me at all.

'*Move.*' I forced a guest aside, knocking into another as I picked up speed, but Chet Bell was moving now, too. He skirted the perimeter of the lounge to the dining room, disappearing through a paneled door at the far end of the room. I didn't know my way around the Carlson, had no idea where that door led, so I followed him – or tried to. Gracelyn was talking now, her voice merrily commanding, the guests moving ever closer to the lobby. Blocking my path.

Crossing the room felt like wading through a weedy swamp. When I finally arrived at the door Bell had used and pushed it open, I found myself outside. A wall of sticky air, and then I felt it; a gust of wind off the water. I drank it in and looked around.

The cobblestone courtyard was set up with wrought-iron breakfast tables and cushioned chairs, the high brick wall that surrounded it dripping with vines a brilliant shade of green. A few other partygoers had trickled out into the night, but Bell wasn't standing among them. In the middle of the wall, facing the river, an ornate gate swung on its hinges.

'Well, well.'

I spun toward the voice, already knowing who I'd see. Estella Lopez wasn't dressed like a pirate, but she was dressed up; smoky eye make-up, silky white top, that same gold necklace dipping into her shirt. She looked stunning.

She also looked livid.

'You had no right,' she said, as if no time at all had passed since she came to get her brother from the barracks. 'Javi barely touched you.'

The bone bruise on my chest said otherwise. 'He's lucky I wasn't physically injured,' I told her, 'or he'd be looking at an assault charge.'

'So that's your thing, huh? Intimidation? I didn't expect that, actually. I always figured you for a coward.' Estella watched me through lidded eyes. 'He came back from the bathroom and saw you leaning over me. He was *defending* me. And what's wrong with that? We're from Flatbush, OK? People who look like us learn real early to protect each other, because we damn well know nobody else will.'

Was she not aware I'd cut her brother a break, that I could have had him charged with harassment in the second degree? I contemplated pressing the issue, but the woman had been through enough. 'If you'll excuse me, Ms Lopez—'

'It's *Mrs*. Jay may be dead,' she said, 'but I'll never stop being his wife. But you don't care, do you? Not about him or me.'

I swallowed. Said, 'Of course I care.'

'Like hell you do.'

'What do you want me to say, that I'm sorry? You're goddamn right I'm sorry.' Though my voice was shaky, I told her, 'I'll regret your husband's death for the rest of my life.'

'Yeah? Well, regret didn't pay my funeral bills.'

I nodded, and lowered my head. This wasn't the place for another scuffle, and I needed to get back to searching for Bell. 'Why don't you go enjoy the party?' I said. 'I hear you're staying here at the inn.'

'That's right.' Estella cocked her head. 'You're trying to work out how we can afford it. You think you know us, me and Javi, huh? A poor pathetic widow and a criminal? You don't know a thing about us. Javi made some bad choices – but who hasn't? As for me, go ahead, look me up. I work for a digital agency in Brooklyn that has offices all over the world. I'm in line for a director position. I probably make twice what you do in a year. So yeah,' she spat, 'we're staying here. We order filet mignon and Châteauneuf-du-Pape every fucking night. Only the best for me and my brother on our trip to watch an accessory to murder squirm.'

Estella spun away from me and disappeared back into the hotel. I *was* squirming, because she was right. When, after his death, I learned about Jay Lopez's family, I had pictured a stay-at-home mother with three young kids who sapped all her strength. A woman who was lost without the man whose murder would become a stain on her life, spreading like black mold and leaving her timid and adrift. In my hurry to punish myself, I had jumped to conclusions. I'd underestimated her.

It was a reminder, like a cold hand on my shoulder, that I didn't know the strangers who had come to town at all.

TWENTY-FOUR

The morning sun was a bonfire outside my bedroom window, and I woke up to find the back of my head wet with sweat. *Saturday.* Weeks ago, Tim and I had made plans to spend this one downtown, where Pirate Days would be in full-swing. He was going to show me the sword-fighting group that staged shows around the village, and take me to the ice cream stand for the limited-time flavor, a suspicious combination of banana and black licorice. Instead, I would be spending the day working. I had an obligation to Rebecca's family to find her killer. To Alexandria Bay, too.

It had been a split-second decision to bail on Tim. He'd been expecting me after the party, and instead I'd sent him a weak text claiming I was tired and asking for a raincheck. The revelation about Bogle's drinking had thrown me for a loop. I'd chosen Bogle over Tim, cutting Tim off at the knees in the process, and now I wasn't at all sure I could trust Bogle to perform on what had become a prominent, time-sensitive case.

I'd have to confront Don Bogle, no doubt about that, but I didn't want him thinking I'd nosed around in his personal life. Sometime around two a.m., I made the decision to call him into my office as soon as possible. Make sure he was fit to work the case. If he wasn't, there would be another awkward conversation with Tim in my future. I'd have to fix this, and fast. The last thing this town needed was more bad press.

Reaching for my phone where it was charging on the nightstand, I texted Tim: **You up yet? Got a minute to talk?**

I couldn't promise I'd be free tonight – who could say where the day's leads would take me – but maybe if I gave him a proper apology, my stomach would feel less like a tank of eels.

Before Tim could reply, the device rang in my hand.

'Where'd you disappear to last night, boss?' Bogle's voice was a rake on wet gravel, and in the dead space before I answered I could hear the soft crackle of his lit cigarette.

Did he know his brother-in-law had sold him down the river? That would make this call even more difficult. As it was, I wasn't prepared to have a dialogue about cleaning up his act over the phone. If Bogle was caught under the influence while on duty, I'd need to escalate the situation. Request an assessment from Lieutenant Henderson and a Drug Recognition Expert. Secure both his assigned vehicle and his firearm. Things tended to move quickly in situations like this. 'I struck out with Bell,' I told him, at a loss for how to segue into that conversation. 'I looked for you before I left.'

'Oh yeah? I didn't see you. So Bell was a no-show, huh?'

I'd searched the inn for another hour after bumping into Estella, but as soon as he saw me, Bell up and vanished. We'd blown our chance. Tamping down my frustration, I said, 'Listen, can we meet at the barracks in half an hour? There's something I'd like to talk to you about.'

'Oh,' Bogle said again. 'OK, I guess. Sure.'

'Great. Hey look,' I said, startled, 'Tim's calling on the other line. See you later? Say nine thirty?'

'Sure.'

'Thanks, Don,' I said, and switched to the incoming call. 'Where are you right now?'

Tim sounded breathless, like he'd been pacing. Or running. 'I'm at home,' I told him, swinging my legs off the edge of the bed. 'Why? What's going on?'

'A message came in on the tip line last night.'

'About Rebecca?' We'd received a few crank calls about our suspect since setting up the tip line – we always did – but there had been nothing of value.

'I . . . think so,' he said.

'Well, what did the caller say?'

There was a pause before Tim spoke again. 'They said, "Dead girls tell no tales."'

The words raised the hair on my bare arms. 'What's that supposed to mean?'

'It's a pirate thing. Dead men tell no tales. As in you can't tell someone's secret if you're dead.'

'Dead girls.' I didn't like that at all. 'Wait, girls? Plural?'

'Yeah, plural,' he said. 'And I think I might know why.'

While I'd been tossing in my sweat-soaked bed all morning, Tim had grabbed an early breakfast at the diner downtown. He did that sometimes, didn't seem to mind eating alone in a restaurant. Tim was affable and unreserved, often chatting with a server or some old timer at the coffee bar and having a wonderful time. Only this morning, Tim hadn't been in the company of a stranger.

'I didn't know she was going to be there, obviously,' he said, the words coming fast. 'She came in with a friend and saw me sitting at the counter. We got to talking. She's not doing too great, Shana. I know everyone grieves differently, but it's been four months, and she looked just as dazed today as she did at the funeral.'

Right before Tim and I got together, he had a relationship with a woman named Kelsea Shaw, an obliging local girl who worked in physical therapy. The romance had been brief and relatively uneventful, and they'd parted on good terms. After they broke up, much to everyone's surprise, Kelsea had become engaged to Carson Gates. Tim's ex and my ex were planning to marry. We didn't have long to get used to that strange new reality. The next thing we knew, Carson was dead.

Tim said, 'I don't think she's processed what happened at all.'

'Does she blame me?' I couldn't help it; I had to ask. Out of respect for Kelsea and her family – Carson's, too – I had chosen not to go to the funeral. I hadn't seen Kelsea Shaw in months.

'Honestly?' he said. 'I don't know. But she's gotten totally obsessed with murder – reading about it, watching documentaries. She started talking about this homicide up in Massena last month. Did you hear about that?'

I had, and told him as much. On Independence Day, a woman was found dead an hour and a half north not far from Cornwall, Ontario. Massena was a river town, too, known mainly for its canal locks and cameo in a Jim Carrey movie. Homicides were nearly as atypical there as in A-Bay, but Massena was outside my jurisdiction, and unless a friend was working the case or there was some other connection, crimes that occurred up there were rarely on my radar. On top of that a month ago, when that murder came to light, I'd wanted as little to do with death as possible.

'Shana,' Tim said, 'That case? It's similar to ours. Both women were in their late twenties to early thirties, and both of them were stabbed.'

I put Tim on speaker and opened a browser window on my phone. Another young woman stabbed. A search for 'murder massena ny' revealed the victim had been attacked with a knife in a bar parking lot. The suspect remained at large.

'Kelsea knew all kinds of stuff about the case,' Tim went on. 'It sounds horrible – the vic was a single mom. Kelsea knew her name, too. It was Jessica Greenleaf. Shana, her name was Jess.'

The names. I'd chanted them hundreds of times before, not just to keep their owners' memories alive but to punish myself for failing three women who'd died by my cousin's hand. It was a form of self-flagellation, the flogging I felt I deserved. Over time, the names had melded together to become one long, sorrowful moan. Now, though, I gave each one the credence it deserved.

Becca.

Lanie.

Jess.

Jessica Greenleaf.

Rebecca Hearst.

My feet were rooted to the rug, but I felt like a tree in a windstorm. 'It's a coincidence,' I said. 'It has to be.'

'Becca,' said Tim. His voice hitched. '*Jess.*'

'But he's dead.' My face was hot, my vision blurred. 'Bram didn't do this.'

'It isn't just the names.'

He was right. There was more. But this couldn't be Bram. He hadn't come back from the dead to kill again. This wasn't a ghost story or some stupid zombie flick. And yet, I couldn't quiet my mind. *Two murders. Two women with the same names as Blake Bram's victims.*

When I inhaled, it felt like I was breathing through a clogged straw. 'Dead girls tell no tales.'

Bram's crimes were public knowledge now, his victims' names splashed across three columns in bold black ink. His violence had been snuffed out. And now, someone was bringing it back.

For two years, I had known my cousin was a killer. For most of my life, I'd worried about what Abe Skilton would do next. When Bram died, I thought I was finally free.

I wasn't counting on him taking more lives from the grave.

TWENTY-FIVE

I t was a full house in the barracks that morning, and the common space shared by my investigators hummed with tension, every one of us on high alert. Tim's eyes darted around the room, alighting like a dragonfly on the on-duty troopers and each of his fellow back room investigators. They lingered, half-lidded, on Bogle, whose gaze was firmly locked on me.

There were others in the room, too: Lieutenant Henderson in Oneida, and the Utica PD who'd been following leads on Rebecca Hearst in her home city, were on speakerphone, along with the state police out of Massena. We were independent organizations, each with our own protocol, but today we'd united for a singular purpose, one that made me queasy. They were waiting for me to make my statement and issue instructions, fill them in on a development that had changed everything. I rolled my shoulders back and shook out my hands.

'OK,' I said. 'Here's what we know.'

A copycat killer. The term dated back to turn-of-the-century England and Jack the Ripper. The media coverage of his brutal crimes inspired others to slay women like he had. News stories were something Bram's crimes had in spades. The idea that someone would try to replicate his unspeakable brand of violence, here in the county that had barely survived his attacks before, was sickening. Still, the similarities between the killings couldn't be ignored.

On the night of Tuesday, July third, Jessica Greenleaf, aged twenty-seven, left her cashier job at the Massena JCPenney for the Rusty Anchor on Willow Street. According to her mother, Patty Greenleaf, Jessica had a blind date. She was getting together with a man named Ben G. Dool, a personal trainer in his early thirties. A man she had met on Facebook.

Jessica, a single mother of two, left her children at home with their grandmother and promised to be back by eleven. Patty worked a stressful job at a nursing home and fell asleep on the couch around ten, not waking again until five a.m. when the youngest of Jessica's boys, just three years old, began to cry for his mother. When she realized her daughter hadn't come home, Patty called Jessica's cell phone, and got no answer. Seven more tries and two hours later, she called the police.

'Jessica's body was found in the dumpster behind the Rusty Anchor the morning after her date, with stab wounds to the abdomen. ID on her person, but no phone to speak of,' said Damon Ameer, a senior investigator with Massena's Troop B unit. 'I just sent through a photograph.'

'Print that, would you, Don?' I said. Bogle nodded and headed to the computer at the nearest desk.

'Based on interviews with the staff and patrons,' Ameer went on, 'we believe the two never made it inside the bar that night. Either he killed her straightaway, or they went someplace else for their date and ended up back at the parking lot. The area's sparsely populated, and the bar backs up to a copse of trees and beyond that, the river. That means no witnesses, and no CCTV, either. This is as small-town as it gets.

'We have very little information on Dool, which we're assuming is an alias. The bar was hopping inside, but we've been unable to find a witness. The suspect's profile pic is a logo for Save the River, a local environmental nonprofit. The mother never saw a pic of the perp either, but she assumed he was Caucasian, says white guys are Jess's type. She also says that according to her daughter, Dool approached Greenleaf online prior to the homicide.'

Ameer and his team had determined that Dool's Facebook profile was set up in late June. There was little to it, a shell of a typical page. 'No telling why the vic agreed to Friend this guy in the first place,' Ameer said, 'but Jessica had more than two thousand Facebook contacts; suffice it to say, she wasn't discerning. Maybe he used an unsolicited message to go fishing, and happened to get a bite. If that's what happened, the message was later deleted. They didn't interact much on Facebook at all, far as we can tell,' he went on. 'We found a few messages planning the date, but that's it. And after that night, Dool never messaged her again.'

Across the room, Bogle was standing at the printer, staring at the photo in his hands.

'Pass that around,' I told him before taking the lead again. 'There's no clear connection between Jessica Greenleaf and Rebecca Hearst. The question is whether Rebecca knew Dool. We had our team search all her social media accounts for signs of unusual activity, but we'll want to revisit her Facebook page. He could have been using a different name when he connected with her. Which brings us to the issue of a copycat.'

I shifted my weight where I stood at the head of the room. 'Things that stand out as signs we're dealing with an imitator,' I said. 'First, the names. Blake Bram's known victims in New York were named Jess Lowenthal, Becca Wolkwitz and Lanie Miner, all of them between the ages of twenty-six and thirty-two. Now we've got a Rebecca and a Jessica here in Jefferson and St Lawrence Counties. If we're dealing with a serial – and that's still a big if – the names could be the reason we've got victims in A-Bay and Massena. If our perp needed someone with a particular name of a particular age to agree to a date, he had a pretty small pool of targets to choose from.'

The image of the crime scene had made its way around the room. Tim looked at it for nearly as long as Bogle had before handing it over. Though I knew what I would see, having spoken extensively with Ameer before the briefing, the image of Jessica Greenleaf's body spread out next to a dumpster made my eyes sting.

'The murder sites are similar to the New York crime scenes as well,' I said. 'The quarry where we found Rebecca's body isn't so different from the construction site in the East Village where we found Jess Lowenthal. Becca Wolkwitz, Bram's first victim, was left in an alley behind a coffee shop, while Jessica Greenleaf was abandoned behind a bar. And then there's the proximity of these killings to each other. The murder sites are a little over an hour apart, both along the river. Both were stabbings. And as Damon noted, Greenleaf's mobile device was absent from the scene. And then there's the knife.'

Last spring, in an attempt to piece together Bram's recent past, Tim and I had driven down to Connecticut and interviewed a woman who once had the misfortune of becoming the object of my cousin's affection. She barely managed to escape with her life after Bram pulled a knife on her in an apartment complex parking lot. The woman had referred to it as a pocketknife, which fit the description of the weapon he would later use on Becca, Lanie and Jess in New York. The weapon that matched the one used on Rebecca Hearst and Jessica Greenleaf upstate.

'Talk to us about the LaFargeville perp,' Henderson said when I paused to catch my breath. My lieutenant's voice was hollow on the line. It was amazing how much skepticism could be conveyed by a few innocuous words.

'We don't have much on him,' I confessed, which was embarrassing. Damon Ameer and his team were a long way from unearthing their guy's home address, but I still worried it looked like I was asleep at the wheel. 'The message on the tip line – "dead girls tell no tales" – was recorded using a voice-altering app. Those things are a dime a dozen in the app store, so there's very little to work with there. What we do have is a pattern that appears to be similar to Bram's. Bram was known for ensnaring his victims by way of a dating app. According to the vic's mother, Ben Dool found Jessica through Facebook. Dool's the prime suspect in the Greenleaf case. I think we need to consider him a suspect in Rebecca Hearst's murder as well. Dool could be using different aliases, just like Blake Bram did.'

'You mean Abraham Skilton,' Henderson said.

I drew a breath through my nose, grateful my supervisor couldn't see my face. Getting in good with the boss had been a struggle. I suppose I didn't make the best first impression, kicking off my state police career with a suspension, but the mention of my cousin's real name was a slight of the highest order. I didn't expect Henderson to hold my hand through ordeal after horrible ordeal, especially given the negative impact those experiences had on our troop, but I'd rarely heard him sound so angry. The copycat theory was just one more reason for him to resent me. 'Right, Skilton,' I said. 'AKA Bram. He's dominated the news around here for months, as you all know. It sounds like we could be dealing with another charismatic predator who knows how to groom a woman online.'

'How did he know Hearst would agree to come all the way upstate?' asked Ameer.

'I've seen Rebecca Hearst's Facebook page,' I said. We didn't have her account password, and Godfrey Hearst wasn't a

Facebook user, so we were limited with what we could view, but some of her posts were public, and Bogle had pointed me to the most relevant ones. The images were carefully curated, and they told the story of how the woman spent her days. 'Rebecca was pretty candid about her life. Anyone who was paying attention could glean some insight into her emotional state, including the fact that she wasn't entirely happy in her marriage. Something else,' I said. 'Godfrey Hearst said it was Rebecca's idea to come to A-Bay. She told her husband a friend recommended the Admiral Inn, but didn't give a name. We've been throwing around the theory that Rebecca Hearst was meeting someone in A-Bay.' Never would I have imagined she was meeting a predator on a killing spree.

'So, where does that leave us?' my supervisor asked.

'There must be dozens of Jessicas in Jefferson County. So why this Jessica?' I said. 'Bogle, look into that, will you? Anything you can find that might link the two women.'

'You got it, boss.'

'We need to adopt a rough and ready approach to this one,' I went on. 'I've always been of the mind that crimes don't crop up in groups without a reason.' It didn't matter if we were talking an uptick in graffiti or a series of assaults; I believed in taking a thirty-thousand-foot view of the local community. More burglaries than usual? Check to see if any known class C felons recently moved to town. Reports of a sexual assault? Find out if any known sex offenders were just released from Ogdensburg Correctional Facility. More often than not, we discover a link. But that link isn't always obvious, which is why we talk to people, too. Members of the community who might notice an unfamiliar face.

'What's changed around there recently?' asked Damon Ameer, his voice expectant. As my gaze traveled the room, I noticed Bogle jogging his knee. Watching me.

Changes. An unfamiliar face. If I took my own advice and assessed the community, there was only one perceptible change.

The arrival of Javier Barba and Estella Lopez.

TWENTY-SIX

'Bait and switch, is that what you're saying?' asked Tim, his eyebrows tightly knit. 'Estella Lopez and her brother show up in town claiming they're here to punish you for your cousin's crimes, and all the while Barba's committing atrocities of his own?'

Tim, Bogle, Sol and I had been huddled around a table cluttered with Diet Coke cans and loot from the vending machine for almost an hour, expounding on the hypothesis and throwing around ideas to see what stuck. We were over-caffeinated and jumpy, and I was having a hell of a time quelling the tremors in my hands.

And yet, when I pictured Javier's face, first red with anger, then stone cold as he told me he'd only come to town for vacation, I felt we might be getting somewhere.

'It's a possibility,' Bogle said, clearing his throat. 'Based on my research, the timetable fits. We know they were in the area at the time of the murder in Massena on July third, and also last weekend.'

But Tim wasn't convinced.

'We've got nothing concrete to tie either of them to Rebecca Hearst or Jessica Greenleaf. As for their movements, they came up here for Fourth of July and Pirate Days, just like hundreds of other vacationers. Nothing inherently strange about that. And there's a lot that doesn't make sense about their behavior,' Tim said. 'If Barba's our man, why would he assault you in public, Shana? He and his sister walked right up to you and introduced themselves. Dumb move for a killer who's trying to stay hidden.'

'He fits the profile, though,' Bogle replied. 'He has a record, and trouble controlling his emotions. Maybe he snapped at the restaurant without intending to.'

'And that face-off outside the Bean-In?' Tim said. 'Again, the behavior makes no sense if Barba's trying to lay low, and if he killed those women, why wouldn't he be?'

I thought back to my conversation with Estella at the party. 'Estella said Javier made some bad choices. It's possible confronting me wasn't part of the plan.'

'Anger management issues,' Bogle put in. 'That fits the profile, too.'

'And the sister?' asked Tim. 'Where does she come in?'

I said, 'She could be his cover. An excuse to come up here, in case he accidently called attention to himself.'

'Well, whoever did this, I don't like the timing,' Tim said.

'Meaning?'

'It took a long time for us to make the connection between these murders and Bram,' he said. 'The perp had us on a wild goose chase looking for a bridge jumper for half the week. As for Greenleaf, the clues were there – her name, the similarity of the kill site to New York – but she wasn't in our jurisdiction, so we couldn't put it together until we found Hearst – all of which brings us to this weekend. Now Pirate Days is in full swing, and the killer leaves that creepy message on the tip line. It's crowded in town, busy. Good time to take another victim if this is about finishing what Bram started.'

My breath caught in my throat. Tim was right: the killings did seem to lead up to this high-profile event, an event that brought hundreds of tourists to town in spite – or maybe because – of Blake Bram. And here was Ben Dool, teeth bared and waiting.

If we're right, and he's imitating Bram, he'll kill again. That was the unspoken statement, the fact none of us could ignore. Bram killed three women in New York. If our hunch about a copycat was right, it meant our perpetrator could be plotting a third assault somewhere along the shores of the St Lawrence River.

It meant he wasn't done.

TWENTY-SEVEN

Hands on his hips, chin tucked into his chest, Bruce Milton looked at me and Mac over spindly rimless glasses. Scenic View Park lived up to its name, but none of us were paying any mind to the river or Heart Island and beautiful Boldt Castle, built by a millionaire hotel magnate, dead ahead. There was something about the heat and the water and the mayor's downturned mouth that felt familiar, and when it finally hit me, I almost laughed. Sheriff McIntyre and I were Hooper and police chief Brody, trying to convince a stubborn mayor to close the beaches of Amity Island on Fourth of July. In the movie, Hooper had called Jaws an eating machine. Well, our suspect was a killing machine – and if Mayor Milton didn't heed our warning, someone else was going to die.

His gaze drifted to the nearby pavilion, where several dozen costumed kids were lining up for the children's parade. 'My grandbabies are over there,' Milton said with a nod toward the shady gazebo. 'It's the little one's first parade. She's been practicing her pirate speak at home for a month, so I'd appreciate it if we could wrap this up, ladies.'

'Due respect,' I said, 'I'm not sure you understand the gravity of the situation.' How could that be? I'd been providing the mayor's office with regular updates on our progress with the Hearst case, and receiving appropriately staid email replies. *How terrible, excellent work, thanks for keeping us in the loop.* 'This is an active homicide investigation,' I reminded him now, 'and we believe our suspect may attempt to abduct a third woman over the course of the festival. The crowds, all these tourists . . . it isn't safe.'

'You *believe*,' Milton repeated. 'Now, what does that mean? Did this fella you're after specifically say he would be here today?'

'No,' I said drily. 'We came up with that all on our own.' What the hell was this? Could Milton really be so dense? 'We're talking about two homicides within a month of each other. Rebecca Hearst was a tourist. Half the people out here are probably panicked as it is, and now our suspect has left a message on our tip line that we're treating as a threat.' I hadn't revealed that we thought we could be facing off against a copycat, and I wasn't about to tell him what that tip line message said. I didn't take Bruce Milton for tactful, and 'dead girls tell no tales' was far too buzzy of a catchphrase for our mayor to keep a lid on.

'So we're going to make the people even *more* afraid by shutting the whole thing down?' Milton said.

'Come on, Bruce,' Mac chided, 'this is the state police asking. Don't you think it would behoove you to listen?' Before she moved to Watertown and was elected sheriff, McIntyre had held my same position leading a team of investigators with the BCI in A-Bay. She knew Bruce personally, had picnicked with his family. It was the reason I'd asked her along. The disappointment in her voice must have served as a reminder of their personal history, because Milton hung his head.

'Ah, Mac, I'm sorry,' he told her, 'but it's an awful big ask. I mean, cancel the reenactment *and* the parade? In two hours' time, this park will flood with folks who've been waiting all year long for this event. Tomorrow afternoon, the streets will be jammed with visitors who have money to spend that we could really use right now.' Here, he shot me a look. 'The invasion and parade are the highlights of this whole darn thing. We've got a live drill and demonstration by the Brockville Infantry, band performances and skits and birds of prey. Chet and his committee have been planning it all for months, and the Chamber of Commerce spent a gosh darn fortune on advertising this year to make sure we have a good turnout.'

So I've heard. Milton cut me a look. It seemed Chet Bell wasn't alone in blaming me for the town's economic downturn.

'Look,' he said, 'what happened to those girls, it's a tragedy. But you know what they say, don't you? Fear begets fear.'

'And power begets power. I know that quote too,' I said. 'You have the power to protect these people, sir. All you have to do is make a call. Blame the heat if you want to. Whatever it takes.'

'I can think of quite a few individuals who'd take issue with that,' he said. 'Starting with Chet.'

I thought about telling him Bell had concealed critical information about our case, and decided against it. It wouldn't make any difference now, because Milton's eyes were back on the gazebo.

'They're about to get started.' Behind us, little voices squealed with excitement, tiny fists pumping at the heat-wiggly air. 'If you ladies will excuse me, I'd really like to watch my grandbabies walk in the parade.' With the tip of an imaginary hat, the mayor turned on his heel and marched off.

I looked to Mac, who was shaking her head. At a loss, I turned around and scanned the crowd for the Head Pirate. It had only been five days since I sat next to Deputy Sheriff Gorecki at the station, questioning Godfrey Hearst about his missing wife. Now, he was about to have his big moment leading the kids like a modern-day Pied Piper.

If only I had as much sway over this town as he did.

TWENTY-EIGHT

'I need to talk to you,' I told Tim back at the barracks. 'It's about Don.'

In truth, I needed to talk to Tim about a lot more than that, but the situation with Bogle took precedence. I'd instructed Bogle to wait for me in the car and had grabbed Tim on my way out the door. I wanted nothing more than to forget what Amos Barlowe had told me about Bogle's drinking, but this case was getting more complicated by the minute, and I needed a sounding board.

'What about him?' Tim asked, looking genuinely confused.

'Have you noticed any strange behavior lately? I'm going to level with you,' I said. 'His brother-in-law told me last night that Don has a drinking problem.'

Tim reeled back, the news like a blow. 'A drinking problem? Seriously?'

'So you haven't seen any evidence of that? Because I haven't either,' I said, 'but the guy was pretty convinced there was some day-drinking going on.'

Tim shook his head and said, 'Damn.'

A lesser man would have pointed out this was far more egregious behavior than Tim's own habit of being exceptionally compassionate, but there was nothing 'less' about Tim.

'Apparently things are rocky between him and his wife,' I went on. 'Juliet.'

That slanted the corners of Tim's eyes. 'Come on, really? Don and Juliet? Damn,' he said again. 'I thought those two were in it for the long haul.'

Tim knew the man far better than I did, but there were things I'd gleaned about Bogle's life from working with him this past year that had coalesced to leave me with a positive impression. For one thing, Bogle was the only investigator on our team who came from a family of cops; both his father and grandfather had worked in law enforcement in Jefferson County before him. Like

Jay Lopez, Don Bogle's police work was colored by his desire to uphold his family's legacy.

What I hadn't known, not until Tim told me in the station's small lobby, was how hard it had been for Bogle to breach Juliet Barlowe's world.

'He talks about how awkward it is when her wealthy friends and exes swan around the Barlowes's parties,' Tim said. 'Especially when someone brings up Don's roots.' Bogle was working class through and through, with four siblings and a mom with a chronic back problem who hadn't been able to work in years. His upbringing, Tim told me, was a far cry from Juliet and Amos's silver spoon life.

Bogle and Juliet met in town when Bogle was fresh back from the training academy, on a night when the shipping heiress and her Vassar College friends were on a self-proclaimed bender and determined to 'slum it.' The local boys, tan and muscled from summers working construction jobs, liked to believe they had an edge over the guys who only holidayed in the islands. Bogle had been delighted when, the next morning, Juliet gave him her number. He had no idea she'd slept with him on a dare.

As I listened, I wondered why I'd never heard this about Bogle before. There was a class divide in the Thousand Islands, that much I'd known even before setting foot in A-Bay. As is common with vacation towns, the locals cater to the needs and whims of the summer people while the latter loll on their multimillion-dollar islands. What I hadn't realized was that Bogle had experienced this socioeconomic bifurcation first-hand.

'A drinking problem,' Tim said, issuing a sigh. 'I hope the guy's OK. That kind of thing doesn't develop overnight. You going to talk to him?'

'Yeah,' I said, cupping the back of my neck with my hand. 'I think I will.'

'All good?' Bogle said when I finally slid into the driver's seat of our assigned Chevy sedan. It was a nine-minute drive to downtown A-Bay. I had to work fast.

'Fine,' I told him as I started the engine, turned up the A/C, and took a left out of the parking lot on to Route 12. 'But like

I said this morning, there's something I've been wanting to talk to you about.'

His bald head tilted. Beyond it, through the window, the clear blue sky twinkled with sunlight. Bogle's fingers twitched and a hand went to his ear.

'No smoking in the Malibu,' I reminded him.

'Yeah.' Fingers drumming on the dashboard. 'I know.'

The radio was on, the volume low, but I recognized the song – 'Psycho Killer' by Talking Heads. I thumped a fist against the dial and plunged the car into silence. 'So look,' I said. 'I need you to level with me, Don, but I also need you to understand I'm here for you. We all are.'

He stiffened. 'What's that supposed to mean?'

'It means that if you need anything – like a meeting with the same kind of counselor I've been seeing for my PTSD – I can help.'

'What am I missing here?' he asked, but he was already avoiding my gaze.

'I saw how much you had to drink last night.'

There was a long beat of silence. Then Bogle started to laugh.

'Jesus, you had me scared. OK, boss,' he said, raising his hands. 'Busted. I was drinking last night. Everyone was.'

There was more traffic on the highway than usual, a cavalcade of cars headed toward downtown. Plates from Massachusetts and Quebec. 'I'm not just talking about last night.'

Bogle thought about that, his mouth twisting. 'Ah,' he said, capping the sound with a dark chuckle. 'I knew I shouldn't have left you alone with my goddamn brother-in-law.'

So it's true. 'I'm glad he told me. This isn't the sort of thing that goes away on its own,' I said, thinking of my conversation with Tim, 'but we can get you help before it becomes an issue at work.'

'Whoa, this has got nothing to do with work.' Those hands again, raised as if in submission or, possibly, fear. 'I don't know what Amos told you, but let me set the record straight right now: in no way is my *issue* going to affect my job. It's like this.' He ducked his head to meet my gaze, and held it. 'Juliet and I, we're having some problems. Things have been tough at home, OK? And maybe I'm reaching for the bottle a little more than I used to. None of that has any bearing on my job.'

I flicked on my blinker and coasted to a stop at the red light. To my left, I could see the blue-and-gold arch welcoming visitors to downtown Alexandria Bay. 'It does if you're coming to work hungover, or drinking during the day,' I said.

'Which I'm not.'

'OK. Good. It's just that Amos—'

'*Fuck* Amos.' Beside me, Bogle went still. He was studying his fingernails. I hadn't noticed before, but they were incredibly short, trimmed down to the quick. Aside from the yellow tinge to his skin left by the cigarettes, his hands were so clean he could have taken a job in a bakery. Performed surgery sans gloves.

After a beat, Bogle released a sigh. 'Juliet is Amos's sister. He may be my brother-in-law, but he's always going to take her side. Right now, my wife is pissed at me, which means he's pissed, too. So do me a favor and take what he told you with a grain of salt. If anyone should know that gossip isn't always true, it's you.'

I felt my cheeks flush. Passing judgment on Bogle's personal life based on a rumor was a shitty thing to do. Yes, he got hammered last night, and it cost us our chance to question Bell, but I hadn't personally seen any evidence that he had a problem beyond his behavior at the party.

'OK,' I said again, 'then how about this: if you ever want to talk about Juliet, my office door is always open.'

Bogle's head jerked in some semblance of a nod as he turned away from me. 'Well, lookie here,' he said, sitting forward in his seat as he stared out the window. 'The party's finally getting started.'

TWENTY-NINE

There was parking behind the post office, and it was the closest we were likely to find, so we left the unmarked sedan in the shade of a leafy maple and made our way toward the river. Even before stepping out of the car I could hear the resounding boom of canons and musket fire. The air smelled of sulfur and gunpowder, and the stink grew stronger the closer we got to the ruckus. It felt like walking into a war zone.

Every business had posters of skulls and crossbones plastered to the insides of their windows, the ice cream stand boasting a chalkboard that read, 'Warning: Thar be pirates ahead'. People in pirate regalia swarmed the streets wearing scraggly wigs topped with feathered tricorn hats, while others had draped themselves in colorful beads. I saw more than one busty woman in a deep-cut lace blouse and gypsy skirt despite the hot noon sun. My hairline was damp with sweat already. I squeegeed it with the back of my hand.

'Over there,' said Bogle, pointing to Scenic View Park.

The reenactment was well underway. Bystanders had gathered along the shore, with a hundred more watching from boats out on the water. Between them, a tall ship packed with would-be renegades and flying a Jolly Roger rocked in the waves of the St Lawrence. There was shouting. Another round of cannon fire. A haze of smoke hung over the water, the crowd.

'That's the *Black Jack*, out of Brockville,' Bogle said of the ship, his face breaking into a grin. It's true what they say about pirates: everyone loves them. 'Looks like we missed the capture of the scouting party over at Sir Robert Peel Boat Tours, but this is the invasion – the best part. See, they're attacking the villagers. Pretty soon they'll come ashore, and the mayor will turn over the key to the town. People usually scatter after that.'

'But until then, he's here,' I said. 'He has to be.' This was Chet Bell's big moment, the culmination of a year of hard work. No way would he miss this.

And I wasn't going to let him get away again.

Nearby, a little girl in a T-shirt that read, 'Why be a princess when you can be a pirate?' threw a tantrum on the grass because her brother wouldn't share his sack of plastic coins. To our left, a group of women who looked fresh out of high school whooped at the show playing out on the water, tan arms adorned with plastic bangles, braids laced with ribbons of red and black. 'Let's split up,' I said. 'If you find him, call me, yeah?'

'Will do.' Bogle headed north and was quickly swallowed by the masses. I made my way down toward the water.

'Ahoy!'

I had only been walking for a minute when I heard the cry. I turned around, expecting to see an overzealous tourist, and found myself staring at Ivan Gorecki. 'Where's your eye patch?' he asked, snapping the elastic that held his own patch in place. 'You're one of us now, Shana. Gotta look the part.'

'Not today. I'm on duty,' I told him. 'The Hearst case?'

'Right, right. Really sorry to hear how that turned out. Let me know if you need any help,' he said, a bit half-heartedly.

'Sure will.' I looked past him, searching the crowd on the northern end of the park for Bell, but all I could see was Bogle. He was moving through the crowd with purpose now, his bald head like a beacon gleaming in the sun. As he paused beside a trash can to drop something inside, I wondered if he was wearing sunscreen. Fifteen minutes out here and he'd be a cooked lobster. 'Hey,' I said, 'I don't suppose you've seen Chet Bell?'

'Chet? Sure, right over there. He's wearing a long black wig and red scarf around his head, Jack Sparrow-style. You can't miss him.'

Yes. 'Thanks,' I said with a smile. I had eyes on Bell now; he was at the bottom of the hill on which I stood, near the water. Watching a group of patriots prepare to take on the pirates with their replica swords.

I rushed the sea of pink faces, not hesitating to push spectators out of my way. Those who weren't already horribly sunburned looked like they might have heatstroke. There were very few trees here in the park, where many of these same folks had watched the fireworks over Boldt Castle on the Fourth of July, and onlookers had packed themselves into patches of shade like fish in a tin. Even so, it wasn't easy to navigate the audience that fanned out across the hillock. When Bell finally spotted me, just a few yards away, panic flitted across his face. I shouted his name once, twice, as I moved in. Several people looked his way. Bell feigned confusion, but it was becoming clear to those around him that my need to reach the man was grave. He turned away from me, searching for an escape route. Too late.

Breathing hard, I said, 'You're a tough man to find, Mr Bell.'

His smile was unsteady. Sweat dripped from his mustache on to greasy lips. 'What can I do for you, detective?'

Approaching a suspect in a social situation is never easy. I didn't have enough on Bell to coerce him into coming to the barracks. He could tell me to get lost, and in a crowded public space like this one, that could be embarrassing. My best bet was to leverage his discomfort with the situation and hope he'd answer my questions voluntarily.

'Congratulations,' I said loudly, watching as Bell's eyebrows slid up his oily forehead. 'This is quite a show you've organized, here.'

'Well, thanks. But as you can see, this isn't the best time to—'

'Ten minutes.' I leaned in close. 'We can talk in the park, or right here.' I took a step back, gesturing at the crowd. 'Your choice, Mr Bell.'

Most of the spectators had refocused their attention on the pirate ship again, but a few were still listening in, looking expectantly at Bell who couldn't have been dressed more conspicuously for a man who, at the moment, wanted nothing more than to disappear.

'Ah, shit,' said Bell.

THIRTY

It was a short walk to the park's pirate ship play structure, which currently sat abandoned under the blazing sun. It didn't have one of those aluminum slides like the playgrounds of my youth – it was a wonder Abe and I didn't sustain third-degree burns on the backs of our thighs – but even the stairs leading up to the crow's nest looked like they could sear a burger.

I sat Chet Bell down at the shady picnic table beside them.

'I was hoping to catch up with you at the Barlowes's party last night. Guess you didn't see me,' I said.

'Hot as balls out here.' Bell adjusted his wig and ran a hand down his beard. It came away wet. 'There were a lot of people there last night.'

'Uh-huh. I need to ask you a few questions about last Sunday.'

'Sunday.' Wary eyes. Tight smile. Chet Bell was an easy man to read. 'What happened on Sunday?'

I pulled in a steadying breath. 'That was the night Rebecca Hearst disappeared.'

For a moment Bell was quiet. His stare was cold, but his artifice remained. 'And that has something to do with me because . . .?'

'As I understand it, you dined at the Bay Point Grill that evening.'

He took his time answering. 'That sounds right. Yeah, yeah. I sat inside because of the A/C, though they do have a nice view of the river.' I waited for Bell to continue. 'I went in to grab a steak. Don't tell the wife, red meat's not part of the diet.' He added a wink that turned my stomach.

'Don't tell the wife,' I repeated dully. 'Sorry to be the bearer of bad news, but it's pretty likely she'll find out your secret. I have a witness who says you sat with a woman who matches Rebecca Hearst's description. She says you two were pretty cozy.'

'Cozy!' The word caught in his throat. 'That's ridiculous.'

Bell was getting uncomfortable. Sweat streamed down his face from underneath his wig and I could almost hear his saliva thickening, the *mlem* of his tongue against the roof of his mouth. I didn't try to be subtle when I leaned away from him. The man was repulsive. 'Are you listening to me?' I said. 'I know you interacted with my murder victim the night she was killed. You withheld critical information from the state police.'

My outburst seemed to startle him. 'Whoa,' he said. 'That woman and I had a quick conversation – that's all. She and her husband weren't getting along. He was in the bar next door.'

As with the drinking, Godfrey Hearst hadn't mentioned anything about arguing with his wife prior to the conflict at the motel. I took out my notebook and pushed the nib of my pen to the page just a little too hard. 'She said those exact words? That they "weren't getting along?"'

'Pretty much, yeah,' he said, eyeing my notes.

'Did you *know* the woman you were talking to was Rebecca Hearst? Did you realize that when she went missing? When you saw her photograph online and in the paper?'

Too many questions. I knew I was confusing him, making it harder on myself to get what I needed out of Bell, but the idea that he'd been sitting on this information when he came into my office made me see red.

'Honestly, the whole exchange was so brief it was hardly worth mentioning,' he said. 'I talked to lot of people that night. What you said about my wife finding out . . . you were joking, right?'

'Not in the least. In fact, I'm thinking of telling her myself.'

The threat landed hard, like a jab to the jaw, and Bell winced in response. I was tetchy and tired, and Rebecca Hearst's murder made me feel hoodwinked. I'd only just survived Bram; how dare someone come here, to my town, my *home*, and pick up right where he left off? How dare this self-important asshole slow me down? *Deep breaths, Shay.* 'Mr Bell, surely you understand this is a homicide investigation – the same investigation you asked me to "wrap up" so you could boost your boat tour ticket sales. We aren't just dealing with a missing person anymore – and you, Mr Bell, are one of the last people to see Rebecca Hearst alive.'

Bell shifted on the warm bench. Based on my own level of

discomfort, I had to assume he was sitting in a puddle. The backs of my own pants were soaked through with sweat. 'It was nothing,' Bell said, though he sounded distinctly more on edge. 'She complimented my shirt, and we got to talking. She said she was in town with her husband. She didn't seem especially happy about that. We could see him in the bar in the other room, chatting up a group of young women. I felt sorry for her. That's the only reason I talked to her.'

A beautiful young woman was willing to give Bell the time of day, and he talked to her out of pity? I didn't believe that for a second.

'What else?' I asked. 'We have reason to believe she made plans to meet someone that night, someone who wasn't her husband. She say anything about that?'

Bell sighed and, in a fit of frustration, tore the bandana and wig from his head. Beneath them, his pompadour was lopsided and flat. 'Maybe,' he said. 'Not in so many words. She ordered a coffee after her wine – the only customer in the place who wasn't still slugging booze. She said something about having a long night ahead. I assumed she wanted to reconcile with her husband and expected to be hashing things out until late. She didn't mention another guy.' He paused. 'Who was it? Is he the one who killed her?'

'OK,' I said, ignoring his question. Scribbling frantically on the page. 'And where did you go when you left the restaurant?'

'Home.' Bell's eyes narrowed. 'You can ask my wife. She had a book club meeting that night, but I got back after she did. I was home by ten and was by her side all night. She's been a little . . . insecure since I lost the weight.' He leaned back against the bench to show off his flat stomach. 'That conversation was completely harmless, OK? Mrs Bell doesn't need to know.'

Mrs Bell was about to get a phone call, and if she didn't confirm her husband's alibi, things were going to get mighty complicated for Chet. 'The husband,' I said. 'Did you talk to him?'

'No. But I saw him through the window. Guy was smashed. He went outside and stumbled around the parking lot for a while, like he was looking for her. She saw it, too. She told me she'd be right back, and went out to talk to him. Soon as she got out there, he grabbed her arm. She didn't like that, I guess. They had a few words and headed for their car. She never came back inside.'

Bell sounded bitter, even a little pissed. Was this the real explanation for his silence? Was Chet Bell punishing a victim of violent crime because she hadn't bothered to say goodbye? It hardly seemed possible, but his charisma and newfound fitness were clearly a source of pride, and there was a sullenness to his expression now that was hard to ignore.

'What about outside?' I asked him. 'Did you see anyone hanging around when they left?'

Bell's eyebrows lifted again, and this time he brought a hand to his lips. 'There was someone.' I could see him reliving the night in his mind, the steaks and the wine in the bustling restaurant. His hungry gaze on Rebecca's backside as she walked out the door.

'I remember seeing a guy sitting outside the restaurant. There's a life-size chess set out there, in a little park next to Bay Point. You know it?'

A board of red and white squares, painted on the pavement. It was a big attraction for visiting kids, whether they knew how to play the game or not. Everyone delighted in maneuvering those massive knights and pawns. 'I know it,' I said.

'He was next to it, sitting on a bench under a tree. I almost didn't notice him, out there in the dark. He was dressed in dark clothes.'

'And he was watching her?'

'Couldn't look away,' Bell said.

I leaned toward him again, repellant mouth sounds be damned. 'Can you describe him for me? Height? Weight? Coloring?'

'It was dark,' he repeated. The three words an investigator is most loathe to hear. 'He was wearing a sweatshirt with the hood up. I didn't get a look at his face, but I think he was clean-shaven.' He touched his own beard as he said it. 'Oh, and he had an eyepatch.'

'An eyepatch? You mean like a pirate?'

'Yeah. Just like that.'

A man dressed for Pirate Days almost a week before the festival started? I'd seen kids sporting pirate paraphernalia early, but the adults hadn't broken out their costumes until Friday. 'How common is that, getting dressed up before the big kick off?'

Bell's upper lip curled. 'For most people around here, Pirate Days can't come soon enough. Let's put it this way,' he said, running his tongue across his teeth, 'Mavis gets out my Johnny Depp wig and our *Pirates of the Caribbean* DVD collection in July.'

I suppressed the urge to gag. *A man in an eyepatch.* Not a bad disguise, if you didn't want to recognized.

'Is there anything else?' I asked. 'Anything especially noticeable about his clothing?'

'I couldn't see much, like I said. He was gone when I left a while later. We through?'

'OK,' I said, nauseated. 'Yes, we're through. I'll be in touch if I have more questions. Give me a call if you remember anything else.'

'I won't.' Bell plucked his sweat-sticky shirt from his abs. 'If it wasn't for the fact that the girl disappeared, I doubt I would've remembered her at all.'

THIRTY-ONE

I t took very little effort to secure video of James Street from the rooftop of the Tex Mex bar across the street from the Bay Point Grill. Days ago, I'd tasked Bogle with hunting down footage of the restaurant, back when we were hoping to find some additional witnesses.

'Why the hell didn't we get this sooner?' I asked him now, not bothering to hide my aggravation. Social media, security videos; Bogle had volunteered to investigate it all, yet it had taken Chet Bell's witness statement for us to locate this key evidence. Tim was actively reviewing the footage, but we'd lost a lot of time.

'Yeah, that was my bad.' Bogle said it with a wince. 'I checked in with a lot of places around the restaurant, you know? This one told me to call back later and talk to the owner. I guess I blanked on that.'

'Jesus, Don.' It was poor work on his part, the effort slapdash. I'd need to have a word with him about that, but now was not the time.

'Come take a look,' Tim called from his desk. 'I think I've got something.'

Bogle and I got to our feet, joints creaking and popping with disuse, and inched up behind him for a better view. I was close enough to Tim that I could see the fine dark hairs on the back of his neck and smell soap on his skin, the grapefruit-scented bar I'd bought for the bathroom at his cottage. The scent made me dizzy with longing, but I pushed the urge aside and focused on the computer screen before us.

There he was, just as Bell had described him: a man on a bench, hunched over in the shadow cast by a tree in the park, his face turned in the direction of the restaurant. Hard to gauge height and weight since he was seated; he didn't look scrawny or significantly overweight. Despite the heat, he wore an oversized hoodie that covered his head. I couldn't make out any facial hair, but beyond that we had little to go on. Where looks were concerned, he was a closed book.

The man didn't move, not so much as a twitch, which made it impossible to identify him based on mannerisms or gait. He wasn't staring down at a cell phone. There was no cigarette in his hand. He was just sitting there, his stare fastened to the door of the Bay Point Grill.

There wasn't a single doubt in my mind that we were looking at Ben Dool.

'Are you telling me my wife knew the man who killed her?' There was flint in Godfrey Patrick Hearst III's voice. Pain, too.

'That's our working theory,' I told him gently, 'yes.' I felt for Hearst. It wasn't enough that the man had lost his wife; now he had to hear her decision to meet another man had likely cost Rebecca her life.

I'd sent him back to Utica the previous day with the assurance that we wouldn't stop looking for Rebecca's killer. Now that Hearst was home, he was able to provide us with the thing we'd been missing, a piece of information that could be critical to our investigation. Rebecca kept the password to her Facebook account in the Stickies tool on her laptop, and an hour ago, at my behest, Hearst had checked her friends list and discovered Ben Dool. When he logged on to her account, he found Dool had liked several of Rebecca's private posts, some of them a month old.

Back in New York, I'd pored over the messages Bram exchanged with Becca, Lanie and Jess through the dating app. I'd been expecting similar interactions here, some evidence that Dool had used flattery to charm his victim, emasculated Godfrey Hearst, planted seeds of doubt in Rebecca's mind about her marriage. If such messages had ever existed, they were gone now, the chat deleted. But the fact that Dool was Rebecca's Facebook friend spoke volumes.

'The name is most certainly an alias,' I told Hearst. 'We believe he's the same man who murdered a woman from Massena, a little northeast of here. She was his first victim – that we know of, at least.' I didn't like to imagine otherwise, but the thought had crossed my mind. I asked Hearst about the man with the eyepatch, whether he'd seen him outside the Bay Point Grill too, but Hearst had been too drunk and distracted to notice. He hadn't even caught on to the fact that his wife spent close to an hour that night talking to Chet Bell.

'This man and Rebecca, were they . . .?' There was a solid pause as Hearst collected himself and marshaled the strength he'd need to hear my answer.

'It's unclear whether they had a sexual relationship,' I said. 'Considering you'd only just arrived in Alexandria Bay, though, I think it's likely things hadn't progressed that far. As you know, Rebecca's body showed no signs of sexual assault.'

Jessica Greenleaf's autopsy had told a similar story: no sexual abuse, no sign of recent intercourse. That was unusual. It was also consistent with Bram's crimes in New York. Bram and Dool weren't sexual predators. Their murders weren't about victimization, or reenacting some deep-seated psychological ordeal. For Bram, at least, women were sentenced to death because they couldn't live up to his expectations. *Because they weren't me.*

But what was driving Ben G. Dool to kill?

'We now know Rebecca came here to meet him,' I told Hearst.

'But you said he was using an alias. That means you don't know who he is.'

With the phone pressed firmly against my ear, my mind went to the families of Bram's victims. They'd had to wait far too long to know who killed their daughters.

'Not yet,' I told Hearst as I dug my fingernails into the flesh of my palm. 'But we will.'

THIRTY-TWO

H ad someone said there would come a day when I'd be asking Jared Cunningham for help, I wouldn't have believed them. And yet, that Saturday afternoon, I found myself driving back to Watertown to make a request I hoped my former nemesis couldn't refuse.

Cunningham had missed lunch, so we met at a New York-style pizzeria a couple of blocks from his old office, parking ourselves at a rickety table on the sidewalk out front. There was a drop of sweat on the tip of Cunningham's nose, and as much as he tried to hide it, a faint tremor of excitement in his hands when he lifted the grease-soaked slice to his lips. The sleeves of his linen shirt were rolled up to reveal forearms fuzzy with golden hair, and he wore a cheap-looking panama hat wrapped with a braided leather cord that looked better suited to giving tours of the Australian Outback than sharing his expertise over thin crust and soda.

My hope was that meeting with Cunningham would give me a fighting chance of getting inside Ben Dool's head. The man knew true crime – serial killers in particular. Predictably, Cunningham was thrilled. Serials weren't common in these parts. They weren't really common anywhere; by the FBI's estimate, less than one percent of homicides were cases of serial murder. The likelihood that a serial killer would stake his claim to our area was slim, the possibility of a copycat even slimmer. And yet, the region was now infamous because of Blake Bram. For another man with a small and pitiable existence, whose wires were so thoroughly crossed that he had no regard for human life – a man like Ben Dool – Bram's arrival must have felt like a visit from Santa Claus.

'The problem,' Cunningham said, dabbing at his lips with a paper napkin while I sipped my ice-cold Coke, 'is that our society worships the ones who should be loathed. We may not admit it, but there's no end to our interest in their crimes, the way they managed to conceal their violence and get away unnoticed. The way some of them walk among us even now.'

It felt different, listening to him make his same argument while knowing someone out there idolized Bram so much that they'd been moved to kill. It changed the way I thought about those true crime books in the box on Cunningham's desk. Crimes may qualify as stories, he had said, but too often they're treated as content, pumped out at an alarming rate for voracious readers to consume. As long as we kept reading and watching and gossiping about the latest Netflix limited series or podcast episode, the media wouldn't stop selling us murder. And the world wouldn't stop wanting more.

'What can you tell me about copycat killers in particular?' I asked. 'What motivates them? How closely do they stick to the original crime?'

When Cunningham tilted his head, a late day sunbeam sliced past the rim of his hat and the orange stubble on his jaw sparkled like neon glitter. 'In most of these cases, we're talking about psychopaths,' he said. 'The apathetic and morally depraved. These people, they often have what's known as an identity disturbance. They haven't got a good handle on who they are, their beliefs, their goals. So, they glom on to the identities of others.'

'Meaning their crimes are about trying to define themselves? Why not copy someone who's done something worthwhile?' I asked.

'Because there's very little glory in that.' Cunningham said it with a shrug. 'It's like this: society's dark passion for true crime started with Jack the Ripper, right? After he killed and mutilated all those women in London, penny papers changed the way they reported the news. They started printing illustrations – a bobby, or peeler as police officers were sometimes called back then, standing over a woman's body in the street. They ran more atten-tion-grabbing headlines, too – and it worked. They sold more papers, thanks in large part to Jack. Later, the Oliver Stone film *Natural Born Killers* inspired more than a dozen copycat killers, or so they say, and the notorious Zodiac killer spawned a copycat in New York City. When a psychopath hears about serial crimes, and sees the news, and takes notice of the world's fascination with those stories, he recognizes himself – or what he wants to be.'

I thought of Bram. Of Ben Dool, whoever he was, poring over reports about my cousin and somehow seeing himself in those stomach-churning stories. 'So the crimes,' I said carefully, not sure I wanted to go down the path I was currently following, 'they're the catalyst for the copycat. Without one, the other wouldn't exist.'

'You're asking if these two women would still be dead if your cousin hadn't killed three other women first.'

I nodded, and to my horror, felt a tear slide down my cheek.

Cunningham reached across his paper plate to put a hand on my arm, and though I flinched, the weight of it there helped me settle. 'I once heard it put like this,' he said. 'Think of the psychopath – *your* psychopath – as a ship. It's sailing. It's *been* sailing since the day it was christened. It's already following a set course. All Bram's crimes and that media coverage did is steer the ship in a new direction.'

The gratitude I felt for Jared Cunningham in that moment was profound. We sat in silence then, him with his hand on my forearm, me gazing at the intersection across the street.

At length, he pulled back his hand and gave me a tentative smile. 'Have you given any thought to the idea of sharing your story?'

I had. I'd been thinking about his proposition a lot, that notion of shedding light on the plight of people who so often went ignored. We weren't victims – nothing like those who'd lost their lives. And yet, somehow, we were still casualties of crime.

'There are a lot of people out there who won't be swayed,' I said. 'Who'll always lump us in with the killers.' Us. *Casey Mitchell. Noah Remus. Me.* I was one of them, now. We were the same.

'Not if I do my job, they won't.'

'Casey and Noah,' I said, tilting my head. 'What happened to them?'

'Ah. Last I checked, Noah moved overseas. In spite of every-thing, his family never forgave him for turning in his brother. And Casey . . .' Cunningham looked away. 'She took her own life a few years back.'

My mouth filled with saliva, the cloying taste of cola bubbling up my throat. Casey had gone on TV with her story, and now she was dead. With his eleven stitches to the head, Noah had chosen to flee the country. 'I just don't know if I can do it.'

'You can. Just start at the beginning,' he said.

I closed my eyes. Almost two years ago, Dr Carson Gates had spoken those same words at our very first session. He'd been trying to coax me into opening up, and I had – enough that he went from my therapist to my fiancé in relatively short order. But there were aspects of my life and my past that I'd kept to myself even then. Carson had gone to his grave not knowing the man who abducted me was my cousin.

Would he still be alive if I'd told him? I couldn't be sure, but a strangling sense of guilt told me that maybe, just maybe, furnishing Carson with that knowledge might have given him a shot at survival.

I wasn't prepared to make the same mistake twice. I'd already opened up to Mac and Tim, Bogle and Sol, and Cunningham's words about wanting to help me be the architect of my own story resonated. This was my chance to set the record straight. To tell Estella and Javier, and Gracelyn Barlowe, and everyone else out there the truth.

When I opened my eyes, I let them settle on the reporter with the fox-colored hair and drew in a breath so deep it hurt.

'Two years ago,' I began, 'I was minding my own business working a hit-and-run case when my NCO supervisor called me into his office and told me to brace myself. Our colleagues in the Seventh Precinct had been actively tracking a killer. And one of the only things they knew about Blake Bram was that he was from Swanton, Vermont.'

THIRTY-THREE

I didn't go home after meeting with Cunningham. Instead, I drove straight to Tim's cottage. It had been two days since I'd sloughed off his efforts to protect me. We'd talked at work, of course, but on an emotional level, I'd been ghosting him. Mac, too, if I'm being honest. Soon I'd be back at the office again, poring over all the evidence we'd collected so far, but I was running on fumes. I needed my friends.

Talking to Jared Cunningham made me realize something: I was lucky, and not just because I'd survived Bram. There were hundreds of people like Casey Mitchell and Noah Remus out there. Violent crime divided families. It had cost me my own family, too.

But I still had Tim and Mac.

Tim met me at the door and eased me into an embrace that lasted as long as I needed it to, which was a long time. I hadn't felt hungry at the pizza place, but when Mac led me to the table and presented me with the early dinner Tim had prepared, pointing out that she'd supplied the dessert, I was suddenly famished. They listened as, between bites of grilled chicken over lemon rice, I filled them in on what they'd missed. I hadn't had a chance to tell either of them about Cunningham's proposition yet – the past few days were a sprint, the finish line still not in sight – but now I couldn't stop talking, the words as constant as the river flowing past Tim's yard. Never again would I allow secrets to hover around us like ghosts. We were better when we could be honest with each other, and in the wake of the discovery that my dead cousin had a protégé, I needed all the better I could get.

When I explained about Cunningham's new endeavor and what he'd asked of me, Mac was surprisingly receptive to the idea of yet another article centering on 'Blake Bram's cop cousin.'

'It's all about optics,' she said. 'If you can control how you're portrayed, you can gain the upper hand.'

'The upper hand being . . .?'

'The truth, of course.'

'I'm with the sheriff on this,' said Tim. 'It's not actually a bad idea. An interview gives you a chance to finally go on the record with your side of the story and quash all those conspiracy theories about why you handled things the way you did.'

I collected our empty plates and tipped them into soapy water in the kitchen sink. 'From your lips to God's ears, guys. Sit,' I commanded as Mac got up to help with the dishes. I passed the sponge to Tim and snatched a fresh kitchen towel from the cabinet, shaking it open and coming to stand by his side. 'It's weird,' I told them. 'On the one hand, I don't feel like I have to justify my actions. But this also isn't just about me.' There were the families of Bram's victims to think of, and my own family, too. The former needed to know my cousin's behavior was wholly unsanctioned, while the latter needed the rest of the world to understand that was the case.

'What's the over-under on this Cunningham fella?' Mac asked, fluffing her hair as she leaned back in her seat, long legs outstretched. 'Can you trust him?'

Trust was an emotional brain state I struggled with on a regular basis. It had taken me months to confess my abduction to Tim, and I'd only done it because the case we were working was fraught with danger and demanded full disclosure. 'Us against them,' Tim had said, both of our partnership and the suspects we'd been pitted against. If I'd learned anything from the cases I'd worked in the Thousand Islands so far, it was that trust was hard to come by.

'I think so,' I said. 'I didn't before, but I'm starting to realize I may not have given the guy a fair shake.'

With a wink, Mac said, 'Everyone deserves one of those.'

'I haven't been his number one fan, but it's possible I misjudged him. He voluntarily left the paper after the editorial page editor sold me down the river. That says a lot about his character. Speaking of misjudging people,' I went on, 'I can't stop thinking about Estella.' When Tim had asked about her earlier I'd quickly changed the subject, but I couldn't get the woman out of my mind. 'It bothers me that I jumped to conclusions about her. I can't figure her out, though. Is she trying to guilt-trip me, here? Because I couldn't possibly feel guiltier than I already do.'

'Well, I'll tell you what I've always told my nephews,' McIntyre said. 'You can't make people like you.'

'I don't need her to like me. I just need her to not want to skin me alive.'

'Maybe the article will help her come to terms with it all,' Tim suggested.

I nodded, but I'd seen the hatred in Estella's eyes. It would take a lot more than one sympathetic interview to change her opinion about me.

'Well,' said Mac, shielding a yawn with the back of her hand, 'I guess I should hit the road. Whiskey will be waiting.'

'Say hi to that rascal for me, OK?' I missed Mac's Maltipoo. For the few months that I'd lived on her couch post-break up with Carson, the little guy and I had been inseparable.

'Will do,' said Mac, thanking Tim for the dinner. 'Keep me posted on things.'

'Always.' I gave her a quick embrace and watched her saunter down the front path toward her car.

'I have a confession to make.'

Tim had waited until we were back at the sink to say it, the cottage quiet around us, a warm breeze from the open window perfumed with algae and pine and night. I looked up from the plate I was drying. 'Yeah?'

Tim said, 'I've been visiting Carson's grave.'

I didn't realize the dish was slipping until it smacked the counter. Steadying my hands, I carefully set it down. After the calling hour and funeral mass, Carson Gates had been buried at the cemetery behind St Cyril's Catholic Church, in the heart of the town he and Tim grew up in. Just a five-minute walk from all the places they used to go as kids, in the days when Carson was still exploiting Tim's innocence.

'I have to be honest,' Tim said, 'I wasn't OK when I went to his funeral. I did a good job of hiding it – at least I think I did – but I was hurting. I thought his death would wipe all the angry feelings I had away. This horrible thing happened to him, which he didn't deserve, no matter what he did or how awful he could be. Sometimes I still get so furious thinking about how he treated you that I could punch a fucking wall.'

'Us,' I said. 'How he treated us.'

'Us,' he conceded. 'Guess I'm not as compassionate a person as I thought I was.'

'No.' I clutched his arm. 'Tim, no. No one's more compassionate than you are. You and Carson had a complicated relationship, and there was a lot left unresolved.' I paused. 'Does going there make you feel better?'

'Better? Yeah,' he said. 'I think it does. Sometimes, when there's no one else around, I talk to him. Tell him everything I didn't get a chance to say when he was alive, even the stuff that would really piss him off.' He smiled a little. Shook his head. 'I know it won't change anything that happened, but it's comforting, somehow.'

'Then don't question it. Grief is hard,' I told him. 'You need to do what's best for you. Whatever it takes to get through it.'

'One could say the same thing about Estella Lopez.'

'Huh.' I let go of his arm and reached for another wet dish. 'You're sneaky, you know that?'

'Yup,' he said, pulling me into an embrace and pressing his soapy hands against my lower back. The water on his fingers, and those fingers on my skin, sent a shiver of pleasure straight through me. I rested my head against his chest and let my body relax into his.

'So you think I should stop obsessing over her and her brother? Is that what you're saying.'

'I think it's a good idea, yes. I mean, you're right – the timing of their arrival in town, and the fact that they were in the area over July Fourth . . . it's odd. But lots of people make multiple trips here in the summer, and holiday weekends and Pirate Days are the biggest draws. So while their presence may be fishy, we still don't have a shred of proof that either of them was involved with those murders.'

'Who does that leave us with, though?' I asked, stepping away to look at his face.

'Someone you haven't identified yet. The guy Chet Bell spotted outside the bar. If this Ben Dool allowed himself to be caught on camera that night, he may have made other mistakes, too. You just have to find them.'

'I can't believe we're back here,' I said. 'When Bram died, I really thought things would go back to normal.' Instead, once again, we were hunting a killer in our own back yard.

Tim looked down at me. 'It's different this time. This time, we have a sense of what's coming. Bram was a wild card, capable of anything, anytime and anywhere. A copycat, though . . . he's following a blueprint. A blueprint you know inside and out.'

I hadn't thought about it that way. All this time, I'd been cursing Bram for doing what he'd done because it inspired someone just as twisted to carry out his legacy. As frightening as that seemed, this person was following a predetermined path. There was a rhythm to their killings that I had to believe would give us an advantage.

The trouble was, we knew where this road led.

Somewhere, sometime soon, another woman had to die.

THIRTY-FOUR

I t was quiet at the barracks. We'd just missed the trooper's shift change at seven p.m., the busiest time of the day. I typically enjoyed the chance to say hello to our fellow New York State employees, but tonight, I was grateful for the silence.

'Which is more dangerous,' I asked Tim, Bogle and Sol as I paced the room, 'a gun, or a knife?'

I leaned against the corner of Tim's desk, and waited. It was a question most martial arts students were asked early on in their instruction, but I hadn't heard it until I started training in Watertown last year. Sam, my sensei, sprung it on me in class one morning while we were reviewing techniques for disarming an opponent. When I first started taking his classes, I thought Sam's self-defense teachings were redundant. As a graduate of the police academy, I already knew countless tactics for combat. It didn't take long for me to concede that I'd been wrong. The Shaolin Kempo Karate way focused primarily on self-defense, and Sam's approach recalibrated how I thought about subduing uncooperative suspects. It was about using the tools you had – strength, speed, instinct – to your advantage. I wanted my investigators to understand that, too.

'So which is it?' I asked again. 'A knife, or a gun?'

'Gun.' Bogle's answer came quickly. He nodded to himself. 'Definitely gun. It's more powerful. More deadly.'

'Anyone else?'

'Knife.' That was Tim. He gave Bogle an apologetic shrug. 'Guns are dangerous, but it's way easier to evade the barrel of a gun than a knife, because every part of the knife has the potential to be lethal.'

I felt a flush of pride. 'Exactly right,' I said. 'Guns are pretty limited in what they can do, but a knife –' here I grabbed a pen from the desk and slashed at the air – 'can move in every direction, see? Come at you from every angle. Guys, that's what we need to do with this case. Come at it from every possible angle.'

'In other words, be the knife,' Jeremy Solomon said.

'Be the knife,' I repeated, beaming at Sol. From the corner of my eye, I saw Bogle lower his gaze to the floor.

We'd been working closely with Troop B; comparing notes about our cases, and speaking to their team had made me realize there was something missing from our evidence. The Massena police knew Jessica Greenleaf had met up with a man the night she was killed. In A-Bay, we suspected the same could be true of Rebecca Hearst. We knew both Jessica and Rebecca were Facebook friends with Ben Dool, and we had the statement from Chet Bell about the long night Rebecca was anticipating. But none of that had produced enough evidence for us to identify our killer.

'Rebecca's phone was found on a private island near the Thousand Islands Bridge,' I said. 'Why? She could have tossed it after meeting up with her beau so her husband couldn't track her whereabouts. It's also possible the killer ditched it for that same reason. But there's a third possibility. What if the killer dumped the phone because there was something on it that stood to give him away? Remember, Troop B hasn't been able to locate Jessica's phone at all. I'm starting to think there's something there worth looking at.'

It was Tim's comment about our suspect's slip-up with the security camera that got me thinking about the phone again. Ben Dool had been active on social media. It appeared to be his primary hunting ground, and he had to know we'd follow that trail to the bitter end. But his victims' phones . . . those had been ditched. What was he trying to hide?

Text messages, emails, calls . . . we'd scrutinized all of those already, squinting through the cracks in Rebecca's phone screen. What were we missing? 'Photos,' I said. 'Comments Dool may have left on other social platforms. Additional messaging apps that might have been deleted. We need to escalate this, bring in a tech expert and hope to God they work fast. Tim, grab the phone from the evidence closet, will you?'

'On it,' said Tim.

But it took him so long to return from the room down the hall that I checked my watch while he was gone. When Tim finally reappeared, he wore a puzzled expression.

'We've got a problem.' He splayed a hand over his mouth in thought. Tugged at his lower lip. 'Rebecca's phone . . . it isn't there.'

'What do you mean, it isn't there?'

'I searched that thing top to bottom, Shana. The phone's gone.'

'Gone? How could it be gone?' There was a lock on the evidence closet, but that was hardly the point. This wasn't a public space. The only people who had access to the state police barracks were the troopers and my own team. A small group of men, all of whom I knew and trusted implicitly. 'Check again,' I said. 'Maybe it fell behind the shelf or something.'

Tim held my gaze. 'I looked all over. In the other evidence bags. On the floor. I turned that closet upside down. It isn't there.'

I squinted at him, disbelieving. Could someone have misplaced it? How could it be lost? The phone was evidence, more critical now than ever.

'Who was the last to see it?' I looked from Tim to Bogle and Sol. None of the men standing before me were incompetent; they wouldn't be on my team if they were. But if there was a reasonable explanation for what had happened, I couldn't find it.

'Don,' I said with a snap of my fingers. 'Didn't you store it after our initial search?' It was coming back to me, a memory of Bogle carrying an evidence bag down the hall with such care you'd think it was rigged with explosives.

He shook his head. 'I-I don't know. I really don't remember.'

With his clean-shaven head, neck, and face, there was nowhere for Don Bogle's emotions to hide. The lumps and hollows in his skin were a patchwork of heat, some of the blotches such a deep shade of cherry they looked like burns. 'Don,' I said, my voice level, 'I need a hand with something in my office. Would you mind?'

Head aflame, he followed me out the door.

It was cooler in my office than the rest of the barracks, a glitch of the A/C system that I'd always considered a lucky break. Now, the icy air sent a ripple up my arms.

'Is there something you want to tell me?' I asked.

The office door was firmly shut behind us. Bogle loomed over me, his skin clammy up close. He didn't answer.

'Sit down, Don.'

He sunk into the chair across from my desk. 'I'm sorry,' Bogle said. 'I don't know what happened. I put it there. I know I did.'

'When?'

'Right when you told me to.' With a shake of his head he said, 'I just don't know.'

'Don.' I'd never seen him this way. He was tearing up, his face distorted by humiliation. 'We'll find it, OK?' I leaned toward him, and quickly pulled back. 'Jesus, Don, have you been *drinking*?' I could smell the warm bite of liquor on his breath, seeping out of his pores and wrapping him in a sickly-sweet fog.

It was a long time before he spoke again and I watched him all the while, assessing every expression that mangled his face. I happened to know Bogle was of German descent, though with his hooked nose and boxy jaw I'd always thought of him more as a Russian baddie, Drago from Rocky or some other clichéd eastern European thug. Bogle wasn't a thug at all. He was a thoughtful friend who knew just what to say when I was stressed and told me I looked pretty in my party dress.

'I'm sorry,' he said now. 'Ah, Christ, I'm so fucking sorry. I don't know what I was thinking that day. It was an accident.'

I was dumbstruck. Bogle had been drinking at work – and not just tonight. He'd lost key evidence in a homicide investigation. 'The phone.' What the hell were we going to do without it?

'I know, I'm sorry. I know you told me to store it,' he said now, 'but I think I left it on my desk. Maybe the cleaners, or one of the troopers . . .?'

'Don't do that, Don.' There was no way someone had taken an evidence bag from Bogle's desk and not put it where it belonged. We would keep looking. *We have to find that phone.*

'Shana. Please, just let me explain. This isn't me.' He raked at his face. 'It was one mistake – a big one, I know, but . . . you know me. You know I'm trustworthy. I swear to God it won't happen again. Things have been rough lately at home, but I've got this. You have to believe me.'

Alcoholism and anxiety aren't so different. That fight, flight, or freeze response anxiety triggers in our brains is addictive. I had unwillingly trained myself to crave panic like a drug; it was the only way I knew how to punish myself for my blood tie to

Bram. An addiction like Bogle's was skilled at manipulation. It had fleeced him into believing he had things under control.

'I know you and Juliet are having problems, and I'm sorry,' I said, 'I really am. But—'

'Juliet's pregnant,' he said.

I shook my head. 'She's pregnant? That's—'

The look on his face stopped me short.

'We've been trying to have a baby for years,' said Bogle. 'But we're not in the best place right now. I've been living in the guest house for weeks.' He tipped his chin to the ceiling.

'Because of the drinking?'

'She's pissed about that, yeah, but that's not the half of it. I just needed a break. It's her parents,' he said. 'They never approved of us. To them, I'm just some fucking sycophant. A gold digger, I once heard her mother say.'

'That's terrible.' It explained the weird energy I'd picked up on between Bogle and Amos at the party. They may have been Saturday pickleball partners, but Amos's loyalties lay with his flesh-and-blood family.

'Trust me, I'm used to it.' Bogle's laugh was bitter. 'But humiliating me isn't enough for them anymore. They want me gone. I guess they thought there was a chance Juliet would come to her senses and leave me on her own. A divorce doesn't look great for the family, but Juliet's still young; she'd find someone new, they'd make sure of it. It never happened, though. They don't know she's pregnant yet – she's only ten weeks along – but they know we've been trying. And a kid would tie the Barlowes to me for life.'

'Have you talked to Juliet about it? Does she know her family's trying to turn her against you?'

Bogle hung his head. 'She can't see it – or doesn't want to. Every time I bring it up she accuses me of being unfair to them. I couldn't take it anymore, Shana. We live twenty minutes from them and her mother's over all the time, smothering Jules. Judging me. Gracelyn's always been ridiculously protective of Juliet. Jules told me stories about when she was at college – her mom would call multiple times a day just to check on her. Was she exercising enough? Eating her greens? Had she remembered to talk to her therapist? Was she taking care of her cuticles? That's what these people are like,' he said in response to my raised eyebrows. 'Appearances matter. Reputation is everything. As soon as they found out I'd been drinking a bit more than usual, they went from talking behind my back to condemning me out in the open. I can't live this way.'

'They'll come around once they hear about the baby,' I assured him, but I could see that he wasn't convinced. 'Look, Don,' I said, 'we're colleagues, but I consider you a friend. A good one.'

Click. Clack. Those knuckles again. 'I appreciate that more than you know.'

I lowered my eyes. Had I simply caught Bogle drunk at work, I might be able to justify letting him off with a warning. If that wasn't enough, I could have put him in touch with the Drug Recognition Expert. But a DRE couldn't help Don Bogle now. His behavior had severely impaired his ability to do his job, and I knew I had no choice but to initiate a formal complaint. Very soon, the whole thing would be out of my hands. We'd get him through it, but Bogle had to know he couldn't carry on working like nothing had happened. A drinking problem was one thing. Losing evidence was quite another.

'And as a friend,' I went on, 'I'm telling you that you need help. There's a chain of events that needs to happen here. We'll have to talk to Oneida about getting you assessed, and connect you with a counselor. You'll have to go on leave until we can figure this out.'

Bogle's expression clouded. I hoped that he would acquiesce. Acknowledge that yes, he had a problem, and face it head-on. Instead, the realization of what was about to happen hit him like a tsunami.

'No,' he said, eyes wild. 'I can't get suspended. I have to be here.'

'You know that can't happen, Don.'

Bogle pressed one big hand against the other, knuckles snapping like popped gum. 'I need a minute to think.' A nod at the door.

'Go ahead.'

I suspected it was going to take more than a minute for him to accept what was happening, but if Bogle needed to slam a door and splash some water on his eyes before facing his fate, more power to him. He'd seen me go through something similar to this last year, when I was suspended pending a psych eval after it became clear my PTSD hadn't magically resolved itself. I'd been hoping he could take some comfort in remembering that and seeing me now, back at work. But I knew he was thinking about that missing phone. From where I was sitting, the odds that Bogle's critical mistake hadn't been affected by drinking were slim. His mood, his sleep, the ability to concentrate were all colored by his problems at home, and the booze was only making things worse.

The missing evidence made a dog's breakfast of our investigation. A few years ago, in Minnesota, a missing persons case had been cracked when a digital forensic investigation helped police locate two thirteen-year-old girls in their abductor's basement. The manual acquisition of any digital evidence we'd missed was no longer an option. I'd have to file a request with Rebecca's phone provider to extract her data from the cloud. Even under exigent circumstances, that could take anywhere from a few hours to a few days. And Bogle knew it.

'Fuck,' I muttered under my breath as I smacked the desk with my open hand.

THIRTY-FIVE

When Jared Cunningham called my cell phone just after eight p.m. that night, I immediately convinced myself he was having second thoughts. Regrets about his offer to help paint me in a better light. I wouldn't have blamed him; my story had a tendency to scare people off. He didn't want to talk about that, though.

'Got a minute?' he asked. His accent was back. 'There's something you need to see.'

I had already sent Sol home for the night, and Bogle was long gone too; I wasn't surprised when he didn't stop by my office again to say goodbye. Tim and I had been turning the barracks upside down in search of that missing phone. Now, we sat side by side at his desk as I put Cunningham on speaker and stared down at the image on my screen.

Aside from using it last fall to reconnect with my old high school friend Suzuka Weppler, I hadn't so much as glanced at my Facebook account in more than a year. It wouldn't have mattered if I had. The post Cunningham had screenshotted was from a private page, a community group to which I didn't have access. As I scanned the post, two words in particular hit me like a shove.

'*Copycat killer?*' I stammered. 'What the hell?'

'Anyone can post,' Cunningham said sadly, 'as long as you're a member. My sister – she lives in Dexter – saw it and gave me the heads-up. The group's called Moms of Jefferson County. It has just over three thousand members.'

Three thousand people had access to what I was currently looking at, and likely many more would hear about it through word of mouth.

Gracelyn Barlowe strikes again.

> Hi everyone, local mother and businesswoman here. I can't
> be the only one thinking this, but . . . is it possible a copycat
> killer has come to our area?! The tragic murder of a young

woman earlier this week is the second such incident in the Thousand Islands since July. We all know the story of Bram/ Skilton and what he did to poor Carson Gates and all those women in New York, and now, just a few months after his death, we're seeing more violent crime here with similar victims. I don't expect much from 'detective' Shana Merchant – we all know how little she did to help our counties the first time around – but two murders is a pattern, whether the state police cares to admit it or not. I hope that by posting this message I can encourage you to lodge a formal complaint about Ms Merchant with the Bureau of Criminal Investigation. Until then, hold your loved ones close.

'Shana?' said Cunningham. 'You still there?'

'I'm here.' When Tim put a hand on my knee to anchor me, I realized I'd been biting my lip, gnawing it raw. 'Why would she post this?'

'It's looking more and more like a personal vendetta.' This time, he didn't try to wave it off or console me. Instead, Tim said, 'Fuck that she-devil. You have every right to be angry, Shane.'

'There's something bugging me,' I said.

'About the post?' asked Cunningham.

'About the copycat theory.' The post made me furious, yes, but it had also joggled a thought loose in my mind. 'There are very few people who know the details of the cases I worked in New York. The stuff that wasn't in the news, I mean,' I said. 'There are aspects of both Rebecca and Jessica's cases that our copycat killer shouldn't – couldn't – know.'

'Like what?' asked Tim.

'Like what Bram's third victim in New York, Jess Lowenthal, looked like when we found her. Her body was splayed on a pile of gravel.' I could still picture the crime scene photos, the woman's hair bejeweled with bits of rock.

'Just like Rebecca's,' said Tim.

'Right. But the Seventh Precinct, and my guys in Nine, we kept that close to the vest. The press wrote about the construction site, but the project foreman who found the body, the medical examiner, the techs and my team were the only ones who knew about the gravel.' In truth, a few others had found out since, but I doubted that Tim, Mac and my investigators had been gossiping about the cases that almost cost me my life.

'People talk,' Cunningham said. 'Any one of them could have told someone else. Violent crimes make the rounds – believe me, I know. I can't tell you how many times I've had a witness give me an exclusive story only to find out they already spilled their guts to everyone and their dog.'

I said, 'I guess it's possible one of them could have posted the details online.' There were a million message boards on the dark web that traded in just that kind of sick shit. If that's how our perp got the scoop, we'd never track him down. 'I think the way to find our guy is by zeroing in on motive.'

'The *why* of the murders,' said Cunningham, 'since copycat crimes are rarely cookie-cutter deals.'

Tim and I exchanged a glance. The crimes were so similar to Bram's that we'd assumed the killer was going for accuracy. 'Keep talking,' I told him.

'It's like this,' said Cunningham. 'Some copycats envy the media attention lavished on a high-profile murderer. Others are inspired by some aspect of the crime – how a killer succeeded at capturing his targets, or how he disposed of the bodies. It's very unusual for a copycat crime to be an exact replica of the original.'

'They use qualities of the original crime as building blocks, and give the killing their own unique twist,' said Tim.

I pulled a face. The idea repulsed me. 'That means the motive could be unique, too.'

'So, motive,' Tim said. 'The victims are all women. This guy could be a misogynist.'

'Or have mommy issues.' Cunningham's voice crackled as he readjusted the phone against his ear. He seemed to be reveling the opportunity to be in the trenches with me and Tim. I thought back to McIntyre's question about whether I trusted the man. One thing I knew for sure was that, right now, we needed him.

'It could just be about the fame. Bram got a lot of press,' I said. 'If his successor wants attention, associating himself with Bram is a way to get it.'

'Wait.' Tim's hand was on the desk, his arm rigid.

'What is it? Another motive?'

'Kind of.' All of a sudden, he was looking pale. 'There's a common thread between these crimes. Beyond their similarities to Bram's killings.'

It was Cunningham who spoke next. 'It's you,' he said, sounding amazed. 'Holy shit, Shana, the common thread is *you*.'

I opened my mouth to argue, and immediately closed it again.

'Someone keeping tabs on news about Bram would have heard that you're related,' said Tim. 'By every indication, this copycat is an obsessive personality who idolizes Bram.'

'This person, they'd be hungry for every piece of information on his life that they could find, and your connection to him is public now,' Cunningham said.

'But they know something they shouldn't.' Tim looked up at the ceiling, elongating the sinews in his neck. 'That suggests we're not dealing with a random stranger who read about you online. This killer, he could be someone from your life.' His lower lip slipped between his teeth. 'Could they be from New York? Maybe someone you worked with who has a bone to pick?'

Thinking back to my days in the city, I couldn't call up a single person who had a beef with me. There was the usual shit-talking among detectives and patrol officers, sure. I'd heard stories about other precincts, how tough it was for women to rise in the ranks even now. I was the only female detective in the Fighting Ninth, but to my knowledge that had never been an issue for my peers.

'Tim's right,' Cunningham said. 'There has to be a reason why this guy came all the way up here to plot two elaborate murders. So who'd you piss off back in New York, Shana?'

A chill washed over me. There was someone I'd angered. Someone who I knew for a fact had come upstate, and who might have had access to detailed information about Bram's crimes in the city. I'd been trying to put him out of my mind. Stop obsessing, like Tim said, and focus on the evidence. Now, though, I wondered if that was the right approach after all.

I hadn't worked directly with Officer Jay Lopez, but he'd patrolled the Lower East Side. Three murders in as many weeks; there would have been a lot of talk in his department about them. Lopez might have taken that information home. I could almost picture him, falling heavily into bed at the end of the day after pressing a kiss to his sleeping children's faces, their foreheads sweet and soft beneath his lips. Telling his wife the city was going to hell, that he was terrified for their daughter. About what might happen when she grew up and started dating online just like Becca. Lanie. Jess.

Beside him, her long hair loose and face scrubbed clean, Estella Lopez would have listened while she used her fingernails to stroke her husband's bare back.

And maybe, the next morning, she called her brother Javier.

Hours ago, Tim had said there was nothing to tie Javier to Rebecca Hearst and Jessica Greenleaf, but that wasn't entirely true. Javier and his sister were holding a grudge. Copycats tended to have obsessive personalities. Was it possible I was the focus of Javier's obsession because of what happened with Jay Lopez? I remembered Cunningham's analogy about the ship, how Bram's crimes might steer a psychopath on a new course. Could it be that my cousin had become the unholy compass Javier was using to guide himself to port? Could Javier be the man in that video? I glanced at Tim. He looked like he wanted to retch.

I covered the phone with my hand.

'We're still missing the evidence,' I said under my breath.

'But if there's any truth to this at all, we need to keep an even closer eye on you. I'm sorry,' said Tim, 'but it's true.'

I had to wonder, sometimes, if Tim wished he had a girlfriend who wasn't in constant danger of being butchered in her sleep.

He deserved a relationship that was much simpler than this.

THIRTY-SIX

Nightfall should have come as a relief. The sun had set, the sky was dark, but the humidity remained, hanging over the river like a dense fog. In the gold and navy boat, Tim and I mopped our brows and swatted at mosquitoes while Len the ferryman steered us through Carlson Island's South Bay to the rocky shore.

'He's got a record, a history of violence,' Bogle had warned when, days ago, I found the graffiti on my garage door. Tim and I had looked him up ourselves before leaving the station tonight, and Bogle hadn't been wrong about the man's past. He and a friend had tried to burglarize an apartment in Tribeca armed with knives, and he'd spent three years in prison because of it. *Knives.* The word had hit like a ton of gravel tipped onto my head. Since then, it appeared that Javier had kept to the letter of the law. He paid his taxes and his rent. Over the past ten years he'd bounced from job to job, but he did landscaping and snow removal work now, in Brooklyn's Prospect Park.

Did that make him innocent? It was possible the man and his sister had nothing to do with the murders in Jefferson County. It was also possible he'd brutally attacked Jessica and Rebecca on his two visits upstate, and that I was his next target.

We'd come to Carlson Island to find out which of those two theories was true.

In stark contrast to the scene the previous night the lobby stood quiet, all traces of the wild party swept and polished away. Behind the check-in desk, a reedy woman with white hair in a buzzcut beamed at us as we approached. We couldn't search Javier's room without a warrant, but that was fine. All Tim and I wanted for now was to locate the man and have a little chat.

Armed with his room number, we made our way up the central staircase to the second floor, and once again I marveled at the opulence of the place. Of what the property must be worth to Juliet Barlowe's family. On Tern Island, my thoughts had taken a similar course while investigating the Sinclair family at their lavish summer home. Money was never far from my mind when I was working a case, especially if the victim's loved ones had a lot of it. Now, though, I was thinking about Don Bogle, and what it must have been like to marry into a family with sky-high expectations and dripping in wealth.

My knuckles met the door. I rapped once, then a second time before I heard the click of the latch bolt disengage.

Estella stood in the doorway, one arm limp by her side. Her hair was pulled into a ponytail so high and tight it yanked back the outer corners of her eyes, but they would have narrowed at the sight of us all the same. She shifted to the right and pushed the door closed just enough to block our view of the room.

'Your brother around?' I asked it with a smile.

'He stepped out.'

'In that case, we'd like to talk to you. We can do it here or at the barracks,' I said, calling her bluff. 'The choice is yours.'

'No.' The door swung open and Javier stood before us, his nostrils already flared in preparation for a fight.

The siblings' shared room was all windows, and the windows faced the place where the St Lawrence met Lake Ontario. At this time of night the river was a band of midnight blue that sparked under the moonlight, a million lit matches pirouetting on the water. Reluctantly, Javier took a seat next to his sister on the bed. They were almost the same size and shape, and it gave the impression that they were a unit. A matched set. Well, Tim and I were a set, too, and we weren't about to let ourselves be overpowered.

Javier folded his arms across his chest. 'What are you trying to pin on me this time?'

'I'm sure you've heard about our homicide investigation,' I said.

I'd been girding myself for confrontation, expecting to see Estella's face aglow with unregulated anger, but her voice, when she spoke, was chastened. 'It was in the news,' she said. 'That poor woman.'

'*Women*. A month ago, a single mother named Jessica Greenleaf was murdered not far from here in Massena. We believe the cases are related.'

Though Estella was working hard to maintain an expression

of defiance, her mask had slipped. 'You think the same person killed them both?'

'It looks that way, yes.'

'What does any of this have to do with us?' Unlike Estella, Javier was still highly strung, his back ramrod straight where he sat at the foot of the bed.

'We have video footage of our suspect,' Tim said, letting the man draw his own conclusions. 'We're here to establish a timeline so we can eliminate you from our investigation.' When, exactly, had they arrived in A-Bay? Why had they come here in early July? These were details we needed to know.

'Eliminate me.' Javier's mouth curled into a sneer. 'You kidding me with this?'

'If your video footage was worth two shits, you'd be arresting him right now,' Estella said. 'You've got nothing.'

'Not quite nothing,' I said. 'The timing of the crimes lines up with your visits upstate.'

Ever cordial, Tim said, 'All we want is for you to provide us with alibis for last Sunday night and the night of July third. That's all.'

'This is bullshit. So we came up here twice this summer,' Javier said, 'so what? Hundreds of other people did the same thing.'

'Hundreds of other people didn't vandalize my garage and threaten me,' I said, stoking the flames. 'We believe our suspect may have some kind of . . . obsession, and you both made it clear when you arrived in town that you're holding a grudge against me. If you don't have an alibi and a purpose for being in Alexandria Bay, our reasonable suspicion is going to turn into probable cause real quick.'

Estella and Javier exchanged a glance. The movement was almost imperceptible, but she shook her head. A signal for Javier to hold his ground? There was a savageness to the way Estella watched him that made me glad she'd turned her wrath on her brother and away from me. It was hard to imagine Javier could defy her when she looked like this, but he said, 'I'm sorry,' turned his back on his sister, and looked me in the eyes.

'She's filing a wrongful death suit against you,' he said.

'What?' Tim tensed beside me, every muscle straining against his clothes.

'Fuck,' Estella hissed under her breath. Javier reached for her hand, but she shook him off. The jig was up. 'I got three kids,' she said. 'Three kids who deserve a chance to go to college. Who'll never see their father again. Because of you.'

The room tilted. *A wrongful death action.* A civil case against me, maybe even against the NYPD. Estella wanted to see me held liable for Jay Lopez's death.

It was the only thing I could imagine that would generate more negative press than I'd already had. A law suit would prolong the media's interest in me and Bram, but that wasn't the worst of it. It would mean the press would dig even deeper into my trauma bond and PTSD. Expose my mental health struggles to the entire world.

'You can't.' The words were a croak, my voice not my own. 'You can't do that.'

'The insurance policy, it wasn't enough,' said Estella. 'My kids are almost teens, and growing fast. They're always hungry. What the hell did you expect me to do?'

'I was down in that basement for eight days,' I said. 'I didn't know if I was going to live or die.'

'Shana.' Tim's jaw shifted, muscles quivering. 'Don't. You don't have to explain.'

Didn't I? It had taken me a long time to come to terms with it, but the simple fact was that I couldn't have saved this woman's husband. I hadn't even managed to save myself.

So, I told them. About how easy it was to talk to the stranger I met at the pub near Tompkins Square Park, as if I'd known the man who seemed unfazed by my scar all my life. About the Rohypnol in my pint that allowed him to shuffle me outside, and the stale mold funk of the basement cell I found myself in when I woke up, and the terrifying certainty that I would die there like the others. I told them that, for the longest time, I didn't know the abductor who visited me daily and told me stories of his childhood was my own kin, and that when the beastly, unimaginable truth finally clicked into place, I thought dying might be for the best. Better that than have to go home and tell my family what Abe had become.

Estella listened. Fretted her lower lip and watched me with hollow, twitchy eyes. She said, 'I don't care about any of that.

You were *there*. You should have stopped him. But you didn't, because he was your cousin.'

'No.'

'You haven't answered our questions.' There was a cadence to Tim's voice that took me a second to riddle out. He was scared. Scared for me. 'Where were you both on Sunday and the night of July third?' This was him trying to rein her in, get our interview back on track. Estella was about to lose her cool while her brother watched from the corner of his eye, his breathing conspicuously slow.

'Go to hell,' she told Tim at the same time that Javier blurted, 'It was my idea.'

Seething, his sister whipped around to face him. 'Shut *up*, Javi.'

Javier's shoulders slouched and he shook his head. 'It was my idea to sue. I wanted to do it right from the start, as soon as we found out what happened to Jay and that a detective was there when he was killed, but we didn't know who you were. We had no fucking clue. The papers never said your name.'

I had my former department to thank for that. Every news report about Bram had referred to me as an 'undisclosed female officer.' Until now.

'But then in April,' Javier went on, 'Bram died, and you were with him when that happened, too, and your name was *every-where*. Again I told Estella she needed to try and make some bank. Sue you, or the New York police, or both. That time, she listened.'

'I didn't want to do it.' Estella reached for her necklace, and what was hiding down her shirt. The chain I'd seen her wearing was looped through a man's gold wedding band. She fiddled with it as she spoke. 'It's been almost two years since Jay died. The kids were finally starting to get used to him being gone. I was, too. I didn't want to think about that day ever again. I knew how angry it would make me – make *us* – and how long a civil case could drag on. But Javi wouldn't shut up about it.' He reached for her hand again, and Estella dropped her gaze. 'Once I started seri-ously considering it, it was all I could think about. Money for the kids' college funds. Money for Jay's dad. His mom passed last year,' she told us. 'She never got over what happened to him.'

In my lap, my hands grew clammy. My heartbeat was a mallet against my chest.

'I went to talk to a lawyer. Javi came along. The guy said we might have a case, but we would need to show you were responsible.'

By a preponderance of evidence. Beyond a reasonable doubt. Estella and her lawyer would have to prove my negligence was to blame for Jay Lopez's death. But it was my cousin who'd taken Lopez's gun, my cousin who'd left him riddled with bullet holes while I looked on in horror. In shock.

I knew what was coming next. 'He looked into you,' she said, 'and he saw all those news stories about your anxiety disorder. Some psychologists were saying you probably had Stockholm syndrome.'

I hadn't seen those articles, but that theory was nothing new. I wondered how I'd fared, and what the takeaway had been. I wasn't sure I wanted to know.

Estella released the chain and ran the edge of her hand under her nose. 'After that, the lawyer told us there wasn't enough evidence against you. You were the only living witness, and we couldn't be sure about your mental state. He said we had no case. I didn't believe him. I didn't *want* to believe. You're a detective. You could have stopped him.' She brushed a tear from her cheek. 'I didn't want to give up, so I went to another attorney, and another. They all said the same thing.'

'I told her we should let it go.' Javier was rubbing circles on his bristly head, a repetitive motion designed to soothe. 'Like hey, we tried, you know? She wouldn't listen.'

'I couldn't,' said Estella. 'I thought, there has to be a way to prove she's a bad cop. If I had evidence that you were bad at your job, I could go back to those lawyers, and maybe it would be enough.'

You put that bastard first and let him kill an innocent man, Estella had said outside the Bean-In. Javier's accusations at The Dot came floating back to me, too. *You threaten her? Did you?* 'That's why you've been antagonizing me,' I said, looking from one sibling to the other. 'You were trying to set me off. Riling me up so I'd snap.'

Estella's face fell. Though she wouldn't say it, not today and maybe not ever, I knew it had pained her to treat me that way.

'You want alibis?' Javier's voice was rough with emotion. He leaned forward, the springs of the bed creaking under his weight. 'The night before Independence Day was a Tuesday. That day, we found a lady in town who said you liked to hang out at that pizza place by the water. We sat there until closing time, and then we waited on the dock outside until almost midnight. There was an old man in coveralls outside the marina giving us dirty looks the whole time. I'm sure he'll remember.' To underscore his point, Javier flexed his muscles. The tattoos on his forearms rippled.

We didn't need the old man at the marina to validate their story. If Javier and Estella had been on the dock, we'd find footage of them on the same wide-lens security camera that had captured Ben Dool on the park bench. According to Damon Ameer, Jessica Greenleaf left her retail job when the store closed at seven p.m. and went straight to the Rusty Anchor to meet her date. Massena was over an hour from A-Bay.

'Sunday night,' Estella said, holding my gaze. 'We ate dinner at that same pizza place because it was the cheapest meal we could find, and then we came back here to call my kids. You can ask that guy who drives the ferry boat. We never left the island until morning.'

I glanced at Tim. Both alibis would be easy to corroborate. If Estella and her brother were being honest with us, there was no way either of them could have been anywhere near Rebecca and Jessica on the nights of their deaths.

'What can I do to help you?' I said in a feeble voice. I'd misjudged Estella six ways from Sunday, and I felt like a fool. I needed to do something, anything, to show her how sorry I was about what Bram had done.

Tears coursed down Estella's cheeks but she sat tall, her stare keen as a blade. 'If you really want to help,' she said, 'just *go*.'

THIRTY-SEVEN

We were almost back at my place when Jared Cunningham's text came in.

Tell me Tim's with you. Just to put my mind at ease.

Cunningham was checking up on me? The notion was absurd. It took mere seconds for me to realize what was going on. Now that he'd heard my sob story, he saw me as a victim. I was squarely in the sights of his pity. The place I least wanted to be.

Tim *was* with me, and for that I was grateful. He'd agreed to stay over at my place. As much time as I'd spent at that crimson patch of grass in his back yard, the thought of being near it tonight made my stomach clench. I texted Cunningham back while Tim drove, his hand warm on my thigh. I suspected Cunningham had clued into the fact that Tim and I were dating. I also had a hunch that he was jealous. Far as I knew, the man was single, and I'd seen his gaze slide over me and linger when he thought I wasn't watching.

He is, I wrote. **I'm good. Heading home.**

What happened with Barba?

You know I can't tell you that.

But you're heading home, not back to the barracks. So he and his sister are in the clear?

I sighed. I wasn't about to rehash the conversation at the hotel, but Cunningham had gone out of his way to help us tonight. To help me.

That stays between us, I wrote, just to throw the guy a bone.

Really? Wow. Shana, of course. My lips are sealed.

Three dots hovered on the screen before he added, **So now what? Who does that leave?**

That was the question. Without Rebecca's phone data, we were paralyzed. We'd need to reassess everything. Root out the clues we'd missed. Before I could answer, Cunningham was typing again.

No new missing women?

No.

Thank God for that.

Hey, I wrote. **Question for you.** In thinking about copycat crimes, my mind had gotten snagged on one notable truth: in numerous instances, criminals leveraged the media to elevate themselves to heightened fame. **You wrote all those stories about me after the Sinclair case. Ever get any weird letters or requests?**

Like ciphers, Zodiac Killer-style?

Or weird fan mail, I said. The word made me squirm in my seat, in no small part because I thought it much more likely our killer loathed rather than revered me. I was hoping Cunningham would suddenly remember some suspicious piece of mail that could point us to an obsessive suspect. If Gracelyn Barlowe hated me so much that she took the time to write a scathing op-ed and Facebook post, the same could be true of someone else.

Sorry, he typed back. **Nothing comes to mind.**

I blew out a breath. **OK. Gotta run. Appreciate you checking in.**

That's what friends are for. ☺

I read his last message twice. By the time I looked up again, we were home.

Tim and I held hands as we climbed the steps to my back deck, twining our fingers like lovesick teens. I wasn't sure if it was the relief of finally knowing what Estella had wanted from me or the comfort of being in a good place with Tim again, but for the briefest of moments, I felt at peace.

And then I reached the top of the staircase.

I stepped onto the deck. Tripped backward, swiping at the railing, and stood panting on the stairs with my hand clutching at my galloping heart.

'Jesus Christ, Doug, I could fucking kill you.'

THIRTY-EIGHT

The sight of Doug sitting on the back deck, cross-legged in one of my Adirondack chairs, had the same effect on my stomach as jumping off my parents' roof in winter and finding myself waist-deep in Vermont snow. Tim had come to a stop behind me, holding my upper arms in a protective grip, but when he saw Doug all memory of my near cardiac arrest evaporated and my boyfriend pushed past me to pump my brother's hand.

The bugs must have been relentless – I'd left the outdoor light on – but Doug looked perfectly happy to be beside the river under the light of a waxing moon. Despite the smattering of gray at his temples, my big brother still dressed like his teenage self in summer; his cargo shorts were frayed, and though his vintage Soundgarden T-shirt was faded from hundreds of washings, the album's circular logo still looked as sharp as a skill saw. 'What the hell are you doing here?' I asked, working to catch my breath. I was having a hard time believing this was real.

'Wow,' Doug said, and my hand darted to the back of my neck. He was staring openmouthed at my hair. 'You look . . . different. Good different, though. Hey, do I need an excuse to see my sister?' He hugged me then, and for the briefest of seconds, before pulling away, I let my head relax against his chest.

Before my cousin was outed as a killer, I spoke with my family weekly. We talked about the books we were reading, and what we'd watched on TV. I asked after their health, and Dad nagged me to get more sleep. More recently, Mom had started slipping in a question or two about Tim. How were we getting along as partners? Was I listening to his input? Giving him a chance to shine? They issued regular reminders that I couldn't do it all on my own. I'd been a control freak from an early age, forever the kid who takes the reins on every school project and happily finesses the group's unfinished work. My folks knew this about me. They knew everything.

Except they didn't. They hadn't known the murderer I'd been tracking for months was their nephew.

They didn't know how close Tim and I had become, or that I was falling in love with him.

My last visit to Swanton had been for Christmas, and I hadn't seen Doug since. *Eight months*. It was the longest we'd ever been apart. Doug had been adamant about giving each other some space, which was a nice way of saying he didn't want to see me. All the while, I'd fantasized about throwing my arms around his furry neck, thrusting a beer into his hand, and giving him a tour of my new home. Doug would have loved that, once. Yesterday, he'd told me he needed 'more time.'

So why was he suddenly sitting on my porch?

Sighing, Doug flopped back down, his freckled knuckles going pale as he gripped the arm of the chair. 'I didn't like the way we left things yesterday.'

'Up for a beer?' Tim was already on his feet. He knew how to read a room.

Doug nodded and thanked him as Tim took my keys and disappeared into the house. I dragged a chair over to Doug. 'So,' he said when we were both seated. 'You and Tim.'

I blinked. Opened my mouth to ask how he'd found out, and immediately closed it again. Tim was coming home with me after dark. We'd been holding hands on our walk up the stairs. I gave my brother an abashed smile.

'Aw, good for you. I called that, you know,' he said, triumphant, 'ages ago. Back when he followed you to Vermont. You guys serious?'

'Well, we've drafted a joint will and named our unborn children, so . . .'

'Don't sass me, sis.'

'Fine,' I said through a grin. 'We're pretty serious, yeah.'

'So Shay has a new beau. That's great.'

'Sure, as long as I make it through my current case alive. Kidding,' I said quickly as the warmth drained from his face.

'I read about that tourist.' Doug shook his head. 'More murder, after everything that happened here.'

'Yeah. But we're close to finding him.' It was a lie. We *thought* we were close. Tonight had proven us wrong.

'So it's a coincidence?' he said. 'Another murder up here so soon? I mean, it's not the inner city. I just don't understand it.'

He would find out eventually. Back home Della and Wally, my cousin Crissy, and my Aunt Felicia would soon learn someone idolized their nephew, brother, son so much they were taking the lives of more blameless women in his name.

'We think we're dealing with a copycat, Doug.'

The door creaked open and Tim appeared with a can of pilsner. He tossed it to Doug, who caught it easily.

'You guys aren't having one?' Doug asked.

'Long night of work ahead.' Tim stepped back through the door and said, 'I'll give you two a minute.'

Doug nodded. Popped the tab on the can and watched the beer fizz. Took a long, slow sip. 'A copycat.'

'That's what we think.'

'You think someone's imitating Abe.'

'*Bram*,' I said firmly. 'It's the only explanation that makes sense.'

Doug took a second slug, chasing it with a third. 'Does that mean you know what he's going to do next?'

My mouth twitched. Doug always was a quick study. 'We might. So far, the pattern seems to follow the killings in New York. If he stays the course . . .'

'What? What then, Shana?'

'Another woman dies.'

'Jesus.'

'But that won't happen.'

'No,' Doug said and the base of the can hit the arm of the chair with a clunk, sending a spray of beer onto his hand. 'No, it will. I've heard this story too, remember? I lived it. He takes a third woman. And then he comes for you.'

His fear, the pain that warped his features, rendered my brother almost unrecognizable. His eyes had become two vacant holes. When I vanished from an Irish pub near the construction site where Bram dumped his most recent victim, Doug drove our parents to the city. The three of them pressed my NCO supervisor for updates relentlessly until I was found. While I was locked away, they'd withered in a hell of their own.

'Every law enforcement professional in the county and the

next one over is on high alert,' I told him, 'and we're going to make damn sure every woman is, too.'

'Are you in any danger? Are you? Because last time—'

'Last time was different.' I closed my eyes and shook my head. 'Why did you come here, Doug?'

He turned the can one full rotation where it sat. It was sweating in the heat. He was, too. 'I'm here,' he said, 'to take you home.'

Home. That word still had power over me. In equal measure, it could evoke the most comforting of memories and images that stoked the fires of my nightmares. It probably always would.

'This is my home now,' I said. Hadn't I explained that months ago? Why couldn't he understand that I would never live in Swanton again? I'd found my way out of there fifteen years ago and followed my path to the police academy in Albany, then New York, and now here. I had my reasons for leaving, and those would never change.

A mosquito alighted on Doug's hand, but despite its stealth Doug sensed the featherlight predator and slapped it away. 'They worry – Mom especially. She never wanted this for you, not any of it. What happened in New York almost killed her, and then he followed you here, and now this? Jesus, Shay, when is it going to end?'

'This is my job,' I said, the words blunt as chips of wood. Working in law enforcement was my calling, and had been ever since I found out my childhood playmate liked to frame his peers for vandalism. Hurt small animals. Deform blood relatives with rusty nails. In a way, it was Bram who'd taught me right from wrong and made me realize I wanted to be a good guy.

'Look.' Doug leaned toward me. 'I know you're trying to create a life for yourself here, but what kind of life is it, really? Everyone knows who you are and what he did. There's no anonymity for you anymore. You're a magnet for attention, and not the good kind.'

'I'm not *trying* to create a life. I have a life, Doug.' And I did. I had Tim, and Mac. A job I loved, despite the risk. 'Everything you're describing? It won't be forever. We're going to find this fucker – and as for all the rest, I'm working on a solution.' He didn't need to know it involved having an unemployed reporter tell my side of the story on an unknown blog about the familial impact of true crime. 'I'm sorry I chose a career that worries Mom and Dad. I'm sorry I didn't tell any of you about Abe. But if you can't see that using every weapon I had to hunt him down was the only way I could keep you and countless other people safe, that's on you. And yes, OK? I'm still in the middle of something that could be dangerous. It's not fair to you guys, and I know that, but you have to accept it anyway.' I was well aware I sounded like I had at five years old, when Doug got the last red popsicle and I threw a fit. At the moment, I really didn't care.

'What you're doing here, it's not living,' Doug said. 'When a normal day is waiting around for yet another psycho killer to kidnap you, it's a sign that your life took a seriously wrong turn. You think I didn't see the graffiti on your garage door? *Guilty*, Shana? What the fuck? You can't keep exposing yourself to this. Come home. Let us help you make things right.'

It was one thing to be alienated by your family, and quite another to hear your only sibling say your whole existence is a total shitshow. I didn't always feel good about the direction my life had taken, but dammit, I still had my pride.

If only I could keep the tears out of my eyes.

'Hey.' Doug got to his feet, and despite my efforts to resist he pulled me out of my chair and into a hug. 'It wouldn't have to be forever,' he whispered in my ear, his breath soft against my bare neck. 'Just long enough for people to forget.'

And that, right there, was why we hadn't talked in months. Doug's world view was so unlike mine that we may as well have lived on different planets. My brother, my parents, my aunt and cousin – they were miles away from the darkness in which I dwelled. Even their experience with Abe had been tempered by distance. He left town before he could do much real damage, and even now they only had an inkling of the harm he'd caused. The horror he'd wreaked on countless lives.

As a cop, as a detective, I lived in a parallel realm. While Doug agonized over what to make my niece Hen for school lunch, I stood over ravaged bodies mouth-breathing to block out the smell of decomposition. As my mother grew frustrated with Dad for spending too much money on imported English tea, I worked for thirty hours straight to identify a rapist before he could attack again. It sometimes felt like my family didn't believe that I, too, preferred blood and bones to stay on the inside where they belonged. Maybe it was too much to hope they'd understand this was the life I'd signed up to live.

But Tim understood. Mac, Bogle and Sol did, too. I'd found my people, and I couldn't – wouldn't – risk losing them.

Doug drained the last of his beer, and for a moment we were silent, listening to the movement of the river and the occasional splash and plop of an airborne fish. And because we were quiet, it was easy to hear the other noises, too.

'You get many bears in these parts?'

Doug had started to smile, the question a joke, but a tingle of fear shot through me. The rustling in the trees just west of the cottage didn't sound like a bear to me.

It sounded like a man.

I listened. Waited as Doug watched me with confusion. My mind flashed to the cemetery out by Clayton, where last April I'd stood shivering between the headstones waiting for my shot at apprehending Bram. The sound was gone now. *Just a beaver in the underbrush*, I told myself, or maybe a coyote, its yellow eyes trained on its prey, muzzle twitching in the dark.

I turned to face my brother. 'You have to help me with Mom and Dad. Please, Doug. You've got to make them understand.' I had Tim and Mac, yes. But severing ties with my family had felt like lopping off a limb.

He sucked his teeth and lowered his gaze. 'I'll talk to them. I'll try.' I could hear the hesitation in his voice, but what I chose to focus on was that he'd driven nearly four hours to check on me because, like always, Doug could sense when something was wrong. I wanted so badly to believe his visit was an olive branch. I didn't get a chance to ask him if he thought he could forgive me. At that moment, something hurtled through the air between us and collided with the front window of my rental, the glass vibrating like a struck drum before shattering with a colossal boom. Splinters exploded across the deck. A million needles, vicious in the moonlight.

'The fuck—' Doug looked shellshocked, his face drained of blood.

I grabbed both his arms and yanked him to the ground. 'You OK? *Are you OK?*'

Doug's head approximated a nod, and then here was Tim,

standing where the window used to be, his hand on his sidearm,
chest rising and falling fast.

'Go,' I croaked as I drew my own gun, and together we took
the stairs at a run. I vaulted over the railing halfway down and
landed so hard on the pavement that I heard my jaw clack. I'd
tweaked my ankle too and it shrieked with pain, but we kept on
running, fueled by instinct and anger, a fierce animal drive to
neutralize a threat. Our bodies pumped in unison through the
trees in the undeveloped lot next door, our movements honed by
countless hours of training and, in my case, nearly two years
of living in a state of forced hypervigilance that had left me
primed for a fight. We ran flat-out in the swampy scrub, weaving
through the thicket that stretched from the river to the road as
we followed the thump of footsteps retreating through the trees.

'Hey!' I hollered the word, but it came out wobbly. Bugs
swarmed my exposed skin and pinged off my lips. Every now
and then I could make out the figure in the darkness, his form
flickering between the trees, but then he'd vanish again, blending
seamlessly with the night. Twigs crunched and crackled in the
underbrush. Behind me, too. The realization hit me like a fifty-
volt current: my brother was following us. I didn't want him
here, not now. Not for this.

It wasn't far to the road. I could already see two yellow orbs
of light bobbing in my field of vision, the sconces that marked
the entrance to my neighbor's driveway on East Riverfront Road.
We were close – but he was closer. I saw the car next – a truck,
parked on the roadside in a hank of shadow just beyond the light.
In a second he'd be inside it, starting the engine and peeling
off in the direction from which he'd come. We'd never catch him
then, not on foot.

The decision made, I skidded to a stop and grabbed a
handful of Tim's shirt. No point in bursting into the light and
exposing ourselves. Better to let him think we couldn't keep up,
or that one of us had taken a spill in the woods and given up the
chase. Crouching low, I locked eyes with Tim and gestured to
the edge of the thicket. Quiet now, we picked our way around
birch trees and maples until we reached the road, and when Doug
arrived, lumbering with all the grace of that bear he'd joked
about, I yanked him down beside us.

There was a time when I would have expected to see Javier Barba burst into the yellow light. There would have been something poetic about him returning to the scene of the crime where that spray-painted word, like a stamp on my skin, remained. But it wasn't Javier I saw on the road.

He'd made it to the truck. The engine was on, tires grinding against gravel. In the cab, for just a moment, the dome light illuminated his face.

I knew that vehicle. I'd seen it in the parking lot of the barracks just that morning.

I knew the face of its owner, too.

I knew it all too well.

THIRTY-NINE

D oling out an apology and a box pizza from the freezer, we'd left Doug at home to board up the hole in my front window and had gone back to the barracks. It felt absurd to be here under the circumstances, like someone was playing a joke on us, yet here we were, with a pile of new evidence and no choice but to stare it in the face.

Standing in the center of the room shared by my investigators, I stared at Don Bogle's desk. It wasn't the tidiest in the place – without exception, that belonged to Tim – but it wasn't cluttered with unfiled papers and candy bar wrappers, either. Nothing about the workspace or empty padded office chair indicated that Bogle was anything other than what he presented himself to be: a detective with nearly six years of experience under his belt. A gentle giant who excelled at carrying out orders and was committed to upholding the law. A humble local boy who valued virtue and friendship over material wealth, and who'd caught the eye of Juliet Barlowe because of it.

But I knew what I'd seen.

Discovering that truck on my street hit hard, and I knew Tim felt the same way I did: like a fool. When Bogle bought his new pickup a month ago, he'd been low-key about it, which, in retrospect, was strange. Bogle didn't brag about its full hybrid system or massive towing capability. When I remarked on his new ride, he thanked me and quickly changed the subject. As far as I knew, nobody at work had asked which dealership he'd chosen. If we had, and one of us remembered that our colleague's pristine Ford F-150 had Goodyear tires that matched the ones on the vehicle used to dump Rebecca's body at the quarry, there was no chance we'd think of it as anything other than a coincidence. Bizarre, yes, but easily ignored.

In the morning, I would call Godfrey Hearst and have him go down to the dealership to confirm it was Rebecca who'd sold Bogle the truck, but I was already preparing for the worst. The recent sale by our murder victim of a vehicle to a man from Alexandria Bay should have sent up a red flag the size of a house – but it was Bogle I'd asked to look into the dealership angle, and he'd reported back that there were no suspicious sales. Not even Godfrey Hearst himself would have noticed a deal Rebecca made with a man from upstate. Hearst oversaw five dealerships. He trusted his wife. Just like we'd trusted Bogle.

Bogle had been the one to investigate the video footage of the Bay Point Grill, too. How effortless it must have been to overlook the inconvenient evidence that would point us in his direction and report back to me that both lines of inquiry were dead ends. And so, as surreal as it seemed, here we were. Taking another look at the video footage of Ben Dool that we now believed might, in fact, be Don Bogle.

'What do you think?' My voice was somber. 'Is it him?' I asked, because on its own the truck wasn't enough. We needed more.

The man on the screen hadn't born much resemblance to Bogle when we first watched the footage. I wasn't sure that would still be the case now that so much evidence led directly to our friend. Tim swiveled his desk chair, the movement so slight I doubted he was conscious of it. I knew that breed of fidgeting well and reached for him, stopping the chair with a hand on his shoulder. Tim held still.

'It's hard to tell. The height, it's . . . hard.'

I leaned closer, but I was squinting through a film of Vaseline, my eyes raw and exhausted. 'The eyepatch,' I said. 'Is there some color on it?'

He zoomed into the man on the bench. It was blurry, but the close-up view revealed the eyepatch was emblazed with some kind of logo, bright blue.

'What is that?'

Tim leaned back in his chair and sighed deeply. 'That,' he said, 'is a skull and two crossed swords. It's an A-Bay patch. You haven't seen these?'

I shrugged.

'The town gets these patches made up to commemorate Pirate Days. Every year, the logo's a different color. The Chamber of Commerce sells them in the weeks leading up to the event, and people collect them. It's kind of a racket – they go for like seven bucks a pop – but it's a badge of honor to have a lot of them, proof that you're a hardcore Pirate Days supporter, I guess. Sales proceeds go to the chamber to help pay for next year's event.'

'Where do you buy them?'

'At the chamber offices, down on Market Street.'

'Yellow,' I said suddenly. 'This year is yellow.' I *had* seen the patches, on countless spectators just that morning, and had taken them for made-in-China tchotchkes bought online. They may well have been – only now, they were being rebranded as a must-have Pirate Days keepsake. A promotional stunt that paid dividends for decades. I would have bet my lunch Chet Bell was behind it.

'Yellow, right,' said Tim. 'Let me make a quick call.'

I waited while he dialed, and listened in as he greeted Ivan Gorecki. *Smart*, I thought. *When you've got a question about an eyepatch, you call the Head Pirate.*

'Blue was 2016,' Tim declared after hanging up. 'Two years ago.'

'And you're saying people buy the new patch every year?'

I heard the old springs on his desk chair catch as he pivoted to face me. 'It's really just the residents. My mom has at least a dozen of them at home. You wouldn't know where to buy them if you didn't live here. But they'd have sold hundreds of the blue ones in 2016, maybe more.'

I thought, *It doesn't matter. That doesn't change a thing.* There was still a suspicious man watching Rebecca the night she disappeared, and he'd still been wearing a collector's item that was two years old. That suggested something impossible to ignore, and it wasn't that he liked to play dress up. 'Tim, I think—' I began, but he'd already gotten there on his own.

'*Fuck.*' He shoved away from the desk and stood up. The chair gyrated across the floor. Plunging his hands into his hair, Tim set to pacing the room.

I didn't stop him. I didn't want what we'd discovered tonight to be true any more than he did. But it was our job to follow every lead, and in spite of its implications, this was the best lead we'd had yet.

The eyepatch told us something. It indicated we weren't dealing with a tourist or itinerant worker who'd stumbled into town on a whim. We likely weren't even searching for a man who'd come here by design. With that blue logo, the eyepatch told us what Tim least wanted to hear.

Our suspect was a local.

FORTY

'It was on the eighth day that I decided to kill him.'

Months ago at Tim's cottage, while twisting the paper napkin in my lap into a stiff lump, I'd told Jeremy Solomon and Don Bogle everything about my abduction. I confessed it all in a spectacular display of martyrdom, while from their seats around Tim's kitchen table they'd worn slack-jawed stares not unlike the ones I'd grown so used to seeing in town. One of Sol's eyes was slightly larger than the other so he always looked like he was squinting, forever cooking up a scheme, and I'd gotten into the habit of taking cues from the shape of his mouth instead. It was a straight line that day, thin as the crease in a folded card. The vestiges of a spaghetti dinner, complete with a snowfall of baguette crumbs and a half dozen empty bottles of Labatt Blue, had filled the space between me and my investigators, but as I waited for them to respond, we might as well have been separated by a river.

I'd heaved a sigh and reached for my beer, room-warm and bubbly on the back of my teeth. I had been agonizing over this speech for days, and wasn't out of the woods yet. There was still the matter of their response. Both Bogle and Sol had worked under me since my arrival in the North Country, and over the past year I'd come to think of them not just as trusted colleagues but as friends. While they were well within their rights to condemn my actions, I was holding out hope that they'd retain at least a shred of the respect for me they once had. I'd have a hell of a time leading them effectively if they didn't.

And so, I didn't stop at my abduction. I talked about Bram's other crimes, too. Some of what I said was new even to Tim, who didn't pump me for information I wasn't willing to give. That night, I unburdened myself completely.

And that included telling all three of them about the knife.

I knew a lot about Bram's knife, thanks to the coroners who conducted autopsies on his New York victims. It had an eight-inch locking blade, probably titanium-coated. It would have cost my cousin less than twenty bucks at Walmart. It was the same type of knife he'd held while threatening the woman in Norwalk. The same kind used to kill Jessica Greenleaf and Rebecca Hearst.

'Wow,' Sol whispered when I was done. He'd been building a tiny pyramid out of baguette crumbs while I spoke, coaxing them into a neat pile. He wouldn't look at me. 'I don't know what to say.'

'I do,' said Bogle.

Don Bogle hadn't seemed ill at ease at all that evening, and at the time I was grateful for his fortitude. Unlike Sol, Bogle met my gaze. 'I can't believe you went through that. Eight days of not knowing if you're going to live or die . . . Jesus, you're as strong as they come.' *Click. Clack.* His knuckle-popping drove the guys crazy at the barracks, but to me, just then, the sound brought comfort. As long as Tim and Sol were annoyed by Bogle's knuckles, they weren't focused on me. 'All those women,' Bogle said, shaking his head, 'and then he went up against you and somehow still managed to walk free. Bastard must have been a fucking magician.'

I'd held those words to my chest like a security blanket. *Bram was good at being bad. Don't blame yourself for letting him get away.* Now, though, I had to wonder if there wasn't just a hint of reverence in Don Bogle's voice. I'd confessed everything to him that night at Tim's, painstakingly walking him through every piece of evidence, every torturous moment of my time with Bram in New York.

In the end, he'd known almost as much about Bram's crimes as I did.

FORTY-ONE

Rigid at our desks, Tim and I took turns trying to reach Bogle. Every call went unanswered, every text message ignored.

'I don't believe it,' Tim said for the third time, and for the third time, I nodded. There were so many things about Don Bogle neither of us understood.

For me, it had started with the drinking. Amos's stories. The sight of Bogle at the Carlson, knocking back three ounces of premium whisky like it was speed rail tequila when he thought no one was watching. I'd written his behavior off as a byproduct of his problems with his wife, but what if the drinking wasn't the half of it?

What if he'd done something far, far worse?

'You have to admit he hasn't been himself,' I said. 'He was all over this case from the start, super enthusiastic and proactive. He volunteered for all kinds of tasks – tasks he didn't complete. And he misplaced Rebecca Hearst's phone. He blamed it on the drinking, but Tim, what if he did it on purpose to cover his tracks? What if the booze was just an excuse?' I couldn't allow that possibility to go overlooked. Two women were dead in the town where Bogle lived and worked, and the best evidence we had in Rebecca Hearst's case had disappeared on his watch.

There were deep creases across Tim's forehead, and more around his mouth. 'You think Don *took* evidence related to an active homicide case? That's criminal obstruction. Misconduct of office. Breach of trust.'

That was the least of my concerns. 'I know. I know it is,' I said. 'I can't explain any of this. But Tim, the evidence is stacking up.'

'We don't know yet that his truck came from a Hearst dealership. There are lots of trucks out there with those same tires.'

'If he has nothing to do with any of this, why was he outside my place tonight eavesdropping on me and Doug?'

'Maybe he thought he was protecting you.'

'Pitching a rock at someone's house is a hell of a way to protect them. He must have seen you there, too – and when we heard him, he *ran*. Why would he do that, Tim? If it was anyone else, you'd consider it suspicious behavior. He acted like a guy who'd done something wrong.'

Again, my mind returned to Amos Barlowe and another accusation about Bogle that, dirty and determined to linger, stuck like gum on a shoe. *She caught him outside her girlfriend's place, watching them through the picture window.* 'His brother-in-law told me that splitting with Juliet really messed him up. He said Don's been following her,' I told him. 'His own wife.'

Bogle had been listening to Doug and me tonight. He knew we heard someone in the trees. About the graffiti on my garage door, too. If he was guilty of more than just spying, the rock would be a way to shift the blame to someone else. Divert us back to Javier.

'But Javier has alibis for the murders,' Tim said when I explained my theory.

'Yeah. But Don doesn't know that yet.'

'We need to talk to him.' Tim had taken to pacing once more. 'We have to find out what the hell's happening.'

That much, Tim and I could agree on.

'I was just about to call you,' Jeremy Solomon said when I gave him a ring at home. I told Sol we were looking for Bogle and hadn't been able to reach him. I was hoping he'd heard something, or knew where Bogle might be. But Sol's need to contact me was born of something else.

I could hear the TV blaring in the background, something with a laugh track, and I imagined Sol's wife Monica beside him, oblivious as she chuckled at the show. Bogle and Sol often teamed up at work. Bogle's connection to our case, whatever shape it took, had implications for everyone.

'I got some interesting information on Jessica Greenleaf,' Sol said now. 'Sorry I didn't call sooner, the email came in while I was walking the dog. Troop B never thought to ask it, because why would they? But it's like you've been saying, Shana – there has to be some connection between Rebecca and Jessica besides just their names. There are lots of women with those same names in Jefferson County. So why choose these two?'

That had been bothering me, too. Why *this* Jessica? There were half a dozen Jessicas in my niece's high school freshman class alone; there must have been plenty for our perp to choose from here. And why target a Rebecca who didn't even live in the same county? 'What did you find?' I asked, my pulse thrumming in my ears.

'OK, so I'm looking over Troop B's case file, and I see this statement from the mother, right? Ameer asks her whether Jessica's been anywhere out of the ordinary lately – a new friend's house, a get-together, that kind of thing. The mom says yeah, Jessica went to a bachelorette party the weekend of June twenty-third. It was an overnight event. And get this, the party was held at the Carlson.'

'You're kidding,' I said, slowly turning to Tim. *The Carlson.* The same posh inn owned by Bogle's parents-in-law. 'Jessica's mother said Jessica met Dool on Facebook. Could Jessica have been lying? Could they have met that night?'

'Anything's possible,' said Tim, but I knew the news had hit him hard. A link to the Carlson was a link to Don Bogle.

Scenes from the party at the hotel flashed through my mind. I pictured Amos in his red seersucker shirt, and his wife Tarryn's slinky silver dress. Juliet and Gracelyn Barlowe. This was a family with a keen eye and a drive to keep their business going strong. If there was a connection between Jessica Greenleaf and the hotel, I had a feeling the Barlowes might know about it.

And there was a logical place to start asking.

FORTY-TWO

Don Bogle and Juliet Barlowe's house had granite-gray trim and shingles the color of waterlogged sand. Inside, the walls and beamed ceiling were whitewashed wood, and between the matching hardwood floor and the cream-colored upholstery, the combined living and dining room was almost entirely monochrome. I wondered if Tarryn had done the decorating. In winter, the home would be cozy and welcoming, but on an August night like this one, all that softness and warmth felt like a choke hold.

Juliet wasn't alone. Same silver bun, same red lips – but this time, Gracelyn Barlowe wasn't smiling. 'It's awfully late for visitors,' she said disapprovingly. She'd been holding my gaze without pause since the moment we walked in the door, and I wanted nothing more than to tell her off. Instead, I packed my rage into a bitter little nugget and swallowed it whole.

'It's fine,' Juliet told me as we settled in the living room. 'I think I know why you're here.'

With her sleek chestnut hair, whisper-light camisole and diamond studs that sparked every time she adjusted her chin, Juliet Barlowe was striking even without her party clothes. Despite her athletic build – I spotted a Peloton bike stationed near one of the windows, a collection of dumbbells in pastel tones on the floor – there was a softness to her face that I found appealing. She didn't look like one of those women who deprived herself to stay thin only to end up a chic skeleton, notwithstanding her mother's insistence on exercise and greens. I wondered if that had something to do with the pregnancy. Juliet's edges were rounded. Her eyes, though – those were tapered and wary.

'Amos told me about your conversation at the party,' she said. 'He shouldn't have said all that stuff about Don. Don's not in trouble, is he?'

The drinking. She thinks we're here because of the drinking.

'It's OK,' I told her. 'Your brother didn't do anything wrong.

Is Don around?' I knew he wasn't. Before coming to the door,
Tim and I had done a cursory search of the guest house where
Bogle told me he'd been living, peering through its darkened
windows. Checking for the pickup around back.

'I haven't seen him since last night, actually,' Juliet said. 'At
the party. You're not mad at him, are you?'

Between her looks and her manner of speaking, I had a hard
time remembering Juliet was in her early thirties, older even than
Amos. Skittish and reserved, she came across as much younger.

'We just need to ask him some questions,' said Tim.

'I'd like to ask him some questions myself,' Gracelyn put in.
'He got horribly drunk at the party and made an ass of himself
in front of my guests.'

'*Mom.*'

'Well, it's true – and *she* knows it.' Gracelyn's finger was long
and bony, and it was pointed at me. 'She was there last night
– uninvited, I might add. Do you think I don't know who you
are? You're that detective who failed to apprehend her own
cousin.'

Easy, Shay. Already, my heart was walloping my ribs.

'Ma'am—' said Tim, but Gracelyn was just getting started.

'I know all about you. The Gateses are close personal friends
of ours. What happened to their son, Carson . . . I can't stand to
think about it. And you were once *engaged* to him,' she went
on, 'weren't you? Funny how trouble seems to follow you everywhere you go.' Casting me a look of disgust, she shook her argent
head. 'It's a wonder the New York State Police superintendent
hasn't seen through your subterfuge. But that will soon change.'

'That's enough, Mrs Barlowe.' Tim fixed her with an icy stare.
'We're here to talk about your son-in-law, and that's all.'

For the time being, at least, that seemed to put the woman in
her place.

'Don's just going through a rough patch,' Juliet told us. 'It'll
pass.'

'It's not just the drinking – he's smoking again as well,
and that's been going on for over a year now,' Gracelyn said.
'Even though he knows Juliet despises cigarettes.'

'That only started with the IVF treatments, Mom. It was
stressful for everyone.'

'Him most of all, apparently.' Gracelyn rolled her dark eyes at her daughter.

'You and Don had trouble conceiving?' I knew a bit about that, not from personal experience but from Doug and Josie. After they got married, it took almost three years for my brother and sister-in-law to get pregnant. They'd looked into In Vitro Fertilization themselves, but at fifteen to thirty-thousand per cycle, they quickly realized that wasn't an option. They'd all but given up when Josie came to Thanksgiving dinner looking positively green. Mom sent Doug out for a pregnancy test that same evening. We had a lot to be thankful for that year.

'Yeah,' Juliet said, 'but it all worked out in the end.' She lay a hand on her stomach, still flat as a plank, and I froze. Hadn't Bogle said Juliet's family didn't know about the baby yet? But here was Gracelyn, looking adoringly at her daughter and reaching out to hold her hand.

I said, 'Congratulations. When are you due?'

'Early March.' She gave a sad smile. 'Just in time for spring.'

'Don has every reason in the world to stop this . . . this *nonsense* now,' said Gracelyn, 'but he keeps right on drinking and smoking. Thank goodness he's no longer under this roof. More than once, I wondered if I should call the police for help.'

'The police?' Tim's voice was cautious, a midnight footstep on a creaky stair. Again Juliet tried to intervene, but her mother took command of the room.

'Some things are personal,' she said, stretching out her neck, the skin there thin but oddly free of creases and lines. 'I believe that family problems should remain private. You keep those to yourself – it's a matter of respect. But when your daughter's own husband is stalking her, that's an entirely different story.'

'Stalking,' I repeated, thinking of Amos Barlowe's accusation once again. 'What exactly do you mean by that?'

'He didn't stalk me,' Juliet said quickly. She was looking increasingly nervous. 'He just wants to spend more time with me, that's all.'

'And less with us. Don's convinced we all hate him,' Gracelyn said with a roll of her eyes. 'Which is ridiculous. I admit we don't have much in common, but we've always made an effort. My son plays pickleball with Don almost every weekend! We try, for Juliet's sake, but Don would rather sit on the dock with a pack of those filthy cigarettes and a bottle of Seagram's, and then he has the nerve to follow Juliet around like a weasel in the night.'

When I glanced at Bogle's wife, I found that her eyes had welled with tears. 'We're finally going to start a family,' she said. 'I can't do it alone.'

I didn't know Juliet well, but the Barlowes seemed like the kind of people who were accustomed to having things go their way. I knew from Bogle that his wife had attended elite Vassar College and worked in the city before moving upstate. Amos was a Princeton grad, and his wife Tarryn had built a career with a prestigious lifestyle brand in New York. The impeccably decorated inn was a huge success. What had this Waspy family thought when Juliet took up with Don Bogle, with his menacing looks and working-class roots? The pressure on him must have been enormous.

That still didn't explain why his behavior was looking more suspicious by the minute.

'How long has Don been staying in the guest house?' I asked. *Weeks*, according to Bogle. We needed more information than that.

Juliet glanced in the direction of the house down by the dock. 'About a month, I guess.'

The guest house had a separate entrance that wasn't visible from the main house, but the parking area was. 'I don't suppose you know if Don was home last Sunday night?'

'Why do you ask?'

Looking pleased, Gracelyn said, 'What's he done now?'

I hesitated. 'We had something go missing at the station, and—'

'You think Don took something?'

'We're just doing our due diligence,' Tim assured her.

'He gets judged a lot, you know,' said Juliet. 'Because of his looks.' That didn't surprise me. Bogle was strong-featured and large, a bit frayed around the edges, all of which conveyed the impression that he lived hard. At times, he was intimidating even to me. Juliet went glassy-eyed as she said, 'I'll never forget the first time I saw him. He always made me feel so safe, and not just because of his job. He's my rock, you know?' She sniffed. Paused. 'What went missing?'

'That's not important,' I said.

'We're looking into everyone,' added Tim. Even now, with Bogle God knows where and responsible for God knows what, he couldn't stand the idea that someone might think badly of his friend.

'Have you noticed if Don's been out more than usual lately?' I asked.

Juliet trapped her lower lip between her teeth.

'I can answer that,' said Gracelyn. 'He absolutely has.'

'What about the night of July third? Any idea where he might have been then?'

'Something's happened.' Gracelyn tapped the toe of her leather flat on the carpet. 'Something has happened, and you want to know if Don has an alibi!' Her voice was triumphant. I had a feeling Tim was starting to loathe the woman as much as I did.

Juliet sucked in a trembling breath and then she was openly crying, rubbing circles on her stomach with a flexed palm.

'Honestly,' said Gracelyn, patting her on the back. 'The drinking and smoking are one thing, but my daughter deserves better than a cheater and a thief.'

What the hell? Tim and I exchanged a fleeting look. It was getting late, and we hadn't gotten much sleep in recent days, but Tim looked more haggard than he should have, so pasty that his dark eyebrows and lashes were astoundingly dark against his skin. 'A cheater,' I repeated, leaning in. Careful now. 'Juliet, do you suspect Don of being unfaithful?'

'Oh, darling.' Gracelyn forced her daughter into an awkward hug. 'Juliet refuses to believe it, but something strange is going on. I've been spending a lot of time here, nights too, and we see him driving off at all hours.'

We listened as she told us about the flash of headlights in her bedroom window that had been waking her up at one, two o'clock in the morning. 'Was one of those nights July third?' I asked.

Juliet was trying to catch her mother's eye, but Gracelyn wouldn't have it. 'Quite possibly,' she said, tugging on her silver earring. 'It wouldn't surprise me at all.'

What was going on here? Bogle and his wife had been trying to conceive for years, and now that she was finally pregnant, he was stepping out on her? Bogle had cited family stress as the reason for his drinking. *They want me gone*, he'd said of his parents-in-law. But what about this alleged affair? Was he trying to force a divorce? And if he'd been involved with a woman other than his wife, could it have been Rebecca Hearst?

'How sure are you, Mrs Barlowe?' I asked. 'About the cheating?'

Ever hopeful, Tim said, 'Could he just be out with friends?'

'Juliet knows all his friends,' said Gracelyn, 'and anyway, she's been tracking him.'

Juliet's shoulders slumped. 'Mom, *please.*'

'She uses one of those apps, which is very wise indeed. If, God forbid, they can't work things out . . .' She didn't go on, and didn't need to. Gracelyn Barlowe was no doubt thinking about her family's money, and the impact that confirmed adultery could have on settlement negotiations. 'Needless to say, he isn't just going to bars. We've watched him on the app. We know.'

'Where else has he been going?'

'The inn, for one, which is just a slap in the face. Parading around other women right under our family's nose? It's despicable. One night, he was all the way in Massena.'

I went cold. 'What? When was Don in Massena, Mrs Barlowe?'

'Just a few days ago. Earlier this week.'

I cocked my head. Our team had known about Jessica Greenleaf for less than twenty-four hours. What possible reason could Bogle have for going to Massena and not telling us?

There was just one question left to ask. I glanced at Tim, who gave a small, sad nod.

I took out my phone, and enlarged the image on the screen. 'Juliet,' I said slowly, 'does this man look familiar to you?'

Gracelyn leaned over her daughter and said, 'Oh my goodness. That's Don.'

'No.' When Juliet handed the phone back to me, I noticed her hands were shaking. 'That's not Don.'

'It absolutely is. That's the sweatshirt you gave him for Christmas last year.'

'It's a black sweatshirt, Mom.'

'With white plastic thingies on the ends of the hoodie drawstring. It's his, I'm sure of it.'

'It's *not.*' Juliet's voice resounded through the open room, her eyes flashing with anger.

Gracelyn's cheeks were tight as she gripped her daughter's hand. 'I'm sorry. It's the hormones. Mood swings are very common during pregnancy. I remember them well.'

'We understand.' Tim dipped his head to catch Juliet's eye. 'This is difficult, and we don't want to upset you. Do you have any idea where Don is now?' We needed to find him. To flush out the truth.

'Get your phone, Juliet.'

Juliet stared at her mother as she reached toward the end table, eyes pleading and desperate now, but Gracelyn only held her gaze. Slowly, painstakingly, Juliet moved a finger across the screen, and Tim and I watched her open the same app Godfrey Hearst had shown me a week ago at the A-Bay police station when he couldn't find his wife.

'He's at the American Legion,' she said miserably. 'His dad was a veteran. Don visits the members sometimes.'

We wasted no time thanking the two women and rushing back to the car.

'Massena,' said Tim, looked harried as he slammed the driver's side door. 'Could he have been following a lead?'

'Whatever Don knows about Jessica Greenleaf, we know, too,' I said, but as soon as the words were out, I realized that might not be true.

Truth was something I could no longer rely on Don Bogle to provide. It felt like we were searching for a stranger now. Just another suspect we needed to take into custody so we could get the facts.

Over the past month, Don Bogle had been drinking heavily. He'd been keeping things from his wife, and roaming the region at night.

He'd been found lurking outside my house, and following around his wife.

Bogle's truck was a match for the one at the quarry crime scene. He'd lied about being unable to obtain video footage of the restaurant. He'd taken an unexplained trip to Massena.

Bogle was the last person to touch missing evidence in Rebecca Hearst's case.

He knew details about Bram's crimes that few others did.

He appeared to have a connection to both victims.

'Tim, I'm so sorry.' I grabbed his arm as I said it, making sure he looked me in the eye. 'I should never have put Don on this case. It should have been you.' I could still picture Tim lying next to me in bed, the hurt in his eyes he'd tried to conceal because he knew it would only upset me. I'd cast him aside in favor of Bogle – Bogle, who was now our prime suspect – and why? Because Tim had been too *nice*?

Tim twisted his body toward me and slid a hand along my jaw. I didn't have full feeling in my scar, and likely never would, but the sensation of his fingers on my skin set every nerve in my body alight.

'Don't worry about any of that,' he said.

'But Don—'

'I know. I know how this looks. But I don't believe it.'

I blinked at him. Pulled back to get a better look at his face. 'I don't want to believe it either, truly I don't. But there's too much evidence against him.'

'Maybe so,' he said, his voice unwavering, 'but Don's not that kind.'

'What kind?' I asked, but I already knew. The kind prone to violence. The kind to harm a woman.

The kind to kill.

FORTY-THREE

A quick online search revealed there was a community dinner at the legion Saturday night from six to eleven p.m. It was ten fifty when we turned on to Rock Street, but the legion's small lot was still parked full. Bogle's truck – black, new, so hard to miss that I felt the stab of guilt deep in my gut – was right outside the white vinyl building with the sea green metal roof. Next to the door, dual American and Canadian flags snapped in the breeze, and I could see A-Bay's iconic water tower in the distance, just beyond the Methodist church. Tim found a spot up the road, and we stepped out of the car.

'They'll be marching in the Grand Parade tomorrow,' he said as we approached the building. 'Old-timers in their suits and post caps. Kids, too. They're well-respected, a staple at all the big events in town.'

'We're not here to cause a scene,' I said, but I couldn't be sure of that, because we might have no choice. If Don Bogle was involved in the killings, we couldn't risk letting him sneak out the back and vanish in a town that was currently swollen to three times its normal size.

Inside, the place was plain, a mix of engineered wood flooring and white walls dotted with pocket-sized plaques and faux brass sconces. In one corner, a statue of a Bald Eagle was displayed on a shelf too high for anyone to see. Folding tables had been dressed up in white linens stiff with creases from months of sitting on someone's closet shelf. The dining room smelled of melted butter, sweet red sauce and hot white bread.

Even though Tim had mentioned the parade, it hadn't occurred to me that these folks would be all-in for a festival celebrating Bill Johnston. I supposed it made sense. Johnston was Canadian-born, but he'd allegedly spied for the Americans during the War of 1812. After he was accused, he escaped to Sackets Harbor, pledged himself to the US Navy in Lake Ontario, and lived out his days in nearby Clayton. It was the reason he was so revered in A-Bay – and the reason the people of the American Legion, with its military ties, sported pirate hats and paisley-print bandanas tonight.

I scanned the mob of sun-weathered men and white-haired women in patterned leggings. Bogle, his head aglow with sweat in the light of the imitation brass sconces, stood out like a heron in a hardware store.

He wasn't jovial like the others, their smiles molded around forkfuls of sponge cake smeared with Cool Whip. He sensed us coming before we got to his table, and a look of disbelief skipped across his face. Here we were, barging into a community supper, Tim wearing a hangdog look and both of us with our hands on the sidearms at our hips. It wasn't long before comprehension dawned like a crashing wave, sending Bogle's eyebrows plunging toward his blunt nose and rearranging his bare-shaven mouth into a bitter frown.

'Boss.' His voice was remarkably steady when he greeted me, but it did nothing to still the insistent hammering of my heart. Around the room, diners were noticing us, gazes pulling away from overloaded plates. Eyes locking on the two outliers who stood like sentinels next to one of their own. 'Everything OK?' Bogle said, all expression wiped clean away.

'Sorry to interrupt.' The clatter of cutlery against unbreakable dinnerware quieted as I spoke, and my voice filled the room. 'Can we talk a minute?' I forced down the dry lump in my throat. 'Outside.'

Bogle leaned back in his chair to get a better look at Tim. Tim, whose face was nothing but expression, pain and remorse and guilt and dread twisting his features into a cliché, a bad performance artist playing the part of the tortured friend. ''Course we can.' Bogle, on his feet now. Looming over me like one of those trees in the woods outside my cottage.

He knows. He had to. Tim and I radiated tension, and now Bogle did, too. What did that mean? What would he do about it? When it came time to take him in, would he go quietly?

For the moment, Bogle kept his cool. He followed Tim back out the front door while I stayed close behind them, fingers twitching near my holster. Aware of the faces, pink and puffy and lined with the agony of war, wheeled in our direction. I'd

almost forgotten that most of these people were veterans, hardened men with names like Walter and Jerry and Lionel and Cliff
who'd served active military duty. Who'd been honorably
discharged, or were serving still. There were women, too, enough
that my skin itched beneath my clothing as they studied me. We
were the same, in many ways. Except that I was escorting their
friend outside for reasons that were clearly not social.

The parking lot was dim, the air boggy with moisture. Bogle
knew better than to slip his hands into his pocket. His arms hung
by his sides, palms swiveled in our direction, and in spite of
everything it hurt to see him cooperate so fully. Easily. Without
a fight.

'You know what this is about.' There was no question in my
voice. 'You know the drill. You know your rights.'

'It's not what you think,' he said.

My mouth hitched up at the corner. 'Come on, Don. Not that
old line.' All three of us had heard it before, more times than
we could count. As irrational as it was, I realized I expected
better from Bogle. An original defense, at least.

'You were in Massena. You need to tell us why.'

'How . . .?' Bogle's face went slack, and he nodded. 'Gracelyn.
She never trusted me, not ever. It's a class thing. Juliet liked that
I was from the wrong side of the tracks when we first got together.
That was exciting to her back then. Next thing you know, her
mother's using the same blue-collar bad boy persona Jules loved
against me.'

'Are you telling us you're innocent? Because if you are,' I
said, 'you better start explaining yourself. Your truck matches
the one at the crime scene. We've linked you to both victims. So
what's going on here, huh? You've gotta know it doesn't look
good, Don. Not at all.'

He nodded then, thick fingers twitching. He wanted to crack
his knuckles or drag a hand across his scalp the way he always
did when he was thinking, but our own hands were still on our
holsters. Bogle quieted his body. He didn't move.

When, slowly, his wide lips stretched across his face, I thought
of a putty knife being dragged through a waxy lump of clay.
Bogle's flesh was as dull as I'd ever seen it. 'I can't tell you
that,' he said.

'Let's talk about this at the barracks, OK?' Tim said.

'And if I don't go with you?'

I sucked air through my nose, and held it in my diaphragm until it hurt. 'Then we take you.'

No sooner were the words out of my mouth than his hands were on my sternum. The blow snatched the breath from my lungs and left me gasping. To his credit, Tim only hovered over me for a second before spinning on his heel and giving chase, but Bogle was already halfway across the lot. There was a second parking area next to the first, belonging to a three-story structure with a foreclosure sign hammered into the brown grass out front.

He was headed for the derelict building next door.

Get up, Shay. Go! I lurched to my feet and stumbled into a run, my chest aflame with pain. I'd cracked a rib, was sure of it, but that didn't matter now. Tim was yards ahead of me, and Bogle had just disappeared into the brick building's back door.

It was unlocked, and my mind raced to explain why. Was this Bogle's hideout? Had he been using this place, next door to the legion and across the street from a church, to hide and slaughter his victims? I'd seen stranger things, starting with four women held captive in an apartment building that was home to dozens of oblivious residents. Why couldn't a man – even a state investigator – commit murder three hundred feet from the place where he ate pasta bolognese and strawberry shortcake with veterans who'd been friends with his dad?

The door banged open and the stench of mold enveloped me, coiling up my nostrils like toxic gas. Panic seized me, the memory like a smack, but I kept moving, coughing out the stink until my throat burned. Footsteps, on the floor above. I ached to scream Tim's name, desperate to know that he was OK, but I swallowed the urge like a bitter pill and moved toward the staircase, treading carefully on the rotted wood floor. I'd always assumed this building was once an apartment complex, but it looked more like a warehouse inside. Open floor plan, hundreds of square feet of splintered wood and weathered brick. And not a man in sight.

He couldn't stay here. Bogle had enough experience chasing suspects to know we wouldn't leave without him. That meant he needed to find a way out – and that left two choices. The garage, or the roof.

The stairs were so dark I couldn't see my fingers in front of my face, but I felt my way up with a hand on the warm, rough wall. It was stuffy in here, the dust thick as fog, and I held my breath as I ascended, waiting – hoping – to find Tim with Bogle in cuffs on the ground. What I discovered instead was another door hanging open, night air streaming into the stairwell.

I hadn't noticed it from the ground, but the building had a widow's walk. A tower, painted white and rising from the center of the metal roof. That's where I found Tim and Bogle, Tim with his hands raised in warning and appeal. Bogle, with the state-issued Glock he was carrying off-duty, trained on Tim's heart.

No. 'Don. Jesus, Don, don't do this.'

'Don,' said Tim, inching forward even as his voice cracked. 'Come on, man, it's me. What the hell are you doing?'

'Tell him to back off. Tell him, Shana!'

'Back off, Tim,' I said, and Tim receded, still showing our partner, our friend, his palms. It wasn't until Tim was next to me that I noticed his own sidearm lying a few feet away.

'You're not doing yourself any favors right now, Don.' I kept my voice steady and firm. 'All we want to do is ask you some questions. That's it.'

'I didn't kill Rebecca and Jessica.'

'Questions,' I repeated. 'That's all.' My hands were raised now, too, and it felt all wrong, like a dream gone rogue.

'Over there. Now.' With the muzzle of the gun, Bogle gestured to the far side of the roof, and I saw the move for what it was. He was planning his getaway. Opening up a path for himself so he could take the stairs back down and slip away while we stood around like fools, watching him go. Tim looked crestfallen, the weight of the betrayal heavy as a hearse.

'Think this through,' I said as Bogle inched toward the door. 'If you run, you know what happens next.' The BCI would use every means available to find him, and at any point along the way Bogle could get hurt, or worse.

'I don't have a choice.' His expression was pained. 'But I swear I didn't kill them.'

'Then come with us.'

'I can't. You don't understand, I *can't*.'

'Rebecca's phone,' I said. 'Where is it, Don?'

His face crumpled. 'In a trash can at Scenic View Park. You'll never find it now.'

'Don—'

Bogle aimed for Tim's sidearm where it lay on the rooftop, and found his mark. The shot resounded through the night, and the Glock spun from us. Tim dove for it, but the shock of gunfire and the split-second distraction it created gave Bogle the window he needed to run.

His footsteps clanged on the metal steps as he descended the way we'd come, the creaky door swinging loudly in his wake. Both of us armed again, we bore down on the staircase, through the building, out on to the empty street. There was no sign of Bogle. I didn't know if he'd streaked off toward the river or into the cluster of restaurants and souvenir shops on the main thoroughfares, still packed with tourists drinking spiked sodas from waxed to-go cups and walking off their rich suppers on this hot summer night.

'We have to find him,' I said, but it was blind optimism. Don Bogle knew every dock and alley of this town. He'd grown up adventuring in and around its bends, kissing girls in the park pavilion and swigging cheap beer next to clinking boats at the river's edge. Now that he knew we were on to him, Bogle wouldn't allow himself to be found so easily again.

I reached for my phone, and made the call.

'Suspect was last seen at Church and Rock, heading in the direction of James Street,' I said, the words gumming my throat. 'Suspect is armed and should be considered dangerous. He's wanted for questioning in connection to the murders of Rebecca Hearst and Jessica Greenleaf. Suspect's name is Don Bogle.'

FORTY-FOUR

It wasn't easy, calling BCI Lieutenant Henderson to tell him I suspected one of my colleagues of being involved in a homicide – a homicide he himself had been investigating under my watch. I'd never personally witnessed the chain of events that would unfold as a result of a call like that, but by and large, I knew what was coming. Henderson would contact the Internal Affairs Bureau in Albany. IAB would conduct an administrative investigation. There would be reports, calls, meetings. Paperwork and bureaucratic procedure. The New York State Police Investigators' Association would get involved. But the criminal investigation? That was ours. Don Bogle would be brought up on charges that would mark the end of both his career and his freedom.

My next call was to Juliet Barlowe.

As expected, she was panicked and resistant. My own attitude didn't help. I was doing a poor job of concealing my distress. No time for the kid-glove treatment now; we had to move fast. We'd rallied the troops, assembling all the muscle we could find at the abandoned building by the legion and making a plan to fan out across the downtown core in search of our perp. *In search of Don.* For once I was grateful when Gracelyn Barlowe butted in, snatching the phone from her daughter to pull up the location tracking app.

'It looks like he took a boat out,' Gracelyn said. 'That's strange . . . Juliet's boat's still here. I'm looking at it through the kitchen window now.'

'He's on the water?' That wasn't good. If Bogle had access to another boat, he might be able to cross over into Canada undetected. We had a good relationship with the Ontario Provincial Police, but if Bogle fled the country it would complicate things. We needed to find him before he did something stupid.

'Looks like it,' Gracelyn said. 'Oh, but the boat's not moving.'

'Where is he?'

'Do you know Collins Landing?' she asked.

'His phone's at Collins Landing?'

'Right under the bridge.'

'He ditched it,' I told Tim, disbelieving, once we'd issued Gracelyn and Juliet a warning to contact us if they heard from Bogle. 'Bogle ditched his cell in the same place where we found Rebecca's so that we couldn't track him. He ditched her phone, too, in a garbage can during today's reenactment.'

On the corner of Rock and Church Street, a wash of golden light from the lamppost on his face, Tim shook his head, baffled. 'What does that mean?'

'It's proof that he knows a lot more about these homicides than we do, and that he always did.'

FORTY-FIVE

The west-facing wall of the barracks was smeared with ash. I saw the black marks on my way in the next morning, my gaze sweeping over the place where, a few days ago, Bogle stubbed out my cigarette and tucked the singed, still-warm filter into my hand. Mashed and desiccated butts littered the ground where we had stood, the smoke-stink of tar and burning leaves baked into the earth. How, I wondered, had I never before noticed the mess he'd made? He'd been carving his mark into this spot for years, always returning to his desk wearing a satiated smile. But isn't that how betrayal works? Rarely do we see the dagger until it's sunk to the hilt between our ribs.

'We have to treat this like we would any other investigation and ferret out his hideaways,' I said. 'Identify friends and family with property he could use as shelter. He's not going to be on his feet for long. Not in this heat.'

The night had seemed endless, and I felt like roadkill. Too much coffee, far too little sleep, and we'd gotten nowhere. Nearly seven a.m. and my stomach was roiling, my limbs buzzing dully in a way that made me want to shake them off my body. With every passing hour the stakes got higher, the odds of recovering our colleague before someone else got hurt shrinking fast. By now, Bogle would be feeling hemmed in, and people did crazy things when trapped. On top of that, the nature of the killings was never far from my mind. If Bogle was bent on recreating Bram's crimes, he wasn't done yet.

'What about other properties?' Tim unfolded his arms and legs as he said it, arching his back in the desk chair. 'Juliet's family has money. Maybe they've got a cottage somewhere that's rarely used. A potential hiding spot.'

Like Tim's, my back ached from hours spent on my feet, but I straightened up at his suggestion. 'You're right. If they've got a cabin or a boat house, Don would be aware of it. What else do you know about him? Who he runs with?' I was thinking about the legion, wondering how close Bogle was to those veterans. How many basements and attics and hunting cabins he might have access to if he decided to call in a favor. For all we knew, the man had his pick of hideouts.

'No family around here that I know of,' Tim said. 'His mother died when he was little and his father passed a few years ago. I went to the memorial.' Tim shifted his gaze to the window before pushing matted hair off his forehead and clearing his throat. 'There's a younger sister in the Midwest somewhere named Paula, but as far as I know Don spends most of his time with Juliet and her family. This is going to take a while,' he added, sounding exhausted. 'You might want to call your brother and let him know.'

'Fuck.' I'd forgotten all about Doug, who'd been sitting alone in my rental all night waiting for me to come home and no doubt worrying about my prolonged absence. He'd be gone soon, if he wasn't already, and our chance to reconnect would go with him.

'The brother,' I said, turning back to Tim. 'Juliet's brother, Amos. He and Don play pickleball together every Saturday. Maybe he can help. Don might have mentioned something to him that could be useful.'

'Worth a try,' said Tim. 'I'll track down his number.'

'He manages the Carlson.' I rose heavily from my chair. Reconciling with Doug would have to wait. 'With any luck, he's working today,' I said.

FORTY-SIX

Rooting out Amos Barlowe proved to be as easy as selling shots of Dark Island bourbon to drunken tourists. We found him at the Carlson, in a room on the second floor that was all gloss and glass.

'Quiet in here this morning,' I said after introducing Tim. Other than the woman who worked the front desk, we hadn't seen a soul on our way up to Amos's cool, sterile office. 'I guess everyone's getting ready for the parade.'

'Actually, I think they're likely to stay in their rooms today. Don't know if you heard the rumor that's been going around.' Amos's mouth pinched with disapproval. In the light of day his teeth were unnaturally white, bleached to translucence in places. I imagined them snapping in half like a cracker, pearly chips strewn across the tufted rug. It was Amos's mother who started the rumor about which he spoke, spitting more lies about me on Facebook. 'People are concerned about this so-called copycat killer,' Amos said. 'We're getting so many requests for room service that I had to call in extra kitchen staff.'

'I don't think anyone needs to worry,' I said carefully, 'but it can't hurt to lay low for a while.'

'Tell that to my kids. They were up at dawn this morning. We narrowly avoided an epic meltdown when the band on Liza's eyepatch snapped – and then I had to tell them it was best to stay home. They were heartbroken. The kids around here, they wait all year for this day. Gossip about murder isn't exactly kid-friendly.'

'I'm sorry,' I said. 'That homicide is actually why we're here. Don's been working it with us and . . . well, we need to find him.'

Amos tilted his head. 'Are you saying he's missing?'

'We haven't been able to locate him,' Tim said. 'We're hoping you can help.'

'Wait,' said Amos. 'This has to do with the copycat?' His

speech was deliberate and tentative. 'Don's not in any danger, is he?'

'No evidence of that,' said Tim.

'Amos,' I said, changing the subject. 'Your mother mentioned Don's been spending a lot of time around here. Have you noticed that, too?'

He ran a hand through his dense hair, letting a hank of it fall across one eye. 'Juliet's pregnant,' he said. 'Did you know that?'

'We're aware of that, yes.'

'I know I speak for my whole family when I say we'd appreciate some discretion.'

'What does that mean, exactly?' I asked. It sounded like Amos had seen some things around the inn.

'Just . . . my sister's prone to paranoia, and the last thing she needs is a scare involving Don. It took a long time for her to conceive.'

Her, I thought. *Not them*. 'We'll do our best. So how often do you see Don around here?'

'I'm usually in my office, but I see him now and then. He likes to spend time in the library. And the bar,' Amos said with a glint in his eye. 'Come to think of it, I guess that's how I first suspected he and my sister were having problems. She used to come here with him after work sometimes, or they'd stop by for a nightcap. Lately, though, he's been coming alone.'

'Your mother said he's been going out quite a bit at night, too, and that he was recently in Massena. Know anything about that?'

Here, Amos shook his head. 'What Don does at night isn't my business,' he said, but his tone had gone black.

I exhaled through my nose. 'Thanks for your time. You'll call us if you see him?' I handed him my card. 'It's important that we find him.'

Something in my face must have given me away, because Amos leaned away from us, his eyes suddenly wary. 'What did he do?'

'What makes you think he did something wrong?' Tim said.

'You're here looking for him, telling me it's important that you find him and asking all kinds of questions about where he's been. You suspect him of something. What did he do?'

There was a little too much glee in his voice for my liking.

As with Gracelyn, the idea that Bogle was guilty of wrongdoing seemed to delight him.

'We can't comment on that,' I said.

Amos's jaw hardened. 'Don's my brother-in-law.'

I studied the planes and angles of the man's face. It was Amos who'd told me about Bogle's drinking and the troubles in his sister's marriage, and now he wanted to know all the details of Bogle's alleged crimes. At Juliet's house, Gracelyn Barlowe had taken every opportunity to sell Bogle down the river.

'Thanks for your time,' I said, turning toward the door. Amos may have been family to Bogle, but we owed him nothing.

And if the Barlowes had anything to say about it, Bogle wouldn't be his brother-in-law for long.

We made our way back down the staircase to the lobby, the varnished black banister smooth under my hand. It was properly sunny now, and light poured through the front windows. I'd been inside the hotel twice already, but I couldn't stop marveling over the trendy wallpaper and artful flower arrangements. The crisp perfection of it all.

'Let's stop here a sec,' I told Tim as we were passing the front desk. The concierge behind it had been at the party. If Bogle spent as much time at the inn as everyone claimed, maybe she could tell us more about what he did here.

She was completing a check-out when we stepped up to the desk, the man she was speaking with the only guest in sight. He was a grandfather in his sixties with a baby in his arms, balloon-animal folds in his podgy flesh. The little guy was dressed as a sailor, navy-trimmed collar and all.

'Careful,' the man warned lightly as we approached, 'he's a big flirt.' Sure enough, the boy reached for me with a chubby fist and doled out a tilted grin. By next summer, Bogle could have a son not much younger than this boy, but where would he be then? Whatever Bogle had been doing, whatever he was hiding, it required a huge sacrifice, and I just couldn't understand why he was so willing to make it.

'How can I help you?' Behind the counter, the concierge smiled. Her shiny white name tag read 'Mary.'

We introduced ourselves and gave her our cards. 'We're looking for Don Bogle. Juliet Barlowe's husband. Have you seen him today?'

'Oh. I'm sorry, I haven't. Is everything all right?'

'Nothing to worry about,' I told her, though I doubted that she believed me. The staff at the Carlson was relatively small, and if Mary knew Bogle, she had to be aware he was an investigator with our team.

'Does he spend a lot of time here?' Tim asked.

A shadow passed over Mary's face, and her lean body stiffened. 'I would love to help you,' she said, 'but the Carlson prides itself on discretion.'

'I can appreciate that,' I said, sensing we were on to something, 'but we're not asking for his social security number, here. I bet you see a lot, stationed out front like this, huh?'

Tim turned to face me. 'Come on,' he said with mock exasperation. 'She's working. It's not like Mary gets to stand around all day admiring the view.'

'Discretion,' Mary repeated, not falling for Tim's games. 'Now, if you'll excuse me, I have work to do.'

'Makes you wonder what's going on in here that requires so much discretion,' Tim said as we left the empty lobby.

'My thoughts exactly,' I said, glancing back at the towering villa of secrets and stone.

FORTY-SEVEN

The day of the Grand Parade was the hottest the North Country had seen in decades. There was talk of a storm on the way, and hopeful whispers of a cooler night to come, but at the moment I could almost hear the asphalt sizzle as we made our way along the side streets to downtown A-Bay. Despite the yellow pesticide flags that spoke of efforts to keep it under control, crab grass grew in clumps all along the sidewalk. I never understood why some weeds looked healthier, thicker, greener than the sod around them. The crab grass was similar to the real thing, but instead of shriveling in the unforgiving sun, it was thriving. Crowding out the good grass around it.

It came as no surprise when, on the trip back to town from the island, we discovered Gracelyn's Facebook post had gone viral. Some enterprising member of the Moms of Jefferson County group had posted the message to Twitter, where it was racking up retweets and likes. But despite what Amos had said about his guests staying in and speculation that a copycat had A-Bay in his sights, there was a strong turnout for the parade. A wall of greasy, Hawaiian Tropic-glazed flesh stretching down both sides of the cordoned-off road.

I gaped at the crowds, oblivious in their baseball caps and eyepatches, highlighter-yellow logos bobbing everywhere I looked. It didn't make sense. In April, when word got out that Bram was back in town, the retreat had been absolute. Residents had locked their doors, some for the first time in years, while business owners all over town flipped Open signs to Closed – yet here they were not four months later giving a killer the red-carpet treatment. *Welcome to A-Bay. Go ahead, do your worst.*

We were only on Market Street for ten minutes before I clued into what was going on. Chet Bell, the sweat on his mustache winking in the sun, was making his way up and down the parade route clapping spectators on the shoulder. Pressing seven-dollar eyepatches into their hands. 'We should get Nan and Pa down here,' I overheard a middle-aged man tell his wife. 'I hear they're doing extra raffles this year. Pepper steak dinners at Chateau Gris.' In the middle of the street, a group of teens wearing Chamber of Commerce T-shirts were tossing coupons and gift cards into the crowd.

At Henderson's directive, we had extra state police patrols in the area, ostensibly to deal with traffic and crowd control. Like us, they were on the lookout for suspicious activity. The parade was the most popular of the Pirate Days events. That made it a beacon for someone determined to steal the spotlight.

There were many things that didn't make sense to me about Bogle's involvement with the homicides. Despite his height, or perhaps because of it, he reviled attention, while copycat killers tended to embrace fame. It was Cunningham who'd pointed out that I might be the link between the killer and these crimes. If that was true, didn't it mean the killer was fixated on me? Harboring some sick obsession or deep hatred that made him want to resurrect my cousin and show me I'd never truly be free? For the life of me, I couldn't imagine Bogle hiding that kind of abhorrence, and I had to think I would have known if I'd been working side-by-side with a psychopath. Why would he resort to murder? Why now? I kept grappling with plausible explanations, but I couldn't gain purchase.

The costumes were more elaborate today, heavy theater-quality garb that looked unimaginably hot. Clutches of pirates marched down Market Street, chanting the refrain from 'Drunken Sailor.' One man who looked like Zorro was lingering near two heavyset women with flowing black hair and leather corsets. On the stoop of an empty storefront, a guy in a frilly purple shirt glanced furtively around him. Two men dressed in Polo shirts, one of whom resembled Godfrey Hearst, sipped beer on the corner, neither speaking to the other as their gazes roved over a group of teen girls. I watched everyone, clocking the distance between them and the nearest woman. Letting my pulse accelerate and the adrenaline build like heat behind an oven door.

A stench wafted my way just as I saw the horses, four of them with brown coats and blond manes towing an ornate wagon. They were followed by the Senior Drum and Bugle Corps that I knew from Tim was affiliated with Bogle's American Legion.

Bogle. Was he here? I couldn't stop thinking about our conversation on the rooftop.

I swear I didn't kill them.

Then come with us.

I can't.

The memory was disturbing, and when a droplet of sweat rolled down the groove of my back, I shivered.

Many an investigator has fallen victim to confirmation bias. If the evidence doesn't fit their theory, they don't pay attention. The danger there, of course, is that it's far too easy to be misled.

The evidence suggested that Bogle was involved in both crimes. We'd been acting under the assumption that this was the case. But where was the motive? Bogle worked for the state police. He was a dedicated investigator with a baby on the way. What possible reason could he have for killing our victims and making the murders look like copycat crimes?

'Tim,' I said. We were standing on the Market Street sidewalk, parting the stream of people like a river shoal. 'There's another possibility here. We've been approaching this as if Don had a hand in these crimes, but what if you're right about him being incapable of murder? What if that's not it?'

'God, I hope it isn't,' Tim said. Then: 'But what's the alternative?'

'He knows who did it. And for one reason or another,' I said, 'he doesn't want to give them up yet.'

I had some experience with lying by omission. I'd chosen to keep what I knew about Bram a secret, not wanting to reveal his identity until I could gather more information on him, his past crimes, why he'd done what he'd done because I knew he'd take those secrets with him to the grave.

'If there is someone else involved,' I said, 'then it isn't just Don we're looking for.'

Together, we turned our faces toward the crowd.

'Us against them,' I told Tim under my breath. It had become our catchphrase, so steeped in our personal history that speaking those three words made my heart hurt. In return, Tim gave me a half-cocked smile. 'There's a better chance that we'll spot something if we split up. I'm going to check things out down by the water,' I said.

Tim's lips parted, the urge to issue a warning cued up on his tongue, but then his mouth zipped closed again. 'Meet me outside Skiffs when the parade's over?'

'Yup.' I let my fingertips brush against his as I turned to go.

The parade route went straight down Market to Fuller, which ran parallel to Scenic View Park. That was the nice thing about Pirate Days: everything was contained within the quarter-mile radius that comprised downtown Alexandria Bay. According to Tim, the event usually lasted about forty minutes, after which Mayor Milton would stand on the horse-drawn wagon with a mic and announce the winners of the raffle. Fifteen minutes had passed since the pirate fanatics had started marching. I ran a hand down the back of my bare neck, suddenly grateful for my short hair and the whisper of wind off the river. I had to believe the air had reached its saturation point; there was rain on the way, I could feel it. Still no sign of Bogle, though, or trouble of any kind.

Spectators stood three-deep along the sidewalk. Kids as young as four with mouths dyed popsicle-blue zagged around my feet. Some of the parade participants threw candy to the little ones on the sidelines, and there were already groups forming, Halloween-style, to negotiate trades based on some system of economics only a child could comprehend. In spite of myself, my mind conjured a memory of Trey Hayes, the nine-year-old who was abducted last fall. *Please don't let whoever's doing the taking this time be into kids.*

I was navigating past a cluster of just such children when I spotted Jared Cunningham. He stood in front of the building that housed the Chamber of Commerce, a stone-clad two-story with an entryway flanked by concrete lions, their mouths hanging open in a way that made them look more insecure than fierce. *Eyepatch central.*

'Community parades aren't exactly your beat,' I said, coming up behind him.

Cunningham startled when he heard my voice, and spun around.

'Actually, this is totally my beat,' he said once he'd recovered. 'If you guys find a serial killer out here today, I sure as hell don't want to miss it. Mind if I tag along, detective?'

You had to hand it to the guy for trying. 'I don't think that would be a good idea.'

Cunningham exposed all his teeth. 'Fine. Just point me toward the action when it happens, OK?'

'Don't hold your breath.'

Cunningham rocked back on his heels. He was in Bermuda shorts today, his short-sleeved button-down printed with tiny black flowers. 'I'm glad I bumped into you, actually,' he said as I looked around. 'I've been, ah, wanting to tell you something. Better that you hear it from me.'

'OK,' I said absently. The sun was in my eyes, but I'd caught sight of a sketchy-looking guy in the parking lot of the motel across the street.

'I'm going to be interviewing your aunt. Felicia Skilton.'

I spun around to face him. 'What?'

'It wasn't my idea,' he said, showing me his hands. 'She reached out after reading my inaugural post.'

'The interview.' I was blinking wildly. 'It's up?' *My story.* Out there for all to see.

'You didn't get my email?'

I shook my head. I hadn't checked my personal email in days.

'Well, you'll look when you can,' he said. 'I added a page to the site that explains my vision, how I want the magazine to be a platform for families of famed killers. Felicia asked if I wanted to talk. I think this could be good for her. Help her heal, you know?'

I swallowed, and swallowed again, but my mouth was sand, the tongue inside it useless. Distanced as I was from my parents, I didn't know much about how Aunt Fee was holding up, but every time someone uttered Bram's name there was a part of me that heard it through Fee's ears and wondered how long I'd be able to bear listening to the whole world call my child a monster. I imagine parents have all kinds of worries about their kids. Will they be healthy? Successful? Kind? Fee's prevailing fear, the product of a lifetime spent battling an anxiety disorder, had been that something horrible would happen to Crissy and Abe. In the end, it had. Her youngest had morphed into a completely different person. Was that how she saw it, too? Was this the tactic she'd been using to cope? It was less of a stab to the spleen than believing Abe had been Bram all along.

'She agreed to go public about Bram?' I still couldn't believe it. 'But he was her son.'

'No,' Cunningham said gently as he bowed his ginger head. 'Abe was.'

The commotion started up the street, close to where the parade had begun. I heard shouting, and stepped up onto the stairs to get a better look.

'What's going on?' Cunningham did me one better and hopped onto the bench by the door.

It was Raymond, one of the patrol troopers, that I saw first. He was blocking someone's path while a group of curious parade bystanders formed a circle around them, obscuring my view.

'Who is that guy?' Cunningham craned his neck, and I hurried over to the bench where I hoisted myself up, one foot on its curved metal arm, so I could see what he did.

And what I saw was Javier Barba.

I was off the bench and running in seconds. The ruckus was louder now, a single insistent voice rising above the din. Bodies, slippery and reeking of synthetic coconut and vinegar, pressed in from all sides, the bare skin of strangers' exposed upper arms sticking to me as I inched closer. The heat and stink pummeled my senses and made my eyes water. There were nearly as many faces turned toward the man now as to the parade, and through the mob I could see several of the marchers watching. Raymond had his back to me, but I caught a handful of his shirt, so wet with sweat that a warm trickle snaked down the inside of my wrist.

'What's going on?' I was panting; the trooper was, too. His hands were clasped around Javier's forearms, encircling his wrists like the chain-link tattoos stenciled on Estella's brother's skin, and he was doing his best to hold on. There was a murderous expression etched into his sunburned face.

'Hey!' Javier had spotted me. His eyes were wild. 'Hey, I need to talk to you! Get your fucking hands off me, *pig*.'

'He went crazy,' Raymond wheezed, still holding the writhing man at arm's length. 'Said he needs your help.'

'Get the *fuck off of me*!'

I grabbed Javier's arm. 'Calm down, Mr Barba. You need to take a breath. What's going on?'

He only thrashed harder. 'It's my sister!'

'Did something happen to Estella?'

'Hell yeah, something happened!' Javier broke free of Raymond's grip and rushed toward me. My hand went to my sidearm, the reflex familiar, but he stopped just short of me and curled his arms over his head. 'Please,' he said, his face crumpling. 'You have to help me. I think someone took Estella.'

'Took?' I said. 'How? Where?'

His head swiveled toward the river. 'Out on Carlson Island.'

FORTY-EIGHT

The boat ride to Carlson Island was excruciatingly slow. It was designed to be a leisure cruise – coast through gemstone-tinted water, take in the clean upstate air and piney island views. I had half a mind to shove the old ferryman aside and drive the boat myself. Instead, I used the time to question Javier about his sister.

They had planned to leave that afternoon. After realizing there was no hope of a wrongful death suit and payout, Estella was eager to get home to her kids, and the siblings were preparing to make the long drive back to New York.

Together, they'd eaten breakfast on the outdoor patio, enjoying a few more minutes of the view. The next river they'd see would be the Hudson. Estella was done first, and went back to the room to finish packing. Not ten minutes later, Javier walked the same steps up to the second floor of the inn.

When he got to the room, it was empty. At first he thought he'd missed her, that his sister had gone back downstairs. Had he misunderstood the plan? He delayed ten minutes more, packing his own bag while he waited for her to return. And then he returned to the courtyard.

Javier searched the whole of the Carlson, but he found no trace of her. It was only when hurrying back down the hall near the kitchen that he noticed the blood. A streak of it, jagged and bright on the doorframe. Completely out of place in the elegant hotel.

The blood was still wet.

Javier didn't call the village police. He figured there must have been countless crank calls to the station in the wake of news reports about the murders, and didn't trust that an officer would believe his account. Instead, he called the state police barracks, and asked for me. When he was told I wasn't in, he drove into town with the intention of camping out in the parking lot until I showed up. On the way, he'd passed the parade, seen the police presence, and chanced a throw of the dice.

My mind was whirring with possibilities about Estella. The blood was strange, but it could have come from anyone. A staff member. Another guest. It didn't make sense to me that Estella would leave the island without telling her brother, but I didn't know the woman well. I couldn't rule that out.

What was more, Estella's disappearance broke the pattern. If she was the killer's third victim, if our suspect truly was replicating Bram's crimes, the next target should have been someone named Lanie, or possibly Elena – Lanie Miner's birth name. Did finding a Lanie in Jefferson County or a neighboring community prove too difficult? Did unforeseen circumstances force him to deviate from the plan?

Len, the man whose job it was to ferry guests, had been trying hard to pretend he wasn't listening to our conversation, and even harder to look unconcerned about the fact that a woman was missing from his employers' hotel. *Len*. I studied the plum circles around his eyes, and the grip of his leathery hands on the wheel. Day and night, Len had the critical duty of taking visitors to and from the island – and he was about to become a godsend.

'Do you know who we're talking about?' I asked as we chugged through the water, dark waves lapping at the bow. 'The woman who accompanied Javier to the island. Do you know who she is?'

'Long hair? Pretty face? I know who you mean,' he said, 'yeah. Of course.'

'Did you take her into town today?'

'Not today. I haven't seen her.'

'Any other way to get on and off the island?'

Len adjusted his cap as he thought about that. 'Anyone could come by boat and dock there, I reckon. Most don't.'

'Really? Not even to have Sunday brunch at the hotel?' I was imagining another vessel, some sort of emergency that had Estella hitching a ride to the mainland with a stranger. But Len was already shaking his head.

'It isn't the kind of inn you visit for brunch. It takes a bit of effort to get out here, and the restaurant's not that big. The Barlowes reserve it for guests.'

'Who else did you take to the island today?' It was early afternoon and I was betting there'd been little activity on the ferry boat.

'It's been quiet today,' he said, confirming Amos's claim. 'Mostly just the family.'

'Including Don Bogle?'

Again he shook his head. 'Haven't seen Don since the party.'

'Who's Don?' asked Javier.

'And you're the only one who drives this boat?' I went on. We were approaching the island's stony shore.

'That's right. When guests need to get on and off the island, they call the concierge, and Mary sends for me.'

No Bogle, then. *He knows who did it, and he doesn't want to give them up yet.* The words I'd spoken to Tim at the parade swept toward me like a storm across the water.

If Estella was truly missing, and Bogle wasn't at Carlson Island, then who was?

FORTY-NINE

With the exception of a few guests braving the heat to walk the grounds, Carlson Island was eerily empty when Javier and I arrived. I had texted Tim on the way over with an update: **Estella's missing. Meet me at the Carlson when you can.** Len the ferryman was already on his way back to the mainland. I hoped Tim would be quick.

'Show me the blood,' I said as we stepped into the lustrous lobby. I'd need to see their guest room, too, but the blood was priority number one. The idea of it trickling down a doorframe in a public hall unsettled me. It meant someone had a need so pressing they couldn't even spare a moment to wipe up.

Javier guided me to the hall, with its painted millwork and deep navy runner. As we passed the lounge, I caught sight of Gracelyn Barlowe's silver bun disappearing through the doorway to the dining room.

The hall ran alongside the staircase, toward the back of what had once been a private home. The door where Javier had seen the blood was at the very end of the hall, next to the kitchen. Through the porthole-style window in the swinging door, I could see cooks scurrying around stainless steel counters, dressing salads and flipping chicken breasts at the stove. Amos's extra staff. It was noisy inside, but through the clatter of pots and pans I could just make out the syncopated rhythm of jazz music crackling from an old stereo. Despite the kitchen's proximity to the door, there was a good chance that whatever happened in the hall had gone unnoticed.

The blood was a dark stain against chocolatey woodwork, which made it difficult to see. Based on its location on the doorframe, I suspected it had come from a head wound. I imagined Estella's temple slammed against the frame's angular edge and the woman, dazed and disoriented now, slithering down to the footworn rug. The blood was about the right distance from the floor to match up with Estella's height. I tried the door handle. Locked.

'That guy.'

Javier's toned arm, blotchy with fresh bruises from his altercation with Ray, pointed down the hall in the direction from which we'd come. There, looking as slick and commanding as ever, stood Amos Barlowe. Javier's body tensed. 'He's the manager, I saw him at the party. He might know something.'

'Wait,' I said, holding him back. 'Let me talk to him, OK?' I knew Javier's MO; he acted on instinct, especially when it came to defending his sister. I didn't want to scare Amos off. I had a few questions for the man myself.

But Javier pulled away from me, chest heaving. 'Hey!' His shout rang out like a shot through the stillness of the elegant inn.

Amos turned at the sound, face riddled with confusion, then indecision, then fear, and he darted around the corner into the lounge. Javier knew, as I did, about the door that led to the courtyard and the rolling lawn beyond. Before I could stop him he'd given chase and he, too, disappeared from sight.

I started toward the lobby, but both men were long gone. Why had Amos run? I thought back to the time I'd spent with the man, conjuring his face and mannerisms. Expressions arranged as carefully as the flowers I'd seen around the hotel. There was something performative about him, like he was working hard to appear agreeable. Fighting to conceal his disapproval of the things that weren't quite to his standards. It took a special kind of sociopath to execute an act like that.

Bogle's brother-in-law was a local, like him. He spent the majority of his time at the Carlson. As manager of a relatively small hotel, Amos must have known that Jessica Greenleaf, the victim of an unsolved murder, had stayed at the inn in June, yet he hadn't brought that up when Tim and I paid him a visit. He'd been entrusted by his parents with overseeing a tourist destination in a community ravaged by violent crime; he must have kept tabs on the news stories, including those about Bram's life, death and victims back in the city. Bogle and Amos spent time together at the Thousand Islands Club. It was conceivable that Bogle had told him what he knew about the murders in New York. And if Bogle had somehow discovered Juliet's brother killed two women here, he might have chosen to keep that damning information under wraps. Might even have ditched the victims' phones if he thought they could lead us to Amos.

My hand was on my sidearm when I felt the draught of air. It swirled around my ankles like a wet tongue, cold seeping through my pant legs to tickle my skin. I turned to find the door behind me was open, a strip of inky darkness running down its length.

A moment ago, this same door had been closed. Not just closed, but locked. This was a hotel, people coming and going all the time, and it was right beside the bustling kitchen, but suspicion had coiled its way up my spine. Something wasn't right.

With one hand on my Glock, I glanced around me. Still no sign of Javier. Had someone slipped out of the kitchen? There was, I realized then, another option.

Whoever unlocked the door might have been secreted behind it all along.

Slowly, I eased myself along the hallway wall, and toed open the door.

The stairs leading down to the basement were wooden with open risers that told of the villa's hundred-and-twenty-five years. Each tread groaned under the weight of my boots, and the farther I descended, the harder it became to breathe. I had trouble with cellars. Ever since New York, I couldn't see them as anything but cavernous maws threatening to swallow me alive. This one was no different.

'State police,' I called into the void. I had reached the bottom of the staircase, and in the feeble light from the open door I could see rows of shelves. Cans of food. Crates of wine. Beyond all that, and behind me, more darkness.

I stepped onto the stone floor and waited to feel something: proof that I wasn't alone down here, maybe. An intimation of knowing. Instead, what I felt was a spark. As kids, Abe and I would sometimes touch our tongues to live batteries just to feel the zing of electricity in our mouths. This was like that, only bigger. A jolt that left me gasping.

A thunderbolt of pain that yanked my mouth into a silent scream.

FIFTY

T*he smell*. It was so potent that I woke up wheezing as a century of damp and rot wormed its way into my nostrils. The room was completely devoid of light, the floor beneath me ice cold. *No*. Memories rushed me like a wave and I was flailing, fighting off the invisible threat that had dragged me down into this hell once more.

It all felt the same – but it couldn't be. How could I be back here again? I was reeling, and when I gulped in a lungful of air my breath came out raspy. I walked my fingers over my limbs in search of the pain. It was everywhere, from the back of my head to my upper arms and knees, but I found the mother lode under my ribs, and as soon as I acknowledged it, a flare exploded behind my eyes. My shirt had been sliced open and it clung to me like a second, gaping skin. The wound beneath was sticky hot and parted with every breath. A tiny mouth pumping blood on to my probing fingers.

What I knew about abdominal stab wounds wasn't trivial. The information in the autopsy reports for Bram's victims had been exhaustive, and all that talk of subcutaneous fat and fascia – the connective tissue, heavy as canvas, that protects our organs from harm – stuck with me. My wound wasn't deep. Most likely my assailant had nicked some blood vessels rather than a vital organ. That didn't mean I could languish down here indefinitely and still make it out alive.

Reaching down to my boot hurt like hell, but I undid the laces, and slipped off my sock. It was damp with the sweat of days on the job, but I balled it up and brought it to the wound all the same, pressing in and biting down against the blazing sting. I groped around for my sidearm, my phone. Both were gone. A twist of the torso to look around made me cry out in pain. There was no point anyway. Nothing to see but stifling darkness here.

I heard something then, a soft hush of sound. The rattle of saliva in an open throat. I held my breath and strained to hear over the slapping of my heart. 'Who's there?' I could sense them now, close by my side. A shuddering presence in the dark.

'It's me.'

Estella's voice was weedy. Two words, and I knew all the grit had been knocked out of her.

But she was alive.

Why? Why hadn't whoever put us here killed us when they had the chance? Did they want to see us suffer? Because it was clear now that this was all about me, a ploy to kill me and finish what Bram never could. Who had done this? I squeezed my eyes shut against the gloom and tried to remember. The inn. The hall. Javier, running off after Amos.

Javier.

Tim.

Where were they?

Estella said, 'Are you hurt?' Asking took effort, so much that it left her winded.

Though I knew she couldn't see me, I shook my head. 'I think I was stabbed. It could be worse.' I shifted on the hard floor, and winced. I was bruised all over, and the skin of my back burned. Whoever had moved me into this room must have dragged me, unconscious, across the stone floor. *Jesus.* 'Are *you* OK?'

'Pushed down the stairs. Something's wrong with my head,' said Estella. 'I feel sick.'

Had she been knocked unconscious, too? I reached toward her voice. Estella was closer than I thought, sitting arm's length from me in the dark. Had she been here all this time? Spent hours here alone, like I had in my prior cell? 'Can I?' I asked as my fingertips brushed her arm.

''Kay.'

I moved my fingers, whisper-light, up her arm and neck until her hair brushed against me. A frisson shot through my arm; I felt the blood that had congealed on her skull at once. The entire side of Estella's head was wet, and the smell of it, so close, left me woozy. When I withdrew my hand and repositioned myself on the floor, the pain in my abdomen made me see stars.

Steeling myself, I got low and, with a guttural groan, extended both arms. I had to find a way out of here, but the effort was agony.

'Don't bother,' said Estella. 'It's locked.'

There was no light here at all. Not even a seam under a door.

'Hey! We need help down here!' I hollered it, gave it my all as the pain ripped through me.

'I've been screaming for hours.'

Don't bother.

I drew a breath through my nose. My eyes were watering, my body cold. I didn't know old houses, but the Carlson had to be at least fifteen thousand square feet, the basement a labyrinthine system of store rooms and corridors, each damper and darker than the last. 'Who did this to you, Estella?' *To us.*

'I didn't see . . . but I heard them talking. That woman, and the manager.'

Every word was a slog, and Estella's strength was flagging. At best, she was concussed. The worst-case scenario was something I didn't want to think about.

'Gracelyn,' I said. 'Amos. What were they saying?'

'Don't know. I passed them going back to the room. He was mad about something. Her, too.'

Nothing made sense. Were Amos and his mother in cahoots? What had they been talking about? Whatever it was, Estella overheard them, and the outcome of that unfortunate fluke was clear.

It was because of me that Estella was in Alexandria Bay to begin with. I may not have been directly responsible for her husband's death, but it was my cousin's sins that brought her here, and the shame of that would never leave me.

But she wouldn't die down here. I'd texted Tim; he was on his way. Somewhere on the floor above us, Javier was realizing I was gone. He would look for us. Neither would rest until we were found, but Estella and I were both badly wounded, and until then we needed to stay conscious. I had to distract her.

'Why the Carlson?' The question had been nagging me for days. Estella had talked a big game about her good job back in the city, but the inn was the most expensive in the area, and she was a widow with three kids at home.

'We had no choice,' she said weakly. 'Everything else was booked, but the Carlson had a cancellation. Even that shitty motel in town was full.'

The Admiral. Godfrey and Rebecca Hearst must have snagged the last room. If Estella and Javier had stayed there instead, would she still be here in the basement with me? 'But why now?' I asked her. 'Why come back?' And on the busiest week of the summer.

'School starts soon. They need things.'

Her words were slurred, her tone listless. It was a bad sign.

'We were going to ask you for money,' she said. 'If the plan failed. Money for my kids.'

A gasp snagged in my throat. What had made her reconsider? *Me*, I realized. *Damaged and pathetic. Begging for mercy in a hotel room.* 'Where are they now? Your kids?'

'With my mother.' She coughed wetly, the sound garbled and echoey in our empty stone cell. She said, 'I had to come.'

Everything Estella had done, she'd done out of desperation. For her family. What happened to her husband wasn't fair, and it wasn't right. Bram had left her alone. Robbed her children of a father. But Bram was gone. Now, there was only me.

Here on Carlson Island, and back in New York, Estella's brother and mother and children were waiting for her to come home.

And I was going to make damn sure she did.

FIFTY-ONE

The hours blurred together as Estella and I huddled in that basement, dizzy with pain and stiff with cold. Just a few days ago, I'd marveled over the ability of these same stone walls to keep the Carlson blissfully cool, but the chill was under my skin now, and spreading. I'd been shivering for as long as I could remember. I couldn't find a way to stop.

I'd lost track of how long Estella had been sleeping, curled in a heap with her head on my thigh. Try as I might, I couldn't keep her awake. The gash on her head appeared to have stopped bleeding, but softly prodding the wound had revealed more hair matted with blood. I couldn't be sure how much she'd lost, and whether the lesion would soon bleed again.

All the while, I'd been thinking about Amos Barlowe. Picturing the stalker in the video, sitting on the bench outside the Bay Point Grill. Gracelyn had been adamant the man in that footage was Bogle. Had he been watching for Amos? Aware even then that his brother-in-law was a killer? Had Amos followed Rebecca back to her motel that night to stab her in the stomach and recreate the crime first staged by Blake Bram?

Again and again, I went over Estella's words in my mind. *I heard them talking. That woman and the manager. He was mad about something. Her, too.* With blood-sticky fingers I stroked my bare neck and tried to piece it all together. Based on Len's account, Bogle wasn't currently on the island. His in-laws' hotel was no place for him to hide out, especially given the bad blood between them. Especially when Bogle was on the run. And yet, here we were in the cellar. Amos was the logical suspect – but something about that assumption didn't ring true.

Another wave of dizziness washed over me, but I squinted hard and fought it off. The answer was so close, all the things I'd seen and heard over the last seven days poking at me like a fistful of burs. The more I squirmed, the deeper their barbed teeth sank into my skin.

Rebecca's phone. Bogle had volunteered to take the lead on Rebecca's email and social media activities, which in turn allowed him to suppress key evidence. He had to know we'd get our hands on her data eventually, but he'd bought himself time. What was he hiding?

And what was it Gracelyn said about Bogle parading other women under the family's nose?

Theories coalesced like whispers: Bogle's drinking, the explanation for why his truck had been at the crime scene, the look of agony on his face when Tim and I cornered him on the rooftop outside the legion.

I didn't kill Rebecca and Jessica.

All at once, it made sense.

Bogle hadn't committed a violent crime. He'd covered up someone else's.

The sound of a key in a lock. I felt like a rabbit in an open field, startling at every sound, but at this one, I eased Estella's head off my lap and propped myself up. My head felt weightless while my body was riveted to the floor. Steadying myself, I turned in the direction of the noise.

In the East Village, I'd let my chance to detain Bram slip away. I'd been unable to right the emotional tailspin he'd sent me into headfirst and kicking. Could I have found a way to kill him that day? I don't know, and I never will. But I'll always believe I should have tried harder to stop him.

This would be an even tougher fight to win. I couldn't gauge the gravity of my wound, but it was severe enough to sap my strength and mettle. I knew how to defend myself. Just like last time, though, the question was whether I could.

The door scraped against the uneven floor.

I held my breath as it swung open to reveal Juliet Barlowe.

'Ladies.' Juliet held my sidearm in one hand and a phone in the other, the latter dousing her face in a cold blue light. Her voice was all false cheer, her smile affected. She looked healthy, and the recollection of her pregnancy hit me like a gut punch. This was Bogle's pregnant wife, hovering over us with a gun.

My eyes darted to Estella. In the diffused light of the smartphone, she looked worse than I'd feared. Her eyelids were cracked open, her eyes gleaming black slits. The strands of hair that had long since escaped from her braid were strewn across her face, and I watched them flutter against dry, cracked lips. *Still breathing.*

I looked up at Bogle's wife. 'It was you,' I said. 'Don was cheating. You killed those women, and made it look like a copycat crime to throw us off the trail.' *We're finally going to start a family. I can't do it alone.* I recalled what she'd told me and Tim at the house. The tears in her eyes.

Juliet's eyes were bright with alarm now, but the fear didn't last. We were no threat to this woman, unarmed and immobilized in the basement of her parents' inn. As far as she was concerned, Juliet had won.

'Now, this is a problem,' she said. 'You two, down here. Knowing what you do.'

My fury was blinding. 'My partner's on his way.'

'Who, Tim? Oh yes, I saw him when he arrived. We had a chat and I told him you were searching the estate. Seven acres is a lot of ground to cover. He won't find you.'

'Javier—'

'Javier is worried about his sister – and he has every right to be. She's been missing for hours, and there's a crazed killer on the loose. I do my research.' She said it with a satisfied grin. 'I know what happens next, only I'm putting my own spin on it. Think of it as closure. Tonight, I'll call your friend Tim and tell him I saw a man and two women down by the water. Tomorrow, the police will arrive to drag the river. All those same divers who searched for Rebecca by the bridge will come looking, and this time, they'll find a body. Actually, they'll find two. And the killer, that clever copycat, will be long gone. Never to be heard from again.'

Every word she spoke crystalized into a vision that I scrutinized from all angles. Juliet planned to drown us. Take advantage of our location, and dispose of our bodies in the simplest way possible. It was why our injuries were superficial. We were too far from the river. Juliet would have to move us. Did she have an accomplice? Would Amos help? The job would be much easier if we could march ourselves to the firing range.

Even so, what she was plotting posed a colossal risk. The inn was located at the tip of Carlson Island, and it had windows on all sides. Risk didn't seem to concern Juliet Barlowe, though. She'd managed to commit two near-perfect crimes, create the ultimate diversion with a fictional copycat killer, and cap off her mimicry of Bram's murder spree by taking both a third woman, and me.

What would happen if Juliet was able to carry out her plan? I couldn't bear the thought of Mac and Sol standing by while those divers heaved our unresponsive bodies from the river. My parents hadn't spoken to me in months, and they'd never forgive themselves for that. And Tim. Tim, whose mere existence sent a current of joy through my body. For whom I felt a searing white hot love that I'd kill to defend if I had to. The idea of him on that shore hurt a hundred times more than the festering wound in my gut, a million. My team would conduct an exhaustive search for Ben Dool, of course they would, but the man didn't exist. For all Juliet's talk of closure, it was something Tim, and Javier, and Estella's children would never have. She knew that. And she couldn't care less.

I didn't always succeed at summoning my training, but martial arts had taught me to quiet my mind, and it was only because of my years in the dojo that I was able to tamp down my fear now. *Breathe.* Focusing on my breathing had served me well in the past, but now every time I inhaled my body shrieked in pain. Estella was barely clinging to consciousness, and Juliet was armed with a gun. How could I defend us both against that?

You have other weapons, Shay.

But she's pregnant.

She's deranged, and she won't hesitate to kill you both.

When I was Bram's captive, he spent hours talking to me in my cell. I became his confidant against my will, and over time his stories pulled me in until I started to conflate the killer in that room with the cousin I'd been so loyal to as a kid. If words could do that, they could do anything.

'There are a few problems with your plan.'

Juliet tilted her sleek dark head. 'I sincerely doubt that,' she said.

Digging my fingers into my wound and the sock I'd been using to stanch the bleeding, I hauled in a shallow breath. Made it sound extra weak. 'For this to work, you need people to believe it was all the doing of a copycat killer. But a copycat obsessed with Bram would never kill me.'

A flinch. Juliet shook her head. 'That's not true. Bram abducted you. He kept you in a cellar just like this one, and the only reason you're still alive is because Jay Lopez botched his plan. Bram gave you that scar when you were kids. He took you in New York so he could finish the job.'

Whether she'd sourced her information from Bogle, or the media, or a combination of both I didn't know, but she had that last part wrong. Everyone did. 'No,' I told her, biting down on the pain once more. 'Bram loved me. He wanted us to be together again. He would never have killed me – and Tim and the sheriff know it. Don does, too,' I said. 'He knows everything, Juliet. He's been following you. *Everywhere.*'

'Bullshit. Don doesn't have a clue.' Her gaze was unfocused now, her wrist bending under the weight of the gun.

'He knows,' I repeated. 'Where do you think he's been all this time? Why we've been looking for him?'

'He's been drinking.' Her mouth turned pouty. 'He's still getting used to the idea of the baby. I can fix all that.'

'No. He's been covering for you,' I said. 'Every member of the state police currently considers him the prime suspect in those murders, and that means there are only two ways this can go. Either Don decides to protect you and takes the blame for the death of two innocent women, or he turns you over to the police. Either your child grows up without a father, or it grows up without you.'

'That's not true.' The position of the phone's flashlight lit her face from below, creating slashes of shadow across her forehead, cheeks, jaw. It turned her eyes into empty black holes, but I could see by the way she'd arranged her mouth that this upset her, and I held her stare.

'It is, and I'll be honest, I don't think he's going to take the heat. I know Don. We're friends. He can forgive a lot, but he won't abide murder. Especially not when the victim is me.'

'You don't know him. I'm pregnant with his child. He wants to be with me. He just got a little off-track.'

'What if it's you who doesn't know him, this man you call your husband who's been sleeping around? He was cheating on you with those women, wasn't he? He chose them over you.'

The slur found its mark, and Juliet sucked in a breath. 'Are you sure you trust him to protect you,' I went on, 'when you can't even trust him to be faithful?'

'Shut up.' The gun was in her hand, but for Juliet – a woman who had willingly driven a knife through tissue and fat and muscle again and again – its purpose was forgotten. She came at me with the pistol raised high and a straight shot at the top of my head, but even sprawled on the floor, even as the wet heat of my wound spread across my torso, this was an attack I knew how to defend against.

I crossed my wrists and blocked the weapon as it rushed toward me. Zipped my right hand along Juliet's arm to clasp a palm over the gun's barrel, and twisted it straight out of her hand.

She's pregnant. A flashbulb vision of the milk-fat baby in the lobby threw me off-kilter. The woman was carrying Bogle's child. I couldn't hurt her.

But when I blinked, it was Bram balanced above me, and Bram's eyes that were dark with rage. Eyes that had watched, smug and satisfied, as the life leached out of others.

Without hesitation, I aimed for Juliet's leg, and I fired.

The sound of her kneecap shattering was lost beneath the roar of the blast, but I imagined I could hear it through the ringing in my ears and the howls coming from the woman now cowering on the floor.

With my sidearm trained on Juliet Barlowe, I reached for her phone.

FIFTY-TWO

After weeks of brutal heat and relentless sun, the sky above the St Lawrence was swollen with soot-colored clouds, and the reprieve they provided was immeasurable. Outside the Carlson, state troopers and the village police coalesced with EMTs while hotel guests looked on from the perceived safety of the inn's vast stone porch. Between me, Estella and Juliet Barlowe, the emergency techs had their work cut out for them, as did the coast guard, which would be transporting us to the River Hospital. One by one.

Juliet Barlowe was the first to go. She'd been strapped to a gurney, wrists cuffed in front of her and both Sheriff Mac and Jeremy Solomon as escorts. Gracelyn Barlowe stood nearby on the shore, sobbing into her bejeweled hands as her husband and Amos beat a path in the velvety grass while shouting obscenities at attorneys on their respective phones. How long, I wondered, had Juliet's family known she was a sociopath? In a few minutes, Tim would be taking them back to the barracks, and I hoped we would find out.

'Look,' he said, his mouth close to my ear, his breath warm and sweet on my skin. He placed a hand on my shoulder where we sat near the front door of the inn. The bleeding had finally stopped, my stab wound deemed nonfatal, so I was stuck here until the coast guard got back. At least there was the view – which now included Javier Barba. He'd been determined not to leave his sister's side until Juliet was off the island. Estella's wound would require stitches, her concussion some medical care, but she'd survive. Javier looked much worse for wear.

He approached me cautiously. I gave him a nod and a small smile. 'Detective,' he mumbled, bowing his head. 'I want to thank you.'

'It's me who should be thanking you,' I said. 'Estella, too. I'm sorry she got dragged into this. But if she hadn't been paying attention to what was going on at the inn, and you hadn't come to find me . . . well, let's not think about that.'

Javier nodded. He said, 'My sister and me, we read that article about you.'

My hands went cold. 'Article?'

'Your side of the story,' he said.

I turned to Tim, who gave my hand a reassuring squeeze as Javier got out his phone.

I suppose I'd convinced myself the interview would take a while to gain momentum. For the time being, Cunningham's new venture consisted of a bare-bones WordPress blog parked at the URL survivingthecrime.com. I knew he planned to post the link on social media, where he had a following from his days with the paper in Watertown. Whatever he'd done, Felicia had already found it. And now, it seemed, others had, too.

'I didn't know,' Javier said as he handed me his phone, the interview cued up on the browser. 'That he cut you' – his eyes went to my scar – 'and all the rest. You hear about people who bond with their kidnappers, but I never thought that was real. It's kind of like he stalked you your whole life, you know? Leaving you with a scar like that?'

The nod I gave him was a reflex; I was staring at the screen. *It Was on the Eighth Day That I Decided to Kill Him: Shana's Story*. The piece started off the same way I had when recounting my experience to Bogle and Sol, and later, Cunningham, Estella and Javier, but there was so much more of me on the page. Words and feelings that, not long ago, only existed in my own tortured consciousness. I braced myself as I scrolled to the bottom, where I found a button displaying the post's current number of Likes. *92K.* Cunningham's story – *my story* – was going viral. And after all those months of hoarding the truth, so determined to suffer in silence, I felt a tremendous, bone-deep sense of release.

I handed him back the phone. 'It was good to meet you, Javier. If there's ever anything I can do for you and Estella, anything at all—'

'We're OK. We've got a backup plan. A tell-all book.' He scrubbed his buzz cut with his knuckles, and smiled. 'We'll be OK.'

'Well, count on me to write the foreword,' I told him. If the popularity of Cunningham's post was any indication, I could help them sell a good many copies, too.

As we watched Javier walk back down the way he came, I sunk my hand into Tim's hair at the nape of his neck and tried to tune out the excited chatter of the guests at my back.

'Bogle's in custody,' Tim said under his breath, angling us away from them. 'He came in on his own, soon as he heard what happened out here.'

How much had Don Bogle really known about his wife? Did he realize how dangerous she was when he married her? What did Bogle have to say about what Juliet had done?

When I looked at Tim's face, and inhaled the scent of him, I couldn't imagine.

FIFTY-THREE

Don Bogle's face was slick under the lights of the interview room, the color and texture of raw salmon gone rotten. Beside him, his delegate from the union – he'd declined the offer of an attorney – wore a stern expression with his cheap brown suit. There was an unopened bottle of water between them, and every now and then Bogle reached out and crunched the plastic between his thick fingers, not drinking, not so much as cracking the cap. He kept looking at me with something between pity and disbelief, eyes zipping from my stomach and the wound his wife had given me to the scar inflicted years earlier by someone equally unhinged. Two days wasn't enough to heal the former, not when the latter had taken a lifetime.

We'd been questioning him for more than an hour, going over his story again and again to get the full account on record. There were a lot of people invested in seeing both cases sewed up tight.

'I cheated on her,' Bogle told us as Tim scribbled in his notebook. The notes weren't necessary, not with Ameer and Henderson watching us on camera from the other room, but it was a tough habit for Tim to break. The sight of that notebook seemed to hit Bogle hard, a reminder that we were no longer on the same team.

'I lost my phone,' he said, grinding the heels of his hands into bloodshot eyes, 'or thought I did. Juliet must have taken it. She sent me off to work without it and promised to look while I was gone. I think that's how she found out about Rebecca. We'd been messaging about our plan to meet. But Juliet knew about Jessica long before that.'

'Messaging.' We'd already pored over Rebecca's texts. Bogle meant Facebook. 'We didn't see any messages,' I told him.

'Deleted.'

'But you took the phone from the evidence closet. You dumped it at the park.'

'I had to be sure there was nothing else that could connect me with them,' he said. 'Jessica. Rebecca.'

Getting rid of the phone had been a precaution, a calculated effort to keep the rest of us in the dark. In my mind's eye, I could see the unbound threads of our investigation weaving together. All the facts that had been niggling me were finally starting to make sense.

'Talk to me about Jessica Greenleaf,' I said. 'She spent a night at the Carlson in late June for a girlfriend's bachelorette party. Is that where you met?'

He nodded. 'We got to talking. She'd been married before, and it ended in divorce. All those stupid party games weren't her scene, so she wound up at the bar. With me. Things weren't going so well at home. I'd been thinking about leaving Jules for a while by then. When she and I first met she didn't give a shit what her family thought of me, but a few years ago, when they opened the inn . . . it was like they took another look and decided I didn't jibe with the image of "the Barlowe family" they wanted to portray. There were a bunch of family photo shoots and magazine features back then, and they pretty much pretended I didn't exist. Which was fine.' He closed his eyes, and when he opened them again, they were glassy. 'The inn had nothing to do with me. But Juliet saw her parents treating me like garbage, and followed suit. They aren't fans of the police, the Barlowes,' he explained. 'When Amos was a junior in high school, Gracelyn and Morton got slapped with a big fine for letting him and his friends drink at the house underage. The money wasn't an issue, but the gossip spread all over town and tarnished their reputations. And right before the inn opened, Gracelyn got pulled over for driving home drunk from the TI Club. They acted like that was my fault, as if I personally tipped them off or something. They blame me even now.

'Jules would make these backhanded comments about my job, my looks,' he went on, 'even though she always picked out my clothes and told me what to say to keep the peace with her parents. It was constant mind games. I started spending more and more time away from the house. She's always been a little . . .'

'A little what, Don?'

He closed his eyes again, and shook his head. 'Different,' he said. 'Unpredictable. I knew she had some mental health problems when I married her. Her family knows it, too.

'I also knew she still wanted a baby – believe me, she made that damn clear. But the thought of raising a family with her and spending the rest of my life tiptoeing around and taking shit from her folks – it was inconceivable. Honestly, the way she acted, there were times when I didn't feel like having a child with her would be safe.' Bogle blinked. Safe or not, it was happening. 'I met Jessica not long after I found out Juliet was pregnant,' he said. 'I was terrified. A kid . . . it bound me to Jules and her family for life.'

That fear, it appeared, went both ways. 'Was that when the drinking started?'

'Whoa.' Bogle's union delegate had wild gray hair and pleated pockets under his eyes, and when I asked about the drinking, he raised his hand and kept it there.

'It's OK,' said Bogle. 'I'm not trying to hide anything, not now that she . . . now that I know what Juliet's capable of.' He turned back to me and said, 'Yeah, that's when it started. More or less.'

'And then what? You got together with Jessica?'

'Not exactly.' Patches of fuchsia appeared on his neck as he shifted in his seat. 'We were both pretty wasted that night at the inn. When her friends went up to the bride-to-be's room, Jessica slipped me her spare key card. I knew it was stupid. Everyone knows me at the inn. Amos spends most of his time in the office, but he pokes his head out now and then, and there's always staff around. Anyone could have seen us. But I guess no one was watching, and honestly, part of me didn't care if they were. I went up to her room – and nothing happened. Well, a lot happened –' he looked away – 'but my world didn't come to a crashing halt. Amos didn't call Jules to tell her I'd slept with a stranger. Mary at the front desk didn't tell Gracelyn and Morton, and Juliet didn't confront me sobbing and livid when I walked in the door. I got away with it. I hated myself for what I'd done, couldn't look in the mirror, but at the same time it felt like maybe I had a shot at being happy again. The next day, I found Jessica on Facebook and asked her out. And she said yes.' Bogle looked as though he couldn't quite believe it himself. 'I was on duty the next weekend, but she was off the night of July third, so we planned to meet up after work.'

I gave him a nod of encouragement. It was little comfort to any of us, but just like at the legion, interrogating Bogle was

child's play. The man knew what information we needed. He'd
had to squeeze it out of many a suspect himself.

'Did Jessica know about your job?' asked Tim.

'Yeah. I wasn't ready to break it off with Juliet – the baby
thing was so new, I didn't know what to do about it – so I asked
Jessica to be discreet. She told her mother she'd met someone
on Facebook, and that she was going on a blind date. What
Damon Ameer and Troop B saw online was the conversations
we had leading up to that night. It was Jessica's idea for me to
create a fake account with a fake job and a profile pic that gave
nothing away. She thought it would help me keep it all from
Jules. The name I used, it's an anagram,' he said.

I'll be damned. 'So you're Ben G. Dool. All the time we were
looking for him, agonizing over his identity, investigating Javier
Barba . . . it was you.'

'You have to understand,' he said with urgency in his voice,
'Jessica and Rebecca were dead. Dead! I couldn't believe it. I
even went back to Massena this week and sat outside Jessica's
house, hoping to see her. Hoping that Troop B somehow got it
wrong.'

'When did you know,' I asked quietly, 'what happened to
Jessica?'

'Not until you did,' he said. 'When Kelsea told Tim about the
murder in Massena, and you told me. When I didn't hear from
her after that night, I figured she'd wised up and realized dating
a married cop who looks like Jaws from *Moonraker* isn't a great
idea. But that wasn't it at all. And I had to figure out who killed
her, because I knew – *I knew* – I'd take the heat for her murder.
For both of them.'

My head spun with so many questions I hardly knew
where to begin. 'Tell us about that date with Jessica,' I said,
working to keep my voice even. 'Where did you meet?'

'The Rusty Anchor, like we planned. But as soon as I got
there, I could see it was jammed, and I didn't want to risk being
recognized. I don't exactly blend in,' he said drily. 'We decided
to go for a walk instead. I liked her. It wasn't just about the sex.
She left her car in the parking area across from the bar and met
me down the street. I drove us to Whalen Park Trail, along the
river. We walked and talked for a couple of hours, until close to

ten, and then I drove her back. Juliet must have tailed me. It's the only explanation I can think of.'

'She was tracking your phone,' I told him. 'Following you everywhere. Just like you followed her.'

That made Bogle wince. 'She didn't trust me. Guess I deserve that.'

I had to wonder how much of Bogle's insecurity stemmed from his marriage to Juliet Barlowe. His self-doubt ran so deep it had kept him from checking in with Jessica, muzzling the only other person with information about the night she died.

'I guess Juliet waited there for her and . . .' He made a fist on the table, his knuckles white as bone.

I caught Tim's eye. He nodded. We had the explanation we'd been searching for. But we weren't done yet. 'Talk to us about Rebecca,' I said.

Bogle inhaled deeply through his nose, and lowered his gaze.

'Rebecca sold me my truck. She was amazing,' he said, sounding wistful. 'We talked a lot the day I picked it up, hit it off right away. A few days later, I looked her up on Facebook using that same fake Ben Dool account. Rebecca totally got it – she was having problems in her marriage, too. Her husband was a controlling asshole. You know that. They'd only been married a couple of years, but she wanted to leave him. You'd never know it from her Facebook page – not even her family knew – but Godfrey was verbally and emotionally abusive. He put her in that job so he could keep an eye on her, then alienated her from friends and tried to control every aspect of her life. I think that when she heard what I did for work, she wanted me to be her savior. And when she found out I lived all the way upstate, she asked me to help her disappear.'

I let that sink in. It was a theory we'd explored early on, the idea that Rebecca had been trying to escape her husband. Never could I have imagined that Don Bogle was enlisted to help.

'I wasn't sleeping with her,' he assured us. 'Not Rebecca. When I realized what was going on with her, I wanted to help. I know a victim of coercive control when I see one. In a lot of ways, I felt like one myself. So, I came up with a plan. I told her she could stay in Lake Placid for a while. Juliet's family has a hunting cabin there, and no one ever goes in the off-season. She could have lived there for at least a month until she found a job and her own place. It's only two hours from here. We planned to meet in town. I was going to give Rebecca some money – Juliet would never miss it – and drive her to the cabin that night.'

I said, 'But her husband wouldn't let her come north alone.'

'Right – so she fed him that story about wanting to get away and reconnect with him. It was my idea for them to stay at the Admiral. She was going to leave after he was asleep and meet me behind the motel.'

'The night she disappeared,' I said. 'That was you sitting outside the Bay Point Grill?'

Another nod. 'She sent me a message saying she and Godfrey had been fighting. He was pissed about the state of the motel. Drinking. She was scared. She thought he might make a scene at dinner, so I told her I'd keep an eye on her. Follow her back to the motel, and wait until he was asleep to make sure she was safe. But while I was driving out to the Admiral, I got a call from Jules.'

And here was where Bogle and Rebecca's plan had fallen apart. His face twisted with the pain of what he had to say next.

'Juliet told me Amos needed help at the inn. I thought that was strange. It was getting late, and Amos never asks me for help – the only time we spend together is when he's humiliating me on the pickleball court, which Juliet forces me into – but what was I going to say? She was so suspicious all the time. I sent Rebecca a message saying I'd be late, and to wait for me. When I got to the Carlson, Amos wasn't even there. He'd gone home hours ago. That was the moment I started to think Juliet knew something unusual was going on.'

'And while you were on Carlson Island,' Tim said, 'Juliet met Rebecca instead.'

'She took my truck from where I parked it at the ferry dock. Write that down,' Bogle told Tim. 'That's important. There was blood on the passenger side door when I finally got back to the mainland – but you've gotta believe me, I had no idea Juliet killed her. How could she? She's my wife. She's pregnant,' he said in an anguished voice.

'Juliet took your truck so Rebecca would think it was you coming to meet her, and then she attacked her. Sent a text to her husband to make him think Rebecca had left him, and dumped

her body at the quarry. Dumped the phone, too.' I had to hand
it to Juliet; the woman had thought it all through. The Thousand
Islands Bridge was just a turn off the highway between the
Admiral Inn and the quarry. By stopping to ditch Rebecca's
phone and the flip-flops, she'd created an effective diversion.
She'd aimed for Allison Novak's island, if I had to guess. Lobbed
that phone with all her might. Born and raised on the river,
Juliet would have known about the currents and that Rebecca's
shoes would float to shore. She knew a message like 'dead girls
tell no tales' would corroborate our theory about a serial murderer.
What she'd done . . . it was unthinkable. 'And all this time,' I
said to Bogle, 'you knew.'

When I'd briefed my team in the barracks, with Lieutenant
Henderson and Damon Ameer from Troop B on the phone, Bogle
had suspected his wife might be involved in the crimes. He'd
listened to me present evidence to support the absurd, improbable
theory that someone was so obsessed with my cousin's murders
that they'd come here, to my town, and killed in his name. Later,
he'd followed me home to eavesdrop. Assess how much Tim and
I had already puzzled out. All the while I'd been sick with worry,
tortured by the increasingly likely possibility that Bram would
never really go away. And Bogle had stood by and watched.

'I'm sorry,' he said now. 'I'm so sorry, but I had no choice.
You chased Bram for months, all over Jefferson County and
across state lines. You don't fucking give up, Shana. If I didn't
throw you off the scent so I had time to prove what Juliet had
done, you were going to pick up on her trail, and that trail led
straight to me.'

'But all the similarities to Bram,' I said, still reeling. 'The
women's names. The quarry crime scene. The knife wounds.'
Uncle Brett, Abe's father, used to have a pocketknife like the one
that killed these five women. I'd always wondered if my cousin
had coveted it as a kid, and whether that was why he'd used the
same kind of knife to commit murder. Build a sick legacy that,
years later, would be carried on by someone else. 'What about
all that?' I asked. 'What about the basement?' How had Juliet
known to hold me there, what recreating my abduction would
do to me?

Beside me, Tim set down his pen.

'I told them, Shana,' Bogle said, hanging his head. 'A couple of weeks ago, we went to lunch at Juliet's parents. They were talking shit about you. They've been reading the articles, all of them.' His voice hitched and he reached for his bottle of water again, only this time he allowed himself to twist the cap and take a messy sip. 'They said you were a blight infecting this town and that it had gone on long enough. They wanted to complain to your superiors. They had no fucking *clue* what you'd been through. Gracelyn started toying with the idea of writing to the paper. I needed to change their minds. I didn't know what else to do.'

'Jesus,' said Tim, raking both hands through his hair. 'How could you do that, Don?'

Bogle scrubbed his forehead until it was crimson. My brain felt addled. It was too much, too fast. I said, 'But the names . . .'

'Coincidence,' Bogle said simply. 'Probably what gave Juliet the copycat idea in the first place. She'd been following the news about Bram for months, just like everyone else. I would never have thought she could do this, never. But if I'm real with myself, if I think back . . . the instinct? It was always there. For years, Jules saw a therapist for all kinds of things,' he told us. 'Impulsive behavior, compulsive lying, aggression. Her family pays the bills and looks the other way. They ignore her mood swings and pretend she's not trying to manipulate everyone around her. I was the only one who had an inkling of how bad things could get.'

'Not the only one,' I said. 'I think Gracelyn and Amos know, too. And I'm pretty sure they were hoping you'd get the blame.'

'It explains why Juliet's mother didn't let her get a word in at the house,' added Tim, 'and everything Amos told Shana at the party. They were covering for her. Shifting the focus to Don.'

It may not have been the easiest way to excise Don Bogle from the family, but the Barlowes weren't about to let their daughter go to prison for murder.

'There is no copycat,' I said, still trying to wrap my head around it all. 'No serial killer taking aim at me to finish what Bram started.' Just a disturbed woman determined to punish her husband and force him back to her.

'There *was* a copycat,' Tim said sadly, turning to me. 'But the only reason you were part of her crimes is that you figured out the truth.'

FIFTY-FOUR

Three weeks ago, there were few places left where I could go without feeling like a public spectacle. A pariah. A grotesque. I never left the house without looking over my shoulder, or chanced meeting someone's eye without wondering if they were judging me for what my cousin had done. I'd pined for the days when going to Tim's cottage felt like coming home and I could roll down the windows of my SUV, punch the gas and savor the grass-scented stream of wind on my face as I hurtled toward him.

I feel a bit of that anticipation tonight. The work day is behind me, and all that lies ahead is a Friday evening in September with cold drinks and good friends.

Tim's been playing coy with me all day. 'Go to the address I texted you at exactly seven o'clock. Resist the urge to investigate and just drive.' The street name isn't familiar, but according to Google Maps it's in Alexandria Bay, down at the edge of Otter Creek. He said to come hungry and bring a sweater. Now that the weather's turned deliciously cool, the suffocating heat of summer is all but forgotten.

'OK, Maxwell Smart,' I'd replied as we got ready to leave the station, 'Hey, I've been meaning to ask . . . how's Kelsea?' Tim had been spending more time with her, trying to steer her interests away from murder and toward something healthier. He was hoping to convince her to get a puppy from the breeder Mac had used down on Long Island. I was comforted to know Kelsea had Tim in her corner. Relatives of victims often struggle with opening up. The sudden, violent nature of death through homicide is humanity failing us in the worst possible way. It disconnects everything we thought we understood about the world, and sends us careening into orbit. To people like Casey Mitchell, and Noah Remus, and Kelsea Shaw, regaining faith in their fellow man is paramount. Happiness, friendship and love are all off the table if you can't allow yourself to believe in something good again.

'She's better.' Tim's smile crinkled his eyes. 'It'll take some time.'

'That's OK,' I said, reaching for his hand. 'Take all the time you need with her. I trust you.' Behind us, Jeremy Solomon cleared his throat and shot us a playful look that said 'get a room.'

I see a mailbox up ahead. I turn down a long, paved driveway, and there before me is the house. It's got a Victorian vibe, with a turret and wraparound porch, and it sits just a few yards from the water. Tim didn't mention we were visiting one of his friends, but I don't mind. I know Mac will be here, too, and if I have the two of them, I can handle anything.

Shortly after it was posted, Jared Cunningham's article got him a call from a reporter with the *New York Times*. The interview had more than a hundred-thousand Likes by then, and the reporter was keen to explore both Cunningham's newly minted magazine and my candid story. Cunningham set up the call, the three of us talked, and the *Times* published our feature the following week. Since then, the encounters I experience in town look a lot more like my last one with Javier Barba. A sympathetic wave. Maybe even a smile.

Cunningham has connected with other relatives of violent criminals, and is slowly expanding his stable of content. From what he tells me, Felicia's story is next in the queue.

I don't pretend that everyone is willing to listen to the truth. The Barlowes are trying to hit me with an assault charge for immobilizing Juliet – Juliet, who held me and Estella hostage in the basement of a luxury hotel after murdering two young women. Despite their team of expensive lawyers, I'm not worried. Lately, my thoughts are more likely to turn to Don Bogle. His child. What his life looks like now.

Where the hell he goes from here.

I park my SUV in the driveway next to Mac and Tim's, and follow the sound of voices to the back of the house. I'm not sure what I'm expecting, would be equally surprised by a three-person picnic as a crowd playing championship cornhole. What I find instead, standing with McIntyre and Tim on a patio by the water, is my family.

I suck in a breath and hold it. It's been months since I've

seen them, and they look different to me. Mom's fair hair is lighter than usual from a summer spent in the safety of her back garden, away from the neighbors' prying eyes. The snowfall of white on my father's head needs a good brushing, and his round cheeks aren't as full as they used to be, but they both look good. Healthy. Doug stands next to Tim, and when he sees me, his face splits into an enormous grin.

'What—'

'We hid the car in the garage to surprise you,' says Mom and then she's crying, holding me so tight that I'm breathless, and Dad's there too with his long, cardiganed arms bracing us in place as if he's afraid I'll spin away in the breeze. We stay like that, cheeks wet, chests heaving with emotion, and then they're both talking at once, telling me they're sorry, they had no idea how much I'd been through, had never wanted to believe it. They marvel over my short hair and exposed neck, and Dad tells me the cut is ace, brilliant. It's pleasant out, balmy even, yet I find that I'm shaking, my body rocked by the shock of seeing them at last and the pure, raw relief of being with them again.

'Hey,' Tim says after we've pulled ourselves together. He takes my hand and kisses me deeply, his mouth warm on mine. His ribs expand against me as he breathes me in. I'm conscious of my family watching us, but somehow, I don't mind.

'Did you do this?' I say, deliciously dizzy.

'I've got your back, Shane. Always.'

'Promise?'

Tim's smile tilts. 'So? What do you think?'

'It's amazing,' I say through a giddy laugh that quickly sets my parents to giggling, too. 'I can't believe it.'

'I was talking about the house.'

I tip my head. 'The house?'

'I'll admit it needs work. It's an antique,' he says, 'built in the twenties. But I did over the cottage. I can do this, too. Plus this time, I'll have help.'

Confused, I turn around to study the house once more. It's slightly less impressive up close now that I see the peeling paint and chipped trim, but striking nonetheless – and it has a view of Boldt Castle, rising like a German fairytale palace on the horizon. What the hell is Tim talking about?

'I made an offer,' I hear him say behind me, 'and they accepted.'
I turn around again.

On the worn flagstone patio, in front of my family, Tim drops
down to one knee.

I blink at him, not comprehending. I've known Tim just over
a year. For most of that time, Bram's been with us too. An eternal
shadow that blackened our days and terrorized our nights.

So why? Why *me*? Tim's entitled to better. An easier life, a
wife that's all sweetness and light. I'm not that – and he knows
it. Tim knows me. I know him, too. Nobody understands what
he went through with Carson better than I do, because I went
through it myself. But must he live out his days with a tangible
reminder of his pain? Looking at a woman who wears hers on
the outside in the form of a ghastly scar?

Tim's watching me. There's a tremor in his eyebrow now. Is
it born of uncertainty? Is he reconsidering? Remembering – like
I am – our friend Don Bogle, and where his marriage got him?

I think of the tree that withered in Tim's backyard, and my
fears about our future. I remember Noah Remus denying himself
happiness as a form of self-punishment.

And then, I remember sitting injured in the basement on
Carlson Island, and the ferocity of my love for Tim Wellington.

I don't know much about marriage. I don't know if I even
deserve it.

But I intend to find out.

ACKNOWLEDGMENTS

I t's hard to fathom that Shana Merchant has four adventures under her belt. That wouldn't be the case without readers like you. My profound thanks to everyone who has purchased, borrowed, recommended, and reviewed my books. I'm humbled that you chose to spend your time with us.

I feel fortunate to have editor Rachel Slatter in my corner, along with Anna Harrisson, Sara Porter, Martin Brown, and Joanne Grant. As always, thank you to my agent and friend Marlene Stringer.

I shudder to think where I'd be without early readers. Thank you to Leila and Karl Wegert, John and Carol Repsher, Dorinda Bonanno, and Elise Hart Kipness for providing frank feedback and flagging plot holes. My gratitude goes out to experts Sheriff Colleen O'Neill, Chris Brock, Dan Ecker, Lou Ecker, Mike Girard, Michelle Sowden, Elsa Shalaveyus, and Naana Obeng-Marnu for making me look good on paper (any mistakes are my own), and graphic designer Jessica Burnie for making me look good online.

One of the unexpected joys of writing crime fiction has been the generosity of other authors, including Danielle Girard, Edwin Hill, Megan Collins, Sarah Stewart Taylor, Wendy Walker, Lynne Constantine, Hannah Morrissey, Samantha Bailey, Hank Phillippi Ryan, and so many others. I'm endlessly grateful for your support. Thank you Barrett Bookstore, Phoenix Books, The Little Book Store, Fairfield University Bookstore, Elm Street Books, The Mysterious Bookshop, libraries, and the bookstagram community (shout-out to Abby of @crimebythe-book, @the__reading__beauty, @gareindeedreads, and Suzy Leopold) for spreading the word about my writing.

I don't think the families of writers get enough credit. The sacrifices they make in order for us to pursue this career are not small, and my own family is no exception. Thank you Grant, Remi, and Schafer for your patience, encouragement, and love.